THE WORLD WITH NO EVIL

PRISCILA K.

Initio Magna

THE WORLD WITH
NO EVIL

Contents

BOOK THREE

To my mother, Maria Shinta
I love you always

BOOK ONE

THE EARTH WITH NO SENSES

I

Chapter One

The First Sense: A Modern Permian

This is the story about how a new world with no conviction was made.

The earth was coming apart at the seams. Fire was raging out of control and out of breath all over the greenwood, water cruising every root and soul from their withered to sleeping ground, involuntary quivering movement nudging every island gently as a sympathy to the globe's anxiety, not to mention furious hurricanes pushing revenge schemes over manmade climate change. In response, the majority was blaming the seemingly hypersensitivity ever long possessed by Mother Nature who finally revealed her wobbling temper where in fact, that was not really the case. The truth, she had had enough of their treachery, as she gained sight of the reality inside and all over her through her windy vision.

Evil in human bodies, living on her skin, she perceived.

It got her thinking, was there ever any possible way to separate between the good and evil on earth, and eliminate those evils once and for all so that the good could live in perfect peace and harmony until death did them part, not only after? She meant it, after all, why did the good get to leave her wounded body to live happily in the glorious heaven, and the bad to rot miserably in hell, while they looked down and up respectively on her coping and bleeding from the everlasting war between the living black and white forces of energy, using her organs as their resources?

Heaven on earth.

Perhaps that could really be not just a metaphor, but an actuality - a literal meaning, if the wicked humankind's time on earth was over without a trace and she could finally be without pain every time she breathed in the air to her lungs and let it out. Maybe, just maybe, it would do both God and Satan a favor too, for killing the time in choosing their citizens, she thought; but then she got to wonder, were they really, entirely to blame?

It all started when the earth suddenly woke up from her deepest and longest sleep since her birth. She neither knew for what cause or reason, nor could she sense anything for she had no such perception being appended upon her creation, but she was certain that something was bothering her, right when she lost her peace round her circle. All she wanted was to go back to her eternal tight sleep once more.

Her father, who had been there long before she had, showed his empathy silently and cried on his bottomless bed, of course without her knowing as she could not hear or see his advanced sympathy, or even nudge his tears. It was at his beholden too that she was not to be blessed with the acknowledgment of the five basic senses for ignorance was her bliss. Being torn apart from the urge to tell the Creator – maker and landlord of all galaxies across the universe, he decided that it might be best to stay quiet for as long as he could for the sake of her sanity, while taking care of his other children.

Once upon o'clock, on the earth's neck of the wood's integer billions birthday, the Creator dropped by the galaxy where she was cluelessly at. He noticed that she was awake and perceived her discombobulation that was yet without the endeavor to complain.

"Think of what you'd ask of me, now that you are awake," the Creator communicated His proposal by means of none of the senses. It was like those words were planted in her brain the moment He thought of it. She could feel it, but she did not even know the name of what she was missing. Nonetheless, did she know of the usance?

"Now that I discover that I have long had the ability to understand these words, as they are what they are called, I want to be able to know the depth of your voice, my Lord," she responded back to the noble being the same way she never understood what or how, yet, which at the same time the effortless gave her the surprise.

"Very well," as His deity force anon swung the hush of cosmos dirt away from her existing shell-like, so quick that she was able to listen to the two concede words as the first ever sound she could irrevocably hear.

As much as she had felt calmness beyond measure of the Creator's own voice, it was all gone at a rate of knots as soon as she heard the indescribable bluster and cry coming in and out of everything and everywhere around her.

As she could then also hear the conversations of the minor and various planets surrounding her she could not before, she learned of their acquaintances' numerous visits to her own dry land, then blamed them of the laments and explosions while being in constant shock upon hearing her own voice for the first time more than the others were, "It is very hard to get to my sleep ever since your alike fell together upon my ground, went off relentlessly across the landmass, and celebrated your visits with grieve."

"It was not us, as if it was the case, there would even be no cry to spare," they responded as straight as a thrown group of dice with holes and holy grounds, but they did not intend to stop rolling their mouth there without telling her what they were witnessing right at that very moment, ceaseless horrible things.

"This is what we are truly seeing," one of them then began his observation after taking a deep whole breath that almost pushed him a few miles to the back.

Living afar and separated by the broad blue blood of Mother Earth, the two groups of lands inside her apparently never stopped building the invisible bridge of hatred in between them. The chief of the east versus the head of the west warfare was escalating in a substantially larger scale from a rather conventional manner to an all-out thermonuclear battle as soon as the latter started to initiate numerous nuclear warning shots across their enemy's border structures that was not intentionally supposed to cost dead bodies of approximately thousands they did not count living and hiding illegally around the area, which the first soon used as an excuse then without hesitation retaliated without mercy in the expense of the life of millions more.

As many other countries followed to take sides for no assuring reason with none acting as mediators, the fight was soon enough becoming everyone's tactical nuclear war with illicit built-in missiles flying there and then crashing explosions constantly in roundabout helpless wanderers of each side and cursing survivors with their prolonged side effects. Even thereafter, multitudinous counterforce and countervalue excuses of forcing more explosions that served as the obvious instrument to the evident cessation to humanity was never going to end. No one and nowhere was safe any longer. No sovereign too would even selflessly surrender, for that would be the ultimate selfish regret and suicide to have their people to pay the price as slaves to colonialism and exploitation for the leader's own fated loss. Just like that, it happened all over again on repeat, just with slightly different subjects and targets while taking turns in authority roles between many countries.

Gaining witnesses of countless cold familiar figures, the rest who lived had to bear the weight of an endlessly deep reservoir leaking out of their eyes. They screamed to the top of their lungs as the death and the living barrier broke their sanity apart. They convinced themselves that there would be no answer to this meaningless tussle and no conclusion to this misery except with their own death, so they chose to give up with more cries while juggling their own time. No solution, they thought; but not to Mother Earth, or so she thought.

"Where is this exactly happening?" The curious earth still in the disbelief of what she could not stroke as there would be nothing she could feel just yet.

"All over inside you," they made their final witness statement.

"I shall unite them together and so to shatter the other's ground would mean to break their own," the earth convinced herself of her own plan based on the stories she heard, yet to the commencement as she waited for the planetoids and asteroids' ditto due to the insecurity channeling from her inexperience and lack of basic senses. Yes, all that - she was aware.

"We ourselves are stronger when we are all together, but those who astray fall into meteorites. If you think you have the power, why don't you give it a try?" Their response motivated the earth that led to a rise in her confidence; thus, she began her way of solution.

With everything in her power, she never knew she could,

but one she did not necessarily have to know to be able to do as she only needed as far as inspired by, she gave a beyond colossal motion to every land she could grasp under her wings and hugged them altogether side by side in a wrap without a single touch of her feel.

Consequently, there was the biggest earthquake across the world with the loudest longing rumble and screeching reverberation in which death tolls surpassed those twice, then thrice, as those deceased from the only reason why she did it in the first place. As a result, too there was only one green land as a whole as she wished - one supercontinent and one vast ocean once more, a rebirth of a Permian period, as the geographical past was reversed in the modern time.

To her joy, the plan seemed to work.

Explosions were no longer heard. There had been the loudest and longest series of howls and cries followed but as they eventually stopped, she was starting to gain her peace again. Nonetheless, something was still bothering her.

In fact, to her, something was still missing, from the things she could finally hear.

II

Chapter Two

The Second and Third Senses: Seven Colors of Tears

"Speak of what you'd ask of me, now that you are able to listen," the Creator who in her surprise never left though His figure was never visible to her, was going to grant her a second wish without any apparent reason why to her, not that she disliked the idea, however.

"Now that I discover that I have long carried the power to shift the land, as they are what they are called, I want to be able to feel the movement of your creation, my Lord," she was sure of her want but not of her need, but the Creator knew it too without her awareness.

"Very well," as His supreme power coerced on her gas-layered skin with a sturdy blow of air bouncing off every direction immediately after. As streaming lights afterward were seen for a quick moment, she could finally touch those voices but to her surprise, they were scorching her body rather painfully.

As she was listening to a group of stars who bragged widely about their glowing up in adversity in the dark universe without even mentioning the sun (they would never because otherwise their dignity would be scarcely hurt), the earth digested the bright source of lights to her skin as their doing and blamed the blemish on them, "It is very hard to get to my sleep ever since your alike mingled together above my atmosphere, shined so radiantly across my skin, and burnt me wholly to the core."

Her temperature was staggeringly rising right when she was begging the stars not to shine so brightly in the hope, she maybe could cool down even just a little, making her surer that she was speaking directly to the culprit. At least that was what she thought at the time, being unaware that it was her unconscious hurt of pride that exposed her to further feel the burn in the deep.

"It was not us, as if it was the case, there would only be warm smiles coloring your surface, only happiness and never any pain," they were straight to the objection of the blame. Similarly with the minor planets, they continued the conversation to reveal what they were really seeing - hot temperature troubles, sourcing from all over her, again.

Mother Nature was having what the stars mentioned to her as a *fever* without her knowledge. She was sweating chemicals from numerous agricultural and industrial activities as the air was flowing gas emissions to her epidermis and irritating her skin barrier which decreased her immunity to the daily sunbathe, while at the same time shivering from the cold melting mountainous glaciers of ice that were drowning to the sea. As the paradox was already keeping her body and mind addled, what came next was never in her expectation. Instead of blaming the exposure variations to their honest contender, the sun, it was humans - some and most, that they objectively condemned. The mortals living on top were once again the center of the attention; this time of the second story she had heard so far, both excruciating her heart deeply.

Not stopping there, another symptom grew on her from just a mild headache to a savage by endless screams of previously unfamiliar wild beasts and crops burning to expiration, leading to familiar bellows of reasoning beings that were losing their instincts due to droughts and famines as its result. Who was to blame for this? She wondered, so she uncontrollably stroked across her fence thousands of kilometers long to find the truth and brought the wind aimlessly as her means of transportation closer to the surface so she could hear better. Was it her blistering heat that tortured them to death? But was it due to humans' unsustainable actions and deforestation that dehydrated and irritated her complexion in the first place?

As she was discombobulated, her wind was heedlessly speeding along with her confusion and twisting without manner following her stormy brush seafaring beyond the saltwater, transforming into extensive slayer hurricanes and thunderstorms as soon as her caress reached the land. Inevitably, cries and screams volumes were reaching their peak that in due course ended with transitory silence. She did all of this with neither deliberation with the stars nor herself.

"What did the blood taste like?" One of the smart little stars suddenly raised his suspicion from the horror things he was seeing, rather too late for the grown-ups to hush him down.

She asked them what he meant by that, but in return, the stars dispersed intentionally and ignored her obliviousness, and so even when they were still revolving not far from her, their silence and her blindness managed to send their nearby presence away from her awareness.

Taste, she wondered, and just when she was about to give up on thinking, the Creator stayed true to His stand and asked, "Speak of what you'd ask of me, now that you are able to feel your pain."

"Now that I discover that I have long holden the curtains to demise, as they are what they are called, I want to be able to taste the life of your design instead, my Lord," she was sick of the death her existing senses had been exposing her to and thus began to yearn for its contrast. The life of the living.

"Very well," His numen weight expanded the middle of her lips wide in the opposite direction to each other and pressed in on her jaw a tongue a mile a minute in a circle.

It was almost like the tongue was growing from the existing seed inside of her mouth. Even before the procedure was fully completed, she could already taste her sweet element organs stronger and stronger upon the construction; but to her surprise, the flavor was tinglingly growing awful to her taste near completion on the surface that if the process were about a minute longer, she would have puked, and no one could predict how it would have turned into - perhaps except the Creator.

The moon nearby who had been staying quiet while moving languorously to the repetition walk along the orbit and being half awake bored for a long time suddenly widened her eyes and opened her mouth hole, then bounced back in anticipation of the earth vomiting towards her. As it turned out, she had been listening silently to the conversation the earth was having, but only acted when she felt necessary.

The moon ran from the anticipation to the potential vomit, taking cover far in front of the sun and reaching in a waste of manner instead as she realized she could not go behind it as far and as fast to hide. The earth gave out a squeal of apologies for she did not expect what she tasted would be so horrible. She made it obvious to the moon of her lack of knowledge that the natural satellite could not help but ask, "Couldn't you already smell the blood before?"

Afterward, the earth demanded an explanation to which the moon surprisingly gladly responded, maybe to distract her while she was slowly keeping her distance grew larger in between when she spoke. No one exactly knew what made the moon forget what they thought of as fondness to neglect and sleepwalking, but soon after, they realized that she too had been all ears on what was going through even in her nap, unavoidable horrendous terrible scenes.

While those wars and natural disasters were giving rise to drought and poverty, the world was briefed but not fully prepared for what was coming. Some people had to endure substantial loss while others were more able to afford the opulent comfort from the war; however, just up to that moment, they too lost everything from the earth's temper phenomenon. No one was really rolling in money anymore, and with more pressure for survival, everyone was pretty much for themselves, even at the expense of others. As a result, various crimes, and cannibalism - the trend of the old world, became the new trend of the modern world as million liters of blood were set free with and without purpose on the loose, which ended up giving Mother Earth more harrowing taste to her tongue as the number grew. Instead of feeling sorry for what they had done, they kept every second of it from their little device and broadcasted it to the whole world whenever they could; thus, the birth of the law of none became justifiable as transgressions grew acceptable.

Simultaneously, the moon's secret run caused an unanticipated soaring tide across the globe and it would have not really been so if she had walked along her designated pace. Nonetheless, the earth could feel it; that as the moon's voice sounded further and further, the taste too was slowly getting bitter then sweeter again, like the worst part was being filtered by the rising water inside her. As it turned out however, the less the earth looked sick, the more the moon turned back to her usual route.

"No, go back!" Mother Nature screamed to the moon's surprise, but she decided to go as far as she could within her orbit with the earth, following the earth's quirky-behavior demand.

It took a shorter time than the moon expected for the earth to invite her back in closer, but the damage she had participated in washing her mouth was greatly irreversible. There had been the biggest flood the globe had ever had to wrestle with. People were striking the water as much as they could to get to the top, reaching for even just a glimpse of air. They had already been losing their breath before the flood, but the disaster made the choking real to their senses; thus, the provenance of another silence on earth that she preferred.

"No more blood, I reckon. That metallic taste is gone now, so thank you," the earth suspected that the moon would be happy and strive to claim the credit herself on the help, but to her surprise, the moon howled, opening cold air upon her breath from each of the hole, and begged for forgiveness to unknown names seven point five billion times long and more.

"Can't you even smell the dead?" The moon cried her last goodbye with similar debate to meditate and took advantage of the earth's lacking sight by ignoring every single word she retaliated.

However, just as the moon turned her back against the earth and remained a peeking trailing shadow in the sky, she missed to witness and report the survivors - crops, animals, and everything else giving birth from the cold and the sun, and multiplied, only because of the disasters shepherding the freedom from interference; however, still leaving the earth perplexed and filled with guilt from the unseen by the sweeter taste she was getting, when everything was restarting and coming back growing to better than before, even normal. She cried according to her feeling that was left uncertain; sad, happy, and confused, shading seven colors of tears as she pleaded for the guilty pleasure motion.

Nevertheless, she was ready for her next wish.

III

Chapter Three

The Fourth Sense: Omuma

"Speak of what you'd ask of me, now that you are full of the flesh and blood," the Creator who only seemed gone for a second the many years the worst part was happening rapidly, had spoken to the planet in pain before anyone could even say her name, that fast.

"Now that I discover that I have long schlepped the force to wash my iniquity, as they are what they are called, I want to be able to smell this generation, my Lord," she initially wanted to say the fragrance of the reconstruction but realized she should be expecting the worst this time.

"Very well," His demiurge capacity's knife stuck through and molded inward instead, the earth's epidermis, unfurling a trapped pair of cavities for the odor to travel through to her encephalon.

For many months, the wiser air assisted her smell to travel every part of all the seas and oceans, and for that Mother Nature was grateful she could roughly sleep through the utterly sweet-scented breeze and salt-calming journey. However, little did she know that her assistance was saving the worst for the last, for it only had the power to delay and courage to pretend, but not at all the capability to avoid her from the peril any longer.

As the air had no more strength to divert the new sense from flowing over the land, moreover, to put a brake on it, the earth awoke from her drowse for a handful of nuisances in the form of smoke was breaking through her nostril. What had been happening over her ground was humans taking control over the source of fire without respect, and in return, fire ruling over their property with no control. Flames were on the loose all over the greens and woods, further forest to cities, but ended when it reached the seashore. As soon as it did, the earth did not feel the blaze on her skin as those scars were products of immunity from all the burning pain and softened with the fumes as she got used to the heat.

The smoke nonetheless served two purposes. First was as a warning sign to those who paid attention from afar, but second, in contradiction, was to smother nearby running life-forms from behind that started to bite the dust as soon as their knees fell off the ground and went back to their fetal position to be reborn into a state of ashes. As a natural side effect to her immunity defense, the earth's system could not help but to cough out the carbon dioxide.

Her internal organs soon developed a pump mechanism that triggered an accelerated volcanic eruption, as the drive of magma causing the grounds breaking simultaneously from the vibration for quite a while, and as it rose and saw the sky, becoming lava explosion that flew and melted through the dry land and mocked the birth of every living creature, on its way to shuffle off their mortal coils. While some of it touched the sea, it gave birth to more grounds in paradox, that grew to become an expansion of those formerly beautiful lands across the shore, which would eventually have its beauty restored as time went by.

Meanwhile though, gases classified as potential hazards were released unconsciously during the eruption. The rest of the particles traveled with the air and contaminated it along the way millions of tons in size, though ironically only mere less than a quarter of what many industrial activities had been accumulating. All these altogether also further triggered her more painful and inescapable cough.

Not stopping there, giant rocks who lived on the outside did not want to miss out on the escape of its liquid sibling, so they fell everywhere as a consequence to their surroundings instead as they eventually realized that their maneuver was rather limited. When they touched the ground, they woke the nation up with their stress vibration and broke worldly goods and constructions without discrimination. When they touched the sea however, water jumped out of the shock unprepared for the sudden visit and thus created giant tsunamis invading the motherland.

It all got better for a long moment whilst humans that survived were recovering from the sequential disasters and the earth was starting to get her peace back. As the calm was strained however, the diabolical cycle repeated by her inhabitants and terrorized her sanity, not one by one, but this time, on the whole senses. So, she tried what she knew best, what she did all over again, only to find out that there was no use. It was all coming back to her again.

The explosion, weep, irritation, fever, bitterness, and stinginess - all her four existing senses were interrupted, and they were all driving her mad. She did not know what else to do other than trying to keep it all together.

"Useless if the others know, they probably don't even understand how this really feels," she thought as she fell into depression. They could have not helped her like she had thought, and based on her own experience, they were only making it worse. Heck, they probably did not even care too, she trusted. Probably she should not bother them anymore. Probably, probably, then thousands more of 'probably' filled her head eventually.

Embarrassed, she tried not to get the others to realize her pain anymore, pretending what they could see did not bother her any longer, and that she was stronger.

Silence. Escaping her senses.

She chose a sotto voce suffering for a whispered toleration from those who really cared, if any.

She shut her mouth closed and tried to stay still, as motionless as possible in the hope that her taste bud would not be able to perceive any flavor of any kind. She held her breath tight closed the same way to avoid any smell, wishing she could pointlessly un-feel the headache and heat rash as well. While she was doing that, too she was trying to hush her ear, but apparently to no luck. Her suffering was overheating her complex and she began to sweat all around her circle.

Hot, very hot. It was a growing heatwave everywhere as it went, and in the fullness of time, her surroundings could tell of her perspiration, but not her concealed hurt and depression. She was burning up, in all kinds of senses.

Seeing there were just thousands of mortals left on earth, they just thought she was having another sunburn, worse than before then.

"Sun...," she heard someone whisper beneath her total quietness.

"The sun, the bigger star...," then another.

"The sun, maybe burning her skin this time...," and another.

Eventually, she heard what her ears could only reach, everyone mentioning the name of 'Sun' ten thousand more.

"I should ask the sun. He's the one who is burning my ground," thus she decided to raise a question to the sun.

She called out to the sun, but to no response. She increased the volume of her voice a decibel more, again, and again, and again - same word, but to no reach. He did not respond, or did he not want to? The others around her who were disturbed could just run away and those who were at least a hundred and sixty million of kilometers away like Mercury did not feel bothered as much as one who was only about three hundred and eighty thousand kilometers far and could not run further again even if she tried, she did not dare to.

As the moon was getting extremely annoyed, she came to the aid by whispering the true distance of the sun, too far away to reach, "So you must shriek one short sentence once to be heard, once! Choose your words wisely," thus she suggested.

Hence, the earth gave it a thought and decided to give it a go with the first five words appearing in her mind, as loud as she ever could, "Sun, you are burning me!"

She waited for an immediate response, or action supposedly, but it took her longer than expected to get a reply from the Sun, just one-word shorter of a sentence later, "It was not me!"

"Aohw, did uoy ees flesruoy?"

A strange voice out of nowhere almost distracted her from her misery, and the vibe he was giving her not at all came close to the word 'familiar'. Mother Nature did not understand at all what this unknown creature was saying. The arrow of her intuition was right in the bull's eye this time, the stranger was not at all from the same solar system the earth was living in. He was just passing by, then was gone, probably, as if he were never even there. Was the earth just, imagining things?

"Whoa, did you see yourself?" The moon broke her ignorance again, apparently with the most sensible translation of the alien of the universe's short sentence, and with the intelligence of the earth that she secretly possessed, she knew immediately that the alien was simply talking in a reversed order.

Apparently, that was how the Creator was making it easier for everyone to tell if one was not one of theirs. The moon and everyone else took notice of this over several visits, some of very few, of the similar while the earth was sleeping. They successfully gained straight confirmation from the Creator when they raised the question upon His coming. "The visit indicates that a new universe is being made," He added, in a flashback story told by the moon.

"By the way, he's still here," the moon added of his mysterious presence, as the alien who called himself Omuma was still in full curiosity over everything he saw on earth, thus the appeared quietness.

Moving forward, the earth gained full understanding of the universe language and was able to have conversations with him, which never sounded quotidian.

The earth asked Omuma of the things he saw, and the word he spoke of was very close to what the others had been telling in summary; "Rorroh," he said plainly. Unfortunately, the hook was not docked at the port as the ship of those foreign words had been sailed to continue its journey once again.

IV

Chapter Four

The Story About a Father, A Son, A Book, and A Seed

Weren't those he witnessing just plain evils, naturally perhaps?

Further forest fires, all over again and it all started sounding a bit boring when she realized of the considerable repetitions; from when all the crops were perfectly growing from previous flood and lava soil, while humans were starting over building their houses and weapons by setting fire to those woods, and when they were running out of food once more, they started to kill each other again. There were not many of them left; the same kind of catastrophe they caused was only a smaller scale than before, but just enough for Mother Nature to still be greatly affected.

"Can't you see it?" Omuma spoke in reverse in which the

earth's brain was able to reverse it back to her understanding much faster, as she was beginning to adapt more quickly to the foreign.

"I can't see it, can't you tell?" The earth responded in a very similar way that got Omuma to understand her too.

"How should I know, I'm not from here. That is why I don't even look like any of them here. Don't the others tell you that?" The alien regardless unexpectedly opened her mind to another seemingly revelation, and the idea of it was not too much to ask again, "Why don't you ask the Creator to give you one?" As he further reinstated her wish.

Mother Nature never complained about not being able to see. Based on her understanding, her surroundings must have already known for she always asked them what they saw in her. So, they probably just assumed she was comfortable with it. However, it did raise another loophole in her mind as to why she never even thought of asking one. The others usually did the seeing for her and she had been making requests based on what they had seen, not what she had seen with her own eyes. Would it have been different if the opposite had happened?

So, why didn't she then ask Him to give her the sense to see instead, so she could herself? The sense she did not know was necessary, since everyone else in her surroundings never really brought it up and had been doing it for her. She only asked for what she could not.

Maybe, just maybe, she could then smooth the earthquake? Slow the hurricanes? Dry the flood? Or burn the right crops, those that could release a hypnotized smell that sent her and everyone else inside to tranquility, rather than firing blindly?

"Some say you don't know you need something until it's gone. I guess you don't know until it's coming too," Omuma had given his closing statement when he felt the Creator's presence smiling at him before he was forced to go far from the earth at his own speed. Even though he knew the earth could not yet see, he was sure she could at least feel his smile too as soon as he saw hers. If they had belonged to the same universe, perhaps their friendship could have been engraved into something more of a stone where no wind could ever move, or bigger, but again, perhaps.

In a moment the Creator would ask her what she wanted, she thought, and she would tell Him the *thing*. She waited and waited but strangely, it felt like forever. She really knew what she wanted at her present, this time, yet why did it feel like the clock was ticking extremely slower than before then? Why had the Creator's voice not been heard yet?

Her anxiety started to burn her more. Knowing she had converted many things into unsuccessful attempts, she began to wonder if there were any more possible steps left she had not done. Anything that could work. Her point of view, but maybe, it should be His instead?

The earth eventually learned to feel the Creator's presence as she moved her focus out from herself, and as everything else had come and gone, she too wondered if He ever left. She seemed to have been giving her what she asked, even the things she was not sure of, but when there came the time that she finally knew, why didn't he? Or at least as quick?

Out of the blue, she finally thought one, the only one right.

Did she even try asking Him? All this time she got what she needed; and without really the effort to ask, He came to her instead to offer her those wishes. So, she called Him, and to answer straight away He was, kind of to her surprise, and to her inmost expectation, that He probably never left.

The curiosity about the Creator's way of thinking then surpassed the knowledge of her wish. Did He, really, never leave? Did He? So, she asked Him, "Were You always there, here?"

"Does the blue sky turn black because it leaves your surface?" His disguised words sounded like a fluffy cloud that could either turn into a comforting rain or catastrophe at any given time but would always show a rainbow either way in the end.

Comforting. He never left.

The earth would stroke her chest three times if she could, but for then, just the feeling would do. She enquired though, still, in her mind, why did He never tell her what to do? On top of that, she even thought He was constantly away for His seemingly ignorance and lack of presence, furthermore, His constant blow upon her wishing candles that fluttered in the wind towards her affliction.

In response to her reserved questions, known to Him that

the earth intended to keep it quiet, He told a story instead about a father, a son, a book, and a seed.

One day, a father called out to his ten-year-old son then put some little, pale, brown-colored seeds on his left palm for him to grow and a gardening book on his right for him to read beforehand. The son asked him what they would grow into, but the father just smiled and let him know that he could ask him anything he wanted to help him grow them, but that.

Excited, the son immediately went out of the house to start the experiment. Arriving in the garden, he was immediately faced with his first confusion from seeing two kinds of soil in front of his eyes. The left one was smooth, almost like ounces of grounded salt immediately sliding through his fingers as he was trying to lift them up, while the right one was firm. Knowing he would not be able to solve the puzzle by himself, he ran back inside to ask his father about which side of land was better. The father, suspecting that he had not read the book, told him to read it as it would tell him to choose the soil that was able to hold its structure. He looked like he was ready for more questions afterward, but the boy had already run outside again to continue his own research. After his fingers were done clawing the grains up and down, he knew that the right side was the one to go for, so he started to dig and put the seed in after a few scoops, then went back to the house to sleep.

The next day however, a terrible storm was raging upon the town and covered all grounds with snow. As he was unexpecting the natural phenomena, the son asked his father when the storm would stop. The father answered in a couple of months, so the boy waited for that long to proceed on his current ambition. Again, the father suspected that the book had not been read as he should have known to watch out for the season, so he demanded him again to read it but still, to his ignorance.

The sky had changed its skin sixty times and the boy ran out into the garden first thing in the morning to witness that the colonial pile of white flakes had surrendered and left the land. Just when he almost reached where his seed was buried, a hard pouring rain suddenly terrorized the calm gloomy sky and shot at the soil simultaneously without mercy its water droplets. Because of it, he ran back to the house to ask his father how to set fire in the rain.

The father excused himself and came outside with only himself, then showed him how to accurately do them with ultimate precautions. He flickered his right-hand fingers to the front and the left ones to the back to no effect, but when he bent his right knee and attempted another flicker with his right hand, a circle of fire showed around the seed and formed a shade like an umbrella on top to keep just enough amount of water into the seed. However, as the boy grew amazed, the father stopped all the fire and reminded him that the fire needed to go out shortly before the rain fully stopped, or the consequence would be severe. Afterward, he took the boy in and suggested the boy wait for the rain to stop instead.

The curious boy ran away to give the new lesson a try without further question to his father, in which the little child succeeded with his seemingly natural-born talent. The boy went back inside leaving the fire unattended and what came next had yet to come forward before his eyes as he dozed off to sleep.

He woke up in the middle of the night with a commotion of an eye-opening heat coming from his open window as well as some loud water-throwing schemes, only to find that his successful operation had accidentally set a small portion of the garden on fire once the rain stopped, which was quickly being put out by his father. Apparently, the wise male had expected and was staying all night long just in case his son forgot to turn them off - his doubt was right.

If the fire had not been put down just in time, it would have of course spread to the death of the livings inside for fire by itself was never within control, and he knew he needed to put it out himself as it was outside of his little child's capability to. Acknowledging that, the son wept down to his knees begging for forgiveness, but the father lifted his arms up and held his shoulders tight.

"Why didn't you read the book that I gave you? Why didn't you listen carefully?" The father looked him in the eyes, "I see, but you should know that I can't read the book for you," he continued as he saw the truth in his eyes.

The father was disappointed. Although he did expect the boy to disregard reading the book, he knew he had to let it happen. Even when that meant he needed to force his face close to the sun-kissed window during the day and also away from the bed at night to protect the child as well as the rest of the family during sundown, for the incident to never leave the boy's memory, so he too would be able to grow from the unforgettable scene he experienced himself not just a stronger tree, but a wiser man, even more than the book could tell. Perhaps the boy would one day share his own knowledge in his own words, more than the book could, to his own, without leaving out what a wise and wonderful father he once had.

Memories would fade and those trees would eventually die, but the lesson would haunt the boy forever, and so would the father's spirit to guide him wise. For as long as the father lived, he promised he was never going to stop sharing what he knew best to his son. He gave another book and seed to the little boy who had then known better not to disregard the first before starting on the latter, with some words of conundrum.

"This time, the fire has to come first," the father hinted at the mystery. The boy had no idea what his father meant, not until he finished reading the book for the vision and completing the task for the visual.

This too the boy would do when he grew older, to his own child. The book, like his father, and the seed, like his little self - revolving in their own cycle of nurture until their gifts were one day remembered again.

"So, are you ready to open your eyes?" The Creator suggested the initiative for He knew, He had already given Mother Nature a pair of eyes if only she had not preferred to keep them so tight closed in her comfort zone. She had been, for too long, that she forgot she had them, moreover, how to open them too. The idea thus never crossed her mind of the simple solution, to open her eyes and begin to grow.

Alas, both lids began to unfold voluntarily.

V

Chapter Five

The Fifth Sense: "The Brain Is Done"

The earth's surroundings, who could already see from the beginning her shut pair of eyes, did not expect that the earth neither even knew that she had them nor how to open them. The set was so obvious to them - mere acquaintances to Mother Nature's own organs, though less on the why, that a stranger of the universe needed to spot both elephants in plain sight with the "Can't you see it?" question to remind them.

Once the earth's eyes were opened, she was able to see everything she had been hearing, feeling, tasting, and smelling. All the fault of mankind in majority, the whole world felt hopeless from the devil circle of power and blood for survival, trapped in the endless violent storms, and she no longer needed anyone else to tell her about them.

Her invisible eyes were set loose and leisurely wandering through the midair while slowly adjusting to the climate in the opposite way. When it got too freezing where they were, the pair became too hot to touch, and when encountered the opposite degree, it quickly turned back to ice cold. They never seemed to fit in with any of the open-air levels, most likely a reflection of their reverence to the other organs that were in irony, but the core was able to strike through the anomaly by defending the grounds with more than they should regardless, to witness what mattered.

The people.

She started to skim through every human and being across the land and water. Those who were growing life out of the ground and those who were burning them down to the sea, many who fought anciently with only skinny branches that they got left to fight for honor and others who paraded their machine guns for the power they already had, and even with countless of mortals claiming themselves as leaders of nations, where they forgot that there was even no mind left to lead.

Where limitless crimes and wars were almost unstoppable everywhere in synopsis, from human to human and consequently human to nature - all in cycle, they were already beyond far in solving them because more were desperately turning selfish. The world broke because of it too thereafter, as their mind was instinctively altered to primeval but only with a boosted advance of tools they called technology, whose holder would have been provided with more eloquence to bend the mind of those who had not.

There was no more country; well maybe one, only if one without any rules still counted as one. One, blended unknowingly from Mother Nature's set of ignoramus and painful tears that were recorded like a journal on the stone of lava as the new history of the world, unexplainable by rational contemplatives from any field, far from unbiased, and closer than ever to subjectivity - Mother Earth's own feelings.

The earth's eyes followed those scientific experts of stones and long-forgotten words, who majored in the historical aspects and futuristic expectations of her, and they did not leave out all her right and wrong doings she had unconsciously brought upon without her voluntary vision, being her response to the life and threat to her senses that defied all the logical congruence. She also managed to see by herself the digital footage of her action, which to her was almost like watching a well-known serial murder documentary, in where: the main culprit turned out to be her all along, the victims were no less of murderers themselves, and she had still not had the slightest clue - well, maybe a little if her organs were not being impulsive to react.

How did she feel afterward? Worst.

She rolled her tongue numb to the water, closed her ears tight from the rumble, held her breath for as long as she could, and forbade her impulse to the pain of her peel, just so that she could trust herself to stay away from initiating another destruction. She wanted to shut her eyes peacefully too, she really did. Heck, she wished that to be the first thing she could have stroked out from the list; but the harder she tried to, the more she could not. She could close her eyes indeed, but she could not avoid pressing her lids overly tight against each other, it was the loose that was impossible to her. Wasn't it weird that what appeared to be easy to do and most sought-after was always the impossible, until it no longer was? She just wanted a simple sleep, like before, trusting that everything happening and coming that was inevitable and unpreventable was bound to happen for her own good, perhaps by empowering the control to those who really could, but the ease of the mind seemed to be the only way to get there, and that was exactly where it got tricky. Then it got her to surrender the closing.

Her right eye continued the journey separately, flying through the breeze of salt-scented pool in response. It finally reached a peculiar stone-built hole floating by itself with odd drawings of long-gone mortals that almost did not make sense to her but felt familiar to her heart. Four men were lifting their hands to the earth the same way; then the first was flickering five fingers to his front and five others to his back, the second pushing his left arm to the left and right one to his right, the third kneeling and placing both of his hands on the ground, while the fourth lifting both arms up high. Afterward, the four of them stood side by side in various positions, and from the first to the fourth, their linked arms formed a peaceful resting heart pulse of a body and soul.

The earth was thinking of a reason, perhaps a story, or even a memory, until her left eye distracted her based on what itself was witnessing far away from the right.

"What could the dead bring to the table more than the living could?" The left eye made its comment, and soon the right agreed to pull itself back beside the left for Mother Nature to see the same thing with both eyes.

One probable hope, one possible solution, just as she had thought moments ago.

As darkness was all she was seeing no matter where her eyes wandered and no matter when it was hot or cold, she almost thought that there was no other side but that, until she saw a light shining through the corridor of her eyes from inside a seemingly pitch-black abandoned premises and heard dancing concealed instrumentals in the wind as her eyes traveled inside. The peculiar site was covered in snow in the middle of a forest - the perfect hideout for someone who was not ready to be found.

Not ready.

The name was Homeron Beckett, and he felt more than pressured to welcome himself and his generation to follow, a different systematic kind of world that would allow a lawful order to be established based on their genetics, alongside an accurate interactive technology judge that would be able to guide them through it and leave the nature at peace, as he believed. That advanced machine was what the genius had been working on in secret for the past twenty-seven years with his middle-age schematics amid vivid terrors nearby, and what had shed a light to the earth as her eyes were intrigued to know

more about what they were seeing. How did it work? She wondered.

The hopeless ambition of the man with the long white fine
threadlike strands growing around his head, a trait he grew unconsciously by putting heavy custom in cutting metal plates
more than even trimming his own hair the very least, was
meticulously blue printed on a wide dusty brown waterproof
fabric that smelled like a thousand years old. On it too, three
odd square pegs were drawn in three colors only: White, Grey,
and Black. They meant so much more than mere segregation
in his mind, clearly, as the Grey one was being crossed for a
knotty reason, while he was singing in his own rustic tune and
self-written lyrics, "Yin and Yang, Black and White, they say
we've all got a bit of both inside of us, but this *brain* of mine
will tell them all that that's a lie!"

Those wrinkles' appearance on both of his hands was
slightly adjusting to the movement of various minuscule spots
of light, and from time to time the pores were absorbing perspiration his pale egg-shaped face had brought upon, half of
the time from the overheating of one lonely furnace. He had
no plan to stop until his idea was fully settled on the not-
so-little odd device, not even plenty of wandering dust and
scorching heat from the manmade brazier as well as lack of
ventilation could burn his ambition to the ground.

The gloomy ambience foxhole became witness to the thirty
degrees hunchback fellow with a grinch stare shining from his
face's windows, grinning to his success in creating the perfect
divider to human's most sacred nature whilst constantly listen-

ing to many instrumentals in the background on repeat like they were relevant to what he was working on, as to his belief, which at that moment was fully vivid only to his mind. Since it was seemingly all done, he laughed sonorously to the beat of his jumping steps and eventually found a way to calm the delirium in his heart. He was proud, proud of himself for being able to achieve what no man ever thought would be able to achieve, but then he remembered that he was to be quiet from the precarious surroundings that might consist of those he thought as clueless mortals who had no other intention but to kill - those his machine would categorize as the 'dark ones'. For that, a silent roar of strangely duologue colloquial filled the air in the room the way he spoke to himself to serene his solitude.

He thought that it was probably best to keep the humble satisfaction for the ignorant and unleashed his proud heart to those who mattered instead; thus, he picked up the old brown telephone that was white in color the first time he arrived at the site.

"The brain is done," he shortly said in a thumping breath right after the line was picked up from the other end.

"Good, but can you add something for me?" A grunge voice vocalized out a request in response. After some words were spoken however, the scientist hung up the phone in reflex.

The atmosphere of a happily rapidly beating heart quickly turned into an enigmatic rush of hiding the dusty fabric that became clear to have on its skin the most salient schematic representation of the *brain* worth the murder. Like the sun that was always designed to set in the west, his blood was pre-destined to splatter all over the peculiar blueprint waiting in plain sight from a single knife driven from his back slashing through the front of his throat speedily in an assassination manner. The butcher in a dark figure could not bear to look him in the eye to do it, as the lamb cried but smiled sensing who it was who killed him and that it was inevitable. Yes, it became clear too that the old man never had the chance for he had been watched from the nearest place unknown to his awareness as the prey, and that his life was scripted to end from an implicit 'no'.

Just as the earth had her past recorded on the stone, his view of the truth too was meticulously written on a wrapper, slipped inside a single paperback; a letter he had successfully inscribed and hidden before his timely death. It served as his contingency plan while his blood flowed over the line of the wood and he was on his way to the spirits realm. The disquisition was still hidden in the little gap of darkness ready to be found as soon as someone with a question or two was ready for a single answer, in time. The whatsit he thought of as a secret, however, he brought to his grave for the sake of potential nobles to try to deduce it.

Meanwhile, the mysterious dark figure was running with both the lack of trust and blood on his hands. He was full of frustration and disappointment, then a wavering ambivalent on how to put his utopian plan to the test.

Your eyes are right, he was one who was about to change the world - one that was holding the *brain*.

Thus, the next story begins.

BOOK TWO

THE WORLD WITH NO SKY

VI

Chapter Six

The Grey Chamber

This is the story about how a single seed of trust could blossom into a heavenly-seen kingdom, seeking their way out of hiding.

A long and plighting cry of a newborn was heard in a small and clean, white-dominated private room that looked just like one in any hospital. The resemblance was uncanny with all those medical gears and antiseptic smell around.

The baby was on his way from his mother's exit to her arms. He stayed on wailing but not for long, on the account of the up and down ride his mother's arms had been motoring with her cosseting nose kisses along the way, simultaneously his father was caressing his bald head in tears and spoke to him words that did not sink in with the infant just yet. These too, did not stay long, for two men in total came in the room with a mission to take him away fresh from the oven as they were instructed to.

"Don't worry, your little one will pass the test, just like you once yourself did. I'm sure you'll get him back in no time," one of the men, the younger one called Bolin, who, just like the mother, was aware that he was once in the baby's place, tried to assure her that everything was going to be alright, something that he was truthfully not entirely sure about.

"But what if he doesn't?" The mother replied and started to cry, not in joyful tears like when she saw her boy for the first time, but in agony and anxiety.

"You know it is not up to us," the older man, Maccush was his name, retaliated her worries for the worse with the voice of great sorrow, but he did not mean to. He just did not want to give any false hope, just like he once himself did. He regretted it and had never once recovered from it.

The mother hugged the boy tight and pleaded to give her and her husband a few more minutes with the baby.

"Two more minutes," the man with the less wrinkle between the two eagerly agreed, much to the silent agreement from the superior next to him, who nodded only because he could not think of anything more kind to say.

Not long after however, another trooper with an odd double pennant shaped moustache and obvious overworked upper body strength (more than the two other men combined could probably ever fight) suddenly barged in where the heart-moving moment was going on.

"What are you two doing? Aren't we all told to bring all babies straight after?"

Bolin and Maccush straight away regretted their discipline that lacked layers and bowed their heads slightly to apologize to their supervisor for their fainted hearts, prompting the full compliance to be effective immediately. They then proceeded to take the precious baby away from his worrying father's caress and crying mother's arms and brought him out to where he was supposed to be from five minutes ago, the Grey Chamber.

The room was almost empty, and nothing was standing in between a long apparatus in the middle and the entrance. The odd machine almost looked like an adult human bed in size to sleep in but covered in a rather confiscated archetypal ceiling. If you were there, as too I was only as far as being told to see it, you might think it looked like one of those white coffins out there - but instead of the dead, the living was to go inside.

Unlike the name, there was nothing silver about the place even when one scanned through the room one day long everything around. Even the machine was all covered in white for crying out loud. So, why would they even call it Grey?

"Please put the baby in here," one junior female scientist with almond eyes behind her spectacles and a small waist behind her oversized white lab coat, in her pride ordered the two troopers, in which they immediately had done even before she finished her sentence. Well, they did this before anyway, many times - the only thing they were allowed to do before being ordered to leave the chamber as soon as possible.

The newborn that still smelled like innocence had fallen gently into the enclosed giant scanner like he was a drop of rain dribbling down a gigantic leaf as his body moved side to side accordingly when the machine detected a living inside. The little boy fell half asleep thereafter, as a soothe-calming lullaby was played and managed to intrigue his tranquil state. Strangely, his body then went on like he was in a nightmare as his body was shaking to the left and right again with a different bustling lullaby, then sweet dreams as he cooled down back to another peaceful lullaby, but afterward back to the familiar cycle and so on about twenty-seven times more. Meanwhile, it was then up to the scientist to further supervise the screen's movements for a result – finalized, generated by the scanner.

Oddly enough, she did not look as excited about this great mysterious task of hers as the person in charge of something important she had thought she wanted. Yes, her expression clearly said, "I did ask for this, but I never thought I would very much hate to do it." She also looked rather tired, not as much as physically, but almost as if the routine bored her to death. Perhaps, because it really felt like that. Actually - let me rephrase that, it must have been so, as I was told.

When the female lab technician first took on the duty, this duty in which details her predecessors had sworn to never tell anyone but the chosen circle, she thought that it would be a challenge, brain teaser of some sorts, because that was what everyone kept talking about. The secrecy, complexity, and seemingly intensity the *brain*, as how they said it in short, had to offer at first invited the young and ambitious mild genius to do whatever it took to get her to the position as close as possible to the *brain*, and she made clear that it was for her surroundings to see how exceptional she was to be one.

The prestige she had received from the title fortunately was more than enough to keep her dejection to the low whenever she stepped out of the chamber, from the fact that it only costed her slight energy given for a touch of a button and not a clever more to operate the brain scanner, and that it was far from complicated unlike perceived by the rest. It was the only upside for her, that no one outside the circle was to know anyway of how she operated them, and since very few were in charge, they could swear on each other to tell, not lies, but of a blurry blossomed truth. Even after many months, she was still far away from knowing even a glimpse of how the brain scanner really worked, or what made its result beyond accurate, which she never told anyone in the pretense of confidentiality.

Yes, being inside the circle was not enough, unless one was a part of those who drew the line. The intention was like so, so that how the brain machine worked, was to remain a hidden parlor of infinite possibilities. The truth was, the brain was always ready, just that its unlimited capacity needed to be fed with more and more results on a daily basis by those like the newborn or even the young female scientist for instance, or rather disobedient troopers, percipient yet oblivious; and what research you might ask?

"He's passed the test," the scientist bellowed out the ruling to herself when the machine showed a familiar coded color, not so much of a shout as her energy seemed to have already been swallowed by the boring routine.

The test was going on for about thirty minutes and to a positive result: the baby was to be brought back to his parents, who called themselves the Daggers. Bolin and Maccush were standing just outside the chamber the whole time, waiting. Their hearts were screaming in joy afterward that their speed was twice as fast and thrice as hazardous on their way back to the anxious parents. Fortunately, the baby made it safely to his parents' arms once again.

The relieved mother and father were so happy, that they almost immediately forgot to ask in detail what the test did to their son. All they knew, his brain was being scanned, but that was pretty much what everyone else had known too whenever a newborn was taken away. Just a few short hours later however, the Daggers realized that they might have been few of the luckiest to have their baby back, as they walked out of the comfortable labor room encountering an unexpected commotion.

"This is not my baby!" A couple was screaming in destruction and throwing a scene, that the Daggers could not help but stop their steps, while at the same time tucking their baby's ears from the drama.

Bolin and Maccush, who were just walking behind the Daggers, did not miss the chance of using their badges, the cool way, to approach the scene right away. As they looked at the couple closely, they realized that they were too the ones who brought their baby to the Grey Chamber and back to the couple.

The mother who in her misery could still discern which trooper's heart was softer than the other, grabbed Bolin by the shoulder and whispered to his ear only, "They took my baby! They thought I would not know, but they were wrong. I'm a mother, mother always knows," that was before three other guards took the outré couple away from the speechless Bolin and Maccush. Maccush felt sorry for Bolin's still-bewildered expression that he gently tapped the young man on the shoulder and said, "Let's go."

As Bolin knew he was one of the tested babies, he started to think if his parents were real and if the place was genuine, as he walked back to the changing room. He began to feel sorry and guilty for the couple too as he could still hear the mother's scream echoing in the hall.

Just before he could spread his arms after all the knobs sewn onto his top garment had been unbuttoned, the speaker had already cried out his and his partner's name. Their presence was anticipated outside the Grey Chamber immediately. After hearing the announcement, Maccush straight away approached the frozen Bolin who had been standing in the back of his own locker all along. While he was still zipping back up his pants, he said his second "Let's go," except this time, he had no idea why.

The two soft-hearted troopers sauntered into the chamber as requested and saw the same female scientist except this time, her expression indicated a lot of enthusiasm. Her voiceless mouthing showed, "This must be important," as she was accompanied by two widely known salient figures, a lead scientist named Gerald Powlett in the room and the captain of the troopers who called himself Gore for a reason. It was also clear to anyone that Gore was not just a leader of the troops, but pretty much everything else after that.

"Failure to a system begins with its part's first neglect of the rules, no matter the cause. You, as part of the system, should have known that better than anyone isn't," the captain spoke in a mixture of rumble and disappointment. The two troopers did not know what to respond except for their sweats quietly sliding from their temple onto their neck in a continuous motion.

Bolin and Maccush were then asked to enter the Grey Chamber and later the machine one by one, the second time for the young and first for the older. The funny thing was, the feeling was the same, exactly, for both; the level of nervousness, they were the same, connecting in between. When the process was going, it was like having the most pleasant dream, followed by a nightmare, but ended with equanimity.

Unexpectedly afterward, both then were taken to another chamber, unknown of the name, to enter a very similar machine with full resemblance in sight, with Bolin came first and Maccush later.

"I've never brought anyone, any baby, to a second machine before," Bolin felt reluctant to the conundrum theory waiting for his apprehension, but the scientist urged him that there was no other way but to move forward. He needed to step into the seemingly twin apparatus, or else, there would not be any ground for him to walk on to; figuratively, she insisted. By this point, he had already forgotten about the probability of him not being the child of whom he always called mom and dad, as he felt the unknown he was about to set foot in was bringing in a greater deal of uncertainty.

As soon as he entered, he asked the female in charge with widened and trembling eyes, "What does this one do?"

In response, she closed the lid of the machine with silence.

VII

Chapter Seven

Almost There

When Bolin came out of the large scanner, two guards were already waiting for him on the other side of the door. The green uniform he was wearing was no longer his as he was requested nicely to swap it out with a brown color, not at all like the guard's outfit he was accustomed to. It was later clear to him that he was to be moved to a different division - that must be the only reason why, he thought.

One guard was walking in front of Bolin while the other at the back, perhaps to make sure he was not going anywhere other than where he was supposed to be. Bolin did not really know them, but he might have seen them once or twice in the break room. Before they reached the unknown destination however, they had stopped by a door very familiar to Bolin.

Why was not it, for inside was where he and his parents slept in.

"What did you do?" His mother, while she was walking, whispered her cured fish roe breath from a fancy dinner she had earlier, and it was tingling enough to Bolin's left ear for him to shake his shoulder off immediately; much to a no comment from his father, an inexplicable big man, who had been voiceless with their fifteen-minute journey, well except for his eyes. His eyes had said it all, that "I swear to God, if you've done anything that makes them kick us out of here, I'm going to kill you myself."

To their surprise, they were taken to a construction division, with a view that hugged Bolin's father by the heart, reminding him of the days he built a small house near a wild giant tree colony that had a shape of a cooked broccoli each. He had always found joy in building things, but as things got hard, really hard, with cannibals on the loose, followed by a burning forest that almost brought the family along with the unborn Bolin to death when the fire swallowed their home, they had no choice but to surrender their freedom to a restricted protection, before Bolin was born, when they got the choice. That included the hopeless thought that Bolin's father had, that he would never have the chance to pursue his long-lost passion again, exchanging it for a green guard uniform that passed down to his only son, until then.

"We're building a new sector here, you two will figure out eventually what to do, and you Mam, you'll be in the kitchen duty just like before," one of the guards told the confused family a very summarized plan the exact same way he was ordered to, and as they were showed into their new room, the exact same size but with a completely different layout to where they had been for the past twenty years, they wondered if the day of all the people there, including them, could finally come out from the safe dark would arrive.

"They're expanding, must be that the world out there is still a hopeless madness," the biggest man in the room spoke up his opinion, and his son and wife seemed to agree with the hypothesis.

The next morning, Bolin and his father made their first appearance in the uncompleted wide space, divided by many potential rooms with the same size. The site was full of people who knew what they were doing, his father could tell too just by looking, but Bolin could not think of a way for him to fit in. He began to grasp that his new contribution would be nothing like what he could do before, bringing a baby back and forth the chamber. That previous duty he had was hard on the mentality, but not so much in the physical state. This one, it would be the other way around, he thought.

The father and son were then brought to an empty room, seemingly the same size as the room they lived in. "This should be a new home unit, and if you're doing a great job, this could easily be yours," the supervisor of the whole construction gave his command and then on his way out to leave the two sinking in his order. He stopped first before letting himself out, however, to say, "Oh, and go crazy."

Bolin was clearly lost in whatever he was supposed to be

doing with the empty space as he looked around, but when he saw his father, he knew that the person he was not entirely sure if he should really call 'Dad' at that moment, was screening the area and adding pictures in his mind of what he wanted it to be.

"What should we do... Dad?" Bolin whispered to the man who appeared to be dreaming in reality, and the man held both of his cheeks with his cold hands and said, "I'm going to tell you the story of how I built a house from scratch; 'Again?' I know, but this time Son, I am going to show you how to do it too. Plus, you're going to help me."

What started out as a theoretical session in a room full of shared construction tools to a practical in the blank canvas of an empty unit, the father and son duo was breaking sweats in joy, and they were forming stronger bonds between themselves as well as around the division more than they thought they ever could, as they were enjoying and treating their duty almost like a hobby. Whenever they went back to their room, they had never been happier as a family sitting down together in a living room exchanging stories of the day.

"I never thought of a construction as an art, really, but now I do. Why have they just assigned this now? Why not, oh I don't know, twenty years earlier?" Bolin's comment lit up laughter across the dining table. Good one Bolin, his parents thought. They all seemed to enjoy doing the new tasks and life they were given, and they were loving each other so much more than before, that Bolin's next opinion warmed their hearts, "I'm so grateful with this downgraded life we're having."

"It's not a downgrade, Son. Why do you even think that? It's never a downgrade if we're still happy and together. It's a good change," his father responded in a very gentle voice, and if Bolin had not opened the sentence with 'I'm so grateful', his tone would have been totally different to an irritated side. How dare his son to think of one of his favorite things in the world as a downgrade. Her mother further responded by holding his left hand and said, "Thus may I say, an upgrade."

Bolin and his father continued talking about the progress they made for the day, and what they planned to do the next day. It was obvious that they were unconsciously excluding the mother from the conversation, but she did not mind, for the moment was the greatest gift the change had brought to her life. When she saw the eyes of both the two people she loved all her life, she could not help but cut the conversation by holding her son's hand again and said, "You are so much like your dad, sometimes it's hard to differentiate between the two of you," as she then looked at her husband to see him gleaming in a forced-hidden smile.

Bolin wished he could tell her how much he needed to hear what his mother had just said, but he could not because he never wanted his parents to know the reason. What was he thinking? Bolin thought to himself, and then he smiled believing immediately that there was no way he was not theirs. The possible character destruction that might occur from the idea of him not being their real son depuffed as soon as his parents hugged him afterward. The love of his parents and the stronger bond they had as a family, as it appeared, made the evil seed blown away from his mind for good, and they continued the dinner with a silence and smile on their face this time. Something the brain scanner had succeeded to discover and advise.

"By the way, what happened with your partner before; Maccush is his name, isn't it?" Her mother spoke of the first thing that occurred in her mind to break the silence. Bolin almost forgot about him, but as he heard his name, he began to wonder if their disobedience also led Maccush to a better life like he did get.

When Maccush came out of the second brain scanner, two guards were also already standing in front of the unnamed chamber. He was only given a warning about how he should have acted according to the order, however then sent to the usual break room instead and was told to wait for a newborn to be delivered. Once they left, the wait seemed just like another day for him except that he was alone and had no idea if things afterward would be as normal as before or not. What happened to Bolin, he wondered, and the uncertainty was the only thing filling his mind to kill the time.

The speaker suddenly spoke of an order for him and his partner to go to a baby delivery room number five, but wait, the announcement did not stop there.

"New partner, Collin," the speaker sounded a bit noisy, but Maccush was sure that he did not hear it wrong. It was confirmed as an unfamiliar guy walked into the room. From the introduction, it was let known that the guy was new in the duty and how he looked forward to it, something Maccush was sure that this new partner of his would grow tired of eventually.

As they walked together, Maccush occasionally stopped familiar guard faces to ask if they had any idea what happened to Bolin, but none of them knew the answer. However, then came one of the guards who accompanied Bolin and his family to the construction side of the hidden premises, but as he was already instructed to never tell, his mouth was correctly enclosed to the order. However, his eyes incorrectly suggested that something bad had happened to Bolin as he was acting out of the ordinary to make sure he was not propounding anything in where, as a result, he was implying the worst.

Maccush turned silent after that. No matter how Collin talked non-stop about every little thing he could think of, trying to get a response from his supposedly mentor (Collin turned out to be an extremely chatty person by the way), Maccush just ignored him thereafter and kept thinking about a possible outcome for the precariousness rising mostly from his worries for Bolin. Who knew? That uncertainty could work and add more fear, better than a fact.

What he was indeed sure of, since then, his brain was scared of disobedience, and he promised himself to never allow him to loosen up on the regulation anymore. This was proven to be right when he immediately took the baby away from that room number five to the Grey Chamber regardless of the infant's parents' cry, and he subsequently warned the new mentee to always follow procedure. The words that he used were not as scary, not so much as the expression when he actually said it, as a deep line creasing his face when he warned Collin, almost like he was telling a horror story that no one ever got to know the ending.

The progress of Bolin and Maccush was reported by two junior scientists who had been secretly following their movement, who then reported it to Gerald, a stubby middle-aged man with round glasses on top of his chubby cheeks, who was one of the two lead scientists. He was informed that the two brain scanners had successfully given the exact same outcome and forecasted the right attitude *once again* for misconduct behaviors to the regulation, as well as the appropriate treatments, in which the latest test was based on Bolin and Maccush's case.

Good news for Gerald was that the brain scanner had then been proven to work not only for babies, but for young children and adults too. As a result, he could not prevent his shady moustache from dancing with the wind as his breath that came out from his pale pointy nose was going in and out of the ordinary sequence from the impatience to tell the big boss what he heard.

Another lead scientist, Meng Holmes was much happier for the fact that he was finally successful in duplicating the chip of the brain that had been threatening his head to go all-bald from a few strands of black hair he got left. His slanted eyes were almost seen as gone even when he chuckled, if it had not been for the eyeglasses he was wearing that had been show-casing all along he had still got them there somewhere behind.

"Would this be enough?" Gerald asked hoping that his co-worker would say yes but considering how much of a perfectionist his lab partner was, it was only expected that Meng would say, "No, we need more samples, just to be sure. However, we're almost there."

Gerald, who had been more on the impatient side to get to the goal, responded, "Alright, but I'll report this anyway to the chief."

"I will do it as always, you just stay here," he added, and Meng just responded with silence.

VIII

Chapter Eight

The Founder

A spacious home unit was free from disturbance. It was set so as the particular area was built on the best side of the whereabouts. Best in accordance with the brain scanner results that showed how probably more virtuous they were compared to their surroundings.

A part of the atelier was dominated with a pile of drafts that focused on something that was almost a potential symbol like. All were drawn in some stone-recycled papers that were with a growing habit of their master to reuse for his precious helpers to spend as little time as possible in the outside world. What it seemed like, living with a growing small population and limited resources had been forcing him unconsciously to think and do like so - recycling, even with the smallest things in life.

The outline drawn on the paper was a round solid figure, and the inside manifested the current land right in the center, shaped like a reniform leaf with no splitting, with only one color - snow instead of the color of a soil. The outside color of the white terra firma was just like the ocean at sunset, dark blue with a sunlight filter. In the bottom right side, two words were handwritten in an italic manner, '*The World*'.

The room belonged to the founder of the substantially large underground safehouse that was divided between functions and brain scanner results. His name was none other than Hayes Beckett for a reason. Just like his father when he was young, the man had the smallest nose and blackest hair, but his oval-shaped face and a slightly rounded jaw had managed to balance them all. His father was indeed Homeron, who first created the brain chip that was ideally invented to make a difference in the world that was going mad with no clarity between who was good and who was evil.

Hayes was turning fifty-two, but never a day went by without him thinking that he was twenty years younger - the point in time in his past where he was getting his vision that was miraculously brought by the wind while he was sitting inside of what seemed to be a cave peculiarly floating under the sky, or it could all just be his own hopeful imagination. The fact became blurry to him as the ex-cave was long gone when he needed to see it again to keep on believing. Not to mention, he was constantly distracted with the need for survival.

Still, he had typed those words months and months into lengthy pages about his quondam belief and spiritual research of why the earth had turned unpredictable and wreaked havoc, further dubious implicit desire for bending powers inspired from a childish drawing on a rock wall, before he realized that his book had been brushed aside by the majority for it was being considered *nonsense* - making him thankful for his insecurity for putting only his initials on the cover. What he did not realize however, the minority existed and grew eventually. They called themselves '*The Earth*' the way Hayes always referenced it in his book, without his full intention to do so.

One once said that you could lose your head if you lost your aim, or that persistence would make all the difference, but Hayes could not say that he never tried his best on both, because he did, the hardest he knew how. Still, he was losing his head as he went out of the forest covered in blood from what he still believed he did right. It was in the middle of hopelessness and loneliness, courage to let himself out to the danger and not afraid to die, that he accidentally found some sort of a secret wide passage underneath the ground.

He was chased by some modern men turning wild, wanting his flesh for breakfast as they ran out of animals who had mostly died from the natural abruption like most of the humans had too. He was so desperate to stay alive that he went back to the dark forest, the one he once swore to never go in again. The panting in the midst of the wind growing cold and hungry for a victim followed by a familiar tenebrosity forced him to go paranoid from the wind that could kill. The next thing he knew was that his cheeks were scratched by the next killer in his mind, twigs, and in one of those bushes the trees had led him into, his back fell first to an uneven ground with a small, rounded metal lump on its surface. As it seemed, the knob had been in a deep-freeze from the cold temperature and the only way to open it was to break the ice from the outside.

Never a day went by without him remembering what he had seen the first time he entered, as he strolled down the hall-way of what was in his present a corridor towards his mega meeting room, he still sometimes saw the safe passage as covered in seemingly countless bodies that had been accidentally trapped and died from hunger. The way he recalled it, he had been nowhere sane before he first entered, that oddly enough he slowly got his mind back seeing what could have been of him, a corpse. He thought that there were so many of the dead that it seemed like he was the only one left on earth and his life was felt invaluable. He trusted that he was regaining hope from seeing the dead, instead of the other way around, simply because he was still standing, very much alive. Little did he know, it was his ambition that kept him strong from his barely breathing physique, a clear goal he visioned when he found the safehouse, that he could still do something to perhaps save the entire new world of good people.

He never knew who first built the bunker with spaces that almost seemed unlimited, one he promised to thank in the afterlife, but he was sure he was at least the second to have the idea of hiding trusted-sane people deep in the ground safely. Alas, he left his old idealistic belief that people could one day control the elements of the earth, the wind for instance, and instead he chose to give in to the wind by persevering through it.

The tall man started by removing those bodies one by one with his bare hands, thousands of them, to the upper ground, and then gave himself a reward by eating one leaf every time a body was successfully lifted to the surface. When he was lucky, there would be a drop of rain left on the leaf to hydrate his dried heart-shaped lip and dehydrated goat moustache. Nevertheless, he did not wish for rain, at least not until he had got all the corpses out of the chamber, since the rainfall would add another weight to the extremely skinny bone lifting another rotten flesh on his shoulder.

One thousand and seventy six was the figure he came into once he got the last body out of every part of the underground passage, assuming his brain did not miss any. Not only that, but he also found out, though such a safehouse below ground looked incredibly capacious and endless, it still led to nowhere as he reached the conclusion that seemed unfinished. He never got to know too if it was built to lead somewhere or simply to hide as many as possible. However, he did not just stop there, as he still needed more things to get the place running. To get the supplies he needed, he had to risk his life by going out of the foul-smelling barrier area he built from the remains he pulled up to the ground, and thus, he never wasted even a single item he brought in.

Most of these corpses had started to rot and multiple times his body could not stand the smell that he just passed out. Forget about spirits, by that point, he did not care anymore if he was to be haunted by ghosts, for all he knew was that he wanted to give the living, more than thousands of them if he could - selected individuals he saw good and trust gleaming from their eyes, a chance to survive. That or he just simply got used to the cold bodies that he fell onto from time to time.

This, all of these, were no longer some words people did not bother to read. These were his new words yet to be spoken but could be taken straight into actions to be heard. A revolutionary, started from his frantic run, blooded hands, and smelly torso which story and evidence had convinced the first few hundred people he ran into hiding to join him instead for a safer life, those who trusted him nimbly as their judgement was already impaired with 'what could possibly be worse'. As decades went by, the story went down in history among them.

It took slowly more than a while from then to what it phenomenally became, including some intellectuals who finally figured out how to avoid being locked up inside by the cold stuck knob, or how to set disguised surveillance in the air to give them eyes in the light while they were hiding, but the underground was eventually seen as a small heaven below surrounded by hell in the upper ground; the hell - not for long they wished. With the good place's own judicial system built by a man trusted to men, they were waiting for the right moment to strike devils. All the good and hopeless men on earth left, tired of being hunted, were dying to know the way to where it was, if they had to first believe in its existence.

"Daddy, daddy?" A chiming voice of a little girl woke Hayes

up from the past as they were walking side by side. She was almost a perfect resemblance to Hayes, if it had not been for the two dimples and brown hair she got from her mother, and much shorter.

He was unintentionally recalling the past as he was walking in the corridor with his family towards one of the bunker's mini dining halls. Not all parts of the story were horror, but he could not help it when a portion of it was so disturbing, that he could not just unsee dead bodies in the currently clean metallic hallway. Luckily, his awareness was brought back to earth by his daughter's calling, who was confused when the figure who had never once said no to her request no matter how bizarre, left her hanging with her wish for a simple ice cream.

The leader, who was now far from both skinny and obese, always enjoyed the company of his dear family. A daughter he would die for in half a second, a wife no man and woman could ever replace her with, his wife's twin that he treated as his own brother, and the son of his so-called brother he loved as one of his own.

Hayes, his family, and twenty other people he called as his beloved friends gathered in one area with the most delicious smell coming from its upper center side of the middle, they called it simply the canteen. There were a couple more there but surely, the one where Hayes and the bunch hung out all the time was the best of all, only because it was unlocked for people that defined themselves as 'angels and associates', such as Hayes the founder, his executives and their relatives as well as philosophers, scientists, heroes and other intellectuals alike.

Some of these academics were developing pioneering ideas in many categories, hoping they would make a quick difference once they could settle in the upper ground. The angels had what they called their warriors too allowed to eat there, but they were never to enter if they looked like one for a reason. As for the rest, who were the inhabitants and inside troopers, they had to stick themselves to the other mess hall.

One might think that the lower part of the 'good' hierarchy who passed the test to stay there was treated worse, with less choices of food and smaller bedrooms et cetera but no, they were not at all. In fact, every single person established as 'good ones' by the brain thus passed the test to live safely in the hidden sanctuary, was eating the same kind of food, with the same portion and even distribution, and living in the exact same size of home unit as the founder. The only difference between them was who really knew the true existence of the *warriors* and *prisoners*, and who did not, and those who did, made them higher because of the horrible things they could see as a consequence, and the higher risk these elites were exposed to as part of their duty. This excluded the mega meeting room, of course, but that was about it.

They were all living with limited resources and to retrieve them would require these warriors' limitless sacrifices, similar to going to a war, but instead, against cannibals and unexpected natural disruptions, and thus even the elites were adjusting. This however did not apply to Siva, Hayes' only daughter, who always preferred to have her long brown hair braided, for her father would constantly give up a portion of his meal for her. He loved her so much, too much to be exact, and he showed the same kind of love to his wife. To her brother, he treated him as if he were his own brother with no ulterior motive, and to his friends, he never wanted to see any of them not having a good time when he was around. He was however a bit hard on Zirilo, his so-called nephew, but that was because he saw himself in the little boy and unconsciously expected him to grow not like his father, but him, for he never had a son. They were all the big family Hayes got left with, the strength for everything he had been working so hard for was charged from their prosperity and safety too, and for that, his lips bended temporarily forming a shape of salted water coming towards the shore as he was looking at them, happy.

His smile stopped briefly, however, when he saw Zirilo, the hazel eyes and black mushroom hair little boy, and his green and red leafy mix salad that was moved around with his spoon and about to take off from the silver plate to a scrap destination. The little boy could tell from the brief look of the man he called 'uncle', that he had no other choice but to finish them, so he did a little trial by 'accidentally' swinging half of the salad to land on the floor.

Knowing how much the chief never wanted anything to be left wasted, plus how fake the 'little accident' was, everyone stopped everything they were doing, which soon gave rise to the quietness of the space. They were all curious about what Hayes was going to do, including the little boy's father.

Hayes stood up silently and brought both of his feet towards the side of Zirilo's chair, with his fork still stuck between his two fingers. He bent down his right knee, picked up those wasted leaves with his right hand, and put them in his mouth. "Next time this happens again, you need to do this," he said, much to a quiet response from the speechless boy.

He got back to his chair, and after taking a deep one or two breaths, continued his apparent disappointment on the behavior by asking, with full eye contact to his plate which still had some food left, "This is the third day of the fourth week, isn't it? So, the timing is just right for you children to come with me."

"They're not ready to see that kind of scene, dear," Hayes' wife issued her worries, but instead of saying anything to calm her down, Hayes briefly touched her left palm and saw through her eyes for a moment. She knew by then; his mind was made up.

"Siva, Zirilo, it is time for you to see the work of our warriors."

IX

Chapter Nine

Four Missions of The Warriors

The underground safehouse was never clear of its floorplan when being looked at from one limited point of view. However, if it were to be seen from the center above, and if these eyes could just penetrate the soil to get a better look, they would be shown of its shape. It was something similar to a sleeping helical staircase that was going nowhere to the right from the entrance, indeed very odd.

What was the architect trying to say?
I too sometimes wonder.

In every metallic tread and riser of the stairs-resemblance, there were many little rooms all in the same size. If it was one unit, it would be for a home of one family - with a small living room even included. Some units are combined to make a public space for all in their assorted classifications such as the canteen, or private prerequisite such as the leader's study room, often used as those decision makers' meeting room.

There was only one entrance to the bunker - one way in and one way out. When one went through, the first room would be found to be used as a waiting hall for potential inhabitants. The executives were always careful on who they chose next to potentially dwell in the safe house, so the room was never cramped. Next to it was probably the cleanest of all, the delivery room fit for five families in labor, for it was instantly scrubbed as soon as a baby was born, ready for the next. Then, there were countless home units for newcomers of the lower part of the good hierarchy, followed by a small infirmary, and then the Grey Chamber, just hiding at the back of a separate door.

Where the chamber was in between, was two wideout-curved door barricades (due to the winding course of every hallway) followed by the same sequence for the higher rank in the hierarchy, where Hayes and his family lived too. The section was then followed by another similar barricade. These blockades made one not able to go to the Grey Chamber or another division so easily, as their task was always limited to which part that they were in. After that, however, was another (but shorter) sequence for the lower pecking order once more who had been moved there for a reason, such as Bolin and his family, making the 'angels and associates' to perch in the middle. The construction was happening on the edge of that last part of the bunker.

At nearly the edge of the glorious middle section, there was a confined room full of darkness. Hayes meant to keep them there regardless, instead of throwing them back out to the cruel world. He still had hope that he could still find the light in them, as long as he did not give up.

This top-secret room was only known to those who lived in the middle, the angels, including the warriors, their associates, who lived in four different rooms, in which that dark room was in between those four warriors' home for a reason. One of their missions, unknown to many others, was to successfully bring those who did not pass the test there, in or out but so far never out, those who the brain classified as 'with evil intentions'. This was harder than it sounded, for umpteen prisoners always rejoiced whenever new ones came, as they always tried altogether to break through the steels like mad bulls when they were opened. In addition, the limited space did not allow Hayes to build a soundproof jail more than one. This was also why the Grey Chamber was located close to the middle, and restricted with doors, so they could still not be seen from the others who had not seen what they had secretly been hearing as rumors.

When those particular people came with their family, it was highly likely that their family would come to the dark with them too, regardless of their own good mark retrieved from the scanner, but not always - if they could swear on keeping the secrets. Although, it had become just a little bit wide known. That was why the executives always preferred those new families with baby bumps, maybe to start fresh they thought.

However, in paradox, that was why too, still, they had to always squeeze their brains very hard in selecting which righteous people to live and work *with* them. It was to seek that hiding wicked standing among the good too, because the machine was, later on, always able to find that impurities were always without guarantees, but if it could still be avoided otherwise, it would have saved them the time, energy, and space.

Never *for*; everyone knew, everyone was working for themselves, in exchange from their contribution to make each other stay alive they got to stay safely underground, and the law and order was what differentiated them from the chaotic world outside - that they knew was the reason for their safety as well.

The warriors' duties were not limited to enforce the law and protect the people underground, with three and a quarter of them not even sure they existed. They were humans too, of course, but it was clear from their appearance what they were fighting against that made them different from the others there.

The eye that was left alone as one, the cheek and arm that was sculpted painfully by the human-form monsters in the upper ground, the leg that was half-rotten from the bite of the devils, even the mental health that was distorted from the nightmares inspired by those terrors they witnessed in their real life. The horror in their giant physical bodies screamed torment just for simple edibles, and how that food scarcity brought about the almost-end of humanity when they were no longer easy to find. Something Siva and Zirilo would soon acknowledge.

In the middle of the night when everyone else had locked themselves from the inside as they were instructed to, Hayes took them both, along with two of his friends and their wives, to one of the four warrior rooms that was closer to the prison from the left. It also just happened that few of the lights were blinking on their way.

While they were getting their battledress and gears ready to literally fight for food in blood as their next mission, it was later revealed that two of the warriors were sons of Hayes' friends he brought along, one of them called himself Pyralis by last name. Their parents could not contain their feeling in how they were both scared and proud of them by hugging them so tight like they were never going to let go.

"Wouldn't those plants we have here be enough? I'm sure that's already enough food for everyone here," one of the mothers was either talking to Hayes or her son that he was looking at the whole time. She was probably right, but her son held the woman's hands gently and moved them from his chest to hers, and replied, "It still needs to be done, Mom, and soon we'll be living out there again, a new world in peace."

Hayes' tears fell onto the iron floor. He formed solid rocks on both of his hands, swore every single time that the moment would sooner or later come when the warriors finally completed their third mission, unknown to even anyone else but Hayes - that they were to kill every single cannibal out there without mercy, even in the midst of unforgiving natural disasters. It was necessary, no matter who they were before their turn, or The World would never see the sunlight again, if there was no heart to end it.

Hayes and the two children, as well as the warriors walked towards the waiting hall quietly. Once they reached, one of the warriors pulled out what looked like a wide handle downward, and one pair of lenses that looked like those in binoculars was unfolded. One anonymous handsome fellow with a long stab mark just at the top of his right dimple (those two small depressions on his cheeks only appeared when he smiled), screened the area as apparently shown by another set of lenses above the ground for any legs - that was how high they could adjust it. He then suggested a clear signal from those dancing fingers on his right hand. The other guy apparently had been checking for any signals the whole time from numerous sensors put in about one kilometer radius length, just enough to give them time to open and close the entrance if there were enemies approaching nearby it. When he too gave a clear signal, they were ready to twist hard the knob and open the round sleeping port.

One by one came out via the ladder but before it was the captain's turn to climb, Hayes grabbed him gently by the arms to remind him something utterly important, "Don't forget to bring that family we've talked about, here," and that was the fourth mission of the warriors, to bring the chosen ones left up there to safety underground.

Once they all set out safely, they closed the portal again

from the outside this time and proceeded carefully and quietly on their assignments. The entrance was hidden in plain sight, camouflaged as part of the soil beneath the bushes, in hope they would never be found or ruined by the bad men and women. Water sprinkler was installed in the surroundings too to prevent or mitigate potential forest fire, because most of the fruits and vegetables were taken from it, also so that the portal could stay hidden by the bushes and trees around.

"The post-apocalypse has brought us limited resources and painful necessity to hunt for food for survival, as what our brave warriors are doing right at this very moment. We will stay here until they return," Hayes' words gave shivers to the two children who still had not known what they were to expect. He held his daughter's hand and walked to the edge of the wall, then sat down with Siva on his lap. Zirilo followed and spread his legs onto the floor too just like what his uncle did, then the three of them waited patiently in nervous silence, while two other junior warriors a couple of meters away from them were on standby guarding the hall.

There were ten warriors in action for the night. Corpse barriers from a long time ago had to be removed because the rotten smell had become deadly and they managed to kill one of their own, as well as many other cannibals. Thus, they had their big weapons ready and steady in their arms for what might come even as soon as they were out of the portal.

Nine of them followed the captain who was leading at the front whilst the familiar sound of dead branches being stepped on by twenty boots traveled to their ears and still startled their brave hearts in every pace. Their sweats were racing to flow down to their necks even though it was cold, before their feet could reach the end and out of the forest, but just a couple steps before they did, two hungry men and one woman suddenly jumped out of the dark from one of the trees onto one warrior's shoulders each. The two men started to hit the two warriors - one was the one in charge of the radar, with their devilish knives, multiple times in the upper body.

One of the three who was that of Hayes' friends' son, the Pyralis, was bit by the woman on the ear instead. Once she started to swallow the thin flesh out of his helix like she was eating sushi, he managed to punch the distracted hungry lady until she fell onto the ground. The young warrior hesitated on firing the bullet onto her head, at a glance she looked like a puppy when she was scared, not until his captain did it himself with that long look of "I've done this before and trust me, it was for the best; thus, you should have too."

The seven other warriors managed to gun the two other cannibals to die quickly. Just after two seconds they had thought that was it, they heard the sound of running steps, a typical sound telling them more than three cannibals were definitely coming.

The captain hurriedly ordered four of his best and luckily uninjured warriors - one of them was that handsome fellow good with the lenses, to run to complete the fourth mission, and the two others to bring the two warriors severely injured by the cannibal men back to the underground.

Down in the safe ground, Siva was already falling asleep

with and in his father's lap while Zirilo was still wide awake, just moving his body front and back on and on. The little boy was still thinking of how one or two salad leaves had come to this, though it was definitely more than that in number. It was not much of the anger that terrified him, but the long disappointment of his uncle, the man he looked up to even more than his own father. The boy had always been impressed with him, how he founded the sanctuary, his vision about the new world, and how he led them all to safety; he too wanted to be just like him one day, or even better if he could, his mind whispered.

That night the boy knew one more thing about Hayes, how much he hated waste, in any kind. His thought was distracted however, when a loud commotion was heard, waking Hayes and Siva. It sounded like the warriors were hopelessly trying their best to open the knob from the outside though it was never locked back, as fast as they could. It was already disrupting until gunshots began to monopolize the noise, much worse.

The two warriors inside had already been climbing to unlock one that was really locked, on the inside, even before the gunshot was heard, but when they did hear it, they whispered to each other, "Gunshots, that means they're near." Their movement unconsciously moved twice as fast from the usual. Once the portal was opened, their motion was thrice faster than before.

Hayes held tight the two children by his sides. He finally agreed with his wife when he eventually thought this was a lot more dangerous than usual, so he ran and led the little boy and girl to get behind the door inside to keep them safe so he could run back to help the two guards.

"Whatever happens, don't open this door on your own," Hayes warned the two children before he closed the door back.

Zirilo, being taller than Siva, managed to do otherwise slightly just for his curiosity to peek at what was still going on. He could see one familiar warrior coming down on his own but with a lot of blood on the side of his face, afterward, two uninjured with two more each at their shoulders being heavily wounded, then finally the captain.

Just when he managed to climb down and about to close round the portal, two cannibals snuck their heads in trying to bite the warrior. Their two hands were with knives too but it was just so lucky that the space was so narrow as it was about to be closed, so their hands and weapons could not reach the captain. He forced the port to close and so did their heads to get in, that what came next was incredibly disturbing when the captain managed to close it at the expense of two of what they called monsters' heads that fell down raining red onto the floor. They were all safe, finally, but still, the image was still incredibly terrifying to Zirilo who was still watching everything. Imagine the unforgettable. The view was out of his control to remain a magnet to his eyes, he discerned, so he screamed in his mind while his hands pressed his mouth tight to keep the silence.

When the door was opened in a dash, Zirilo was almost hit on the forehead for they did not count his peep in the rush. Zirilo hugged Siva to stand close to the wall and covered with his hand both eyes of the little girl who hugged him back, so she would not see what he saw.

The boy thought, after what he witnessed, he would be braver in seeing two injured men being carried away. Well, the other had already walked on his own all the way to the infirmary. When he saw another blood however, he could not stop thinking about the one that was still dripping from the portal, so he closed his eyes on his own terms with a little bit of tears. Hayes came in last and when he saw the two children in fear, he immediately knew he should have listened to his wife - the little boy and girl were not ready.

Why would he force them? They were just little kids. That and other similar sentences were all he could think of as he brought them back to their room to go to sleep. Siva could immediately. Zirilo too, but as soon as he fell asleep, he went down right to the nightmare.

The next morning, Hayes' family gathered again but this time on the small dining table in their home unit. It was just Hayes, his wife, her brother, Siva, and Zirilo. The little boy did not look so good since he opened his eyes that morning and it was all because of the falling heads being replayed over and over in his dream.

Two canteen servers came by the living room with breakfast, and just Zirilo's bad luck, it was meatballs in a soup. His little spoon trembled when two of those were hanging by its edge, and when one of them fell and splashed down the broth, all he could think about was the falling head.

He screamed at the top of his lungs, shocking everybody

around him. He knew when he saw those dying warriors that his perspective about the food on his plate and all would change. Leaving things would not be as easy as before but leaving no waste on them would never be a question. But oh, how it would have been a lot better if he had not seen that, that particular thing he could now never unseen, the horror.

Hayes seemed to get what was going on as he followed the little boy who went hiding in the tiny wardrobe in his room. He opened the wing slowly so as not to scare the one inside who hugged his leg thighs like he was being tied up.

"It's the blood, isn't it?" Hayes whispered as he sat down just in front of him. Zirilo shook his head.

"The noise?" Hayes gave his guess another try, but the little boy turned his head from side to side once more.

"The head, the corpse," the boy softly spoke.

"How do you... But we didn't lose anybody. Did you... never mind," Hayes didn't expect him to see what he thought he saw, "I... I'm sorry you have to see that," he continued with deep sorrow and regret from possibly tainting the little boy's childhood.

The silence lasted for a while before one of them decided to break it, the little one.

"What did you do with them?" Zirilo asked his uncle. He was scared, but apparently his curiosity managed to defeat it at last.

"What do you mean? What are you talking about?"

"The... the fallen heads."

Hayes' heart stopped beating for probably about a second

there. His fear was confirmed, he had his nephew see the worst kind of display anyone would have ever seen. He did not mean for it to happen, but he had to admit, even that was only less than half of the worst that could have happened. His brain got lost there for quite some time, until he realized it was already a while.

"I knew it. They're dead, there's no use of them anymore," Zirilo tapped his right knee while saying that.

"How about fossils? We need that," Hayes replied with uncertainty himself, he knew later that Zirilo could sense that too.

"You mean in ten thousand years? I'm sure, pretty soon the technology you're developing here will soon get rid of that too. There's no use of dead bodies anymore," Zirilo replied with a deeper voice. Hayes sometimes forgot how smart he was for someone of his age, and how interested he was in technology.

"Yet," Hayes responded, with stretched lips upward sincerely. He honestly did not know what he meant by that, and he did not see any use of corpses other than for medical research purposes. Zirilo's eyes however, bewildered by the three-letter word, and his eyes were widened thinking of a way.

Siva interrupted the wardrobe-bonding moment between the two males when she suddenly came into the room and hopped on Hayes' lap, saying "I don't want to be useless." As it turned out, she had been listening from the gap of the door, though she was not sure what Zirilo meant by 'the fallen heads'.

"You won't be, and you still have a long life in front of you, even longer than me. So, you don't have to worry about that now."

"You mean, you're not going to be with me forever?"

"Well, I don't know when my time is going to be up, sweetheart, but even when I'm gone, I'll always be here, in your memory. I'll never leave, there," and Hayes' pointy finger stroked Siva's right temple gently when he said 'there'.

"Do you promise, Daddy?"

"Of course, I do."

The conversation between the father and the daughter had warmed Zirilo's heart to a simmer heat. He somehow started to think about the injured warriors after that, and wanted to confirm himself before they all stood up and walked out of the room, so he asked, "By the way, so, about those dying warriors, they are going to be fine?" Hayes nodded with a tender smile and Zirilo jumped once to reflect his relief.

Zirilo snatched Siva from Hayes to go back to the dining room, and the daughter ran too following the boy's hand, but then she ran back to Hayes a few short seconds later, looking like she was forgetting something.

"And Daddy, I'll always be in here too, I'll never leave there." Siva touched Hayes' head exactly where he first pointed out hers, the same way, while exhibiting her innocent smile that illuminated his day before she ran back to her cousin.

Hayes went to his sleep with that picture of his lovely daughter's smile in his mind, and he too beamed in the dark on his bed with his wife by his side. His dream started out with a beautiful reverie of his daughter running free and safe in the upper ground, all sunny in the world free of miseries and dangers. What he did not expect, the pleasant dream was rigged however, by none other than a memory or a fear. He saw a figure in a shadow.

A strange man's steps were thumping in a hush under three blinking light bulbs as Hayes walked from behind in a chilly granary, but they were not the only ones who were blinking. One too could be seen from that person's hand, a strange object, and it blinked along with his movement following his silhouette. As the hand holding it rose up to visit the target, Hayes knew what it was, a knife.

But it was not just a knife, it looked almost customized if it was not rare. The knife was not as big as those ones that were used in the kitchen, no, this was rather tiny and friendly to any kind of pocket. The blade shaped like a flame in silver with a smooth tip, but the handle was molded from the waning crescent moon figure, with the color contrasting to the light.

Shortly moments later however, the knife was tainted with red spots of blood, as it swung by the part that connected the head to the rest of the body of the silhouette's target.

What was it all about?

X

Chapter Ten

Hayes and His Trusted Men

Hayes' eyes were unwrapped as quick as a bolt winning a race, but he did not seem to be petrified or even showed movement that was just a bit unusual. He had this nightmare almost every day that he did not even remember how it felt anymore not to have it.

One thing that he did only occasionally though was, instead of getting back to his sleep, he forced his shivering legs to get out of the fat blanket, walking slowly in midst of runway lights colony and his utmost silence to stand just in front of the door that led to the secretive prisons in where those who did not pass the test resided. He just stood there silently with his hands in the back and his head looking up just about twenty degrees forklifted. That very same spot in the upper ground he knew, there was an abandoned warehouse almost in complete ruin, where inside leant back a man giving out flesh thirty years long who would never ever see eye to eye on what lay exactly below the ground.

All of a sudden, Hayes could feel something was set on loose in the upper ground. It was the sound similar to a train moving on a track, but he perfectly knew there was not any but trees up there. If it were human beings, it would have not made as much (pressed) noise and quiver as so, unless perhaps it was a whole generation of both the good and the bad in shedload. The vibration though, was unfortunately loud enough to wake up the peaceful sleepers one by one, who mostly woke up from the tremble and not the sound.

His twisted string of reasoning was brought straight when the hallway lights on the wall were suddenly turned on, just a few. Some researchers passing their bedtime were having a hard time trying to choose between going to the left where they headed to or straight where they saw Hayes standing. They were confused whether Hayes was already expecting them, but if he was, wouldn't he just stand in front of their lab?

Hayes, knowing how odd his then predicament was, turned around and made his way to the lab too. There were so many rooms dedicated for testing grounds, something he believed would be of value in his concept of heaven on earth, that he almost walked into the wrong one.

"A... flood? In almost the dry season? Was there even an earthquake?" One scientist spoke of what he could not believe he saw, all covered in questions, from one of the hidden cameras installed on the inside of a tree.

"But it can't be. There's not supposed to be any soon. Is it a tsunami? But it still can't be," the other added with bewilderment.

"The earth is just acting up all weird again," the third of the bunch was fixing his glasses while saying so. He said it rather plainly, like it was normal. He probably got a point though, or he was just giving up in finding the answer. It was not like they had never seen any unexpected natural disaster before that, another before that, and another again before that.

Hayes however, had an explanation he long ago had perceived in his long-lost book, when he was still faintly near to the word nonsensical. Even as empirical as he had become, he still said, "There must be a lot of blood up there, Mother Nature is cleaning up her palette."

It took about a couple of hours until everything was under control. They were lucky enough that none of a single drop of water managed to come in underground and the oxygen stability was not compromised at all amidst the havoc commotion of the perfectly safe inhabitants everywhere they were. Their unified fear was perfectly understandable, considering if the place had gone down, none of them would have survived.

A couple of warriors, one with a long rifle and one without, went inside the hidden prison to check on the bars if they were still strong enough. The latter was barely hearing or looking at the prisoners while he was tapping on those unbreakable rolled steels cooked up by a team of scientists, but unexpectedly, one of those about one hundred inmates was able to seize the opportunity by pulling the warrior's head close to the cell with the intention to speak words onto his ear, saying, "You're gonna leave us all here to die, aren't you?"

The other warrior who was staying away from the cells the whole time with his rifle, quickly pulled his partner back with his left hand while his right waved the weapon at them, scaring them away to move backward from the bars.

"You okay?" He made sure his partner was not traumatized, in which he nodded as a response. Nonetheless, little did he know that the moment those prisoner's words traveled through his ear, he could not bear to ignore their screams anymore.

"Set us free!"

"Better up there in fear than being locked up in here."

Those were just a few of many that combined into one summary of blood-curdling demand, to get them out.

Hayes, who saw the two troopers leaving the prison entrance and said nothing to him but bowing their head a little to the leader, expected that there was no problem from where they were, so he continued his walk to where the construction was happening.

He was greeted by Gore when he entered the incomplete section. Gore looked ordinary if his giant uniform-covered body was not counted. Everyone was sure that 'Gore' was not even his real name. When his face came into the light, and if one looked really closely, he or she would be able to see heavy concealer hiding a big scar on his face. It almost shaped like a big tree covering his whole right cheek with four leafless branches soaring through the sky, with the third from the left almost meeting his right eye, and he wished for no one to see it or know its source.

One could though, even without the light, and it was Hayes whose life was hanging by a thread until Gore, then warrior, risked his life to save him from the cannibals. They both managed to slip away from them, at the expense of Gore's smooth right cheek molded by the knife of the stranger. Since then, Hayes begged him to stay underground with him to lead an underground army he had just established, but not limited to. Hayes ever since trusted his judgement as a best friend and told him almost everything, almost. Furthermore, it was thereupon, that they both had formed the bond no one else even recognized, from an untold scar and unrevealed friendship, hushed by the two.

Gore was never really happy with the decision and privilege, well, other than the bond, for he thought a big scar on the cheek meant nothing compared to all the sacrifices the other warriors had made, even a life. However, he too never questioned the founder's way of thought, and so began to believe leading the underground troopers and being the founder's invisible advisor was necessary.

Hayes continued the conversation by asking how the construction was going. "Going well I suppose," Gore responded, "but don't know how long we can survive living below the ground. Some can, actually have turned crazy," he added.

The construction, once it was finished, was going to provide more rooms for more families that were successfully being brought in by the warriors, amounting to about two families from the same area per year, rescued in two different points in time. However, the renovation had reached its maximum capacity, and afterward, they had no more space to get more of the innocents left out there, in.

"What should we do with those evils? There's too many of them in that one big cell, Hayes," Gore disrupted the founder's deep thinking about the future of the safehouse and how long it was going to last.

Hayes agreed that Gore had a point there. Say, if he had them banished out of the bunker, they could jeopardize the secrecy behind the location of it. However, if he had them all wiped out without mercy - actually, he could not, he just could not, for he still believed there was still a hope to change them from being evil to good. Look at how those two troopers were successfully treated for their disobedience and look how accurate the brain's analysis had been so far, so there must be a way he could treat them well, to be entirely good and not partially evil. Just virtuous. No evil intention, no serial killer's lack of empathy, no wrong perception between what was morally right and wrong.

"Mercy," Hayes spoke softly but to Gore's confusion. Was that his answer for what would happen to all of those prisoners the *brain* had detected with evil intention?

"I asked him to add mercy, you see, but he chose death over living with pity, and that's how he defined it, pity," Hayes continued with a slightly louder voice this time, still did not detach Gore's priceless perplexity look.

Pretending to go along with whatever Hayes meant, Gore asked, "What did you do in response then?"

"What I got to do, the only way to add mercy to it," Hayes answered seriously, but then he forced the edge of his lips to jump from both sides in the end, smiling with still sorrowness, only anyone that was used to his gentle smile could only see, and so Gore knew it was not real.

The next morning, Hayes was already sitting in his study room, thinking, contemplating still of what he had said to Gore the day before. "Will he find out?" He thought to himself over and over.

While he was doing that, he almost forgot why he was there, until his regular guest let himself in from the reporting repertoire that they both got so used to.

"Oh yes, how's everything?" Hayes spoke loudly from afar, mostly from his surprise of the expected, seeing the chubby figure lead scientist getting closer to the desk.

"Never better, Sir, thank you," Gerald was touched by the greeting, until he realized half a second later that it was the bunker, their home, that Hayes was asking about, not how he was doing.

"Ehem, what I meant, Sir, is that the resources are still being gathered, managed, and distributed wisely. Everyone and everything were harmonious, well, except of course for the prisoners, and our *baby trial*, the parents seemed to have noticed," Gerald started speaking with confidence and ended the report with a sense of relief. His practice every night in front of the mirror with various revised report words was always working so far, by all means.

"Hmm, maybe exchanging the *Code Black* baby with the *Code White* one should never be an option after all. We need to find another way to rehabilitate them somehow, without influencing their parents in a bad way. In addition, how's the prototype?"

"The *brain* was successfully replicated, Sir. We have scanned in a hundred more people, the last two were from our own troopers. Fifty more and they should be the last batch to fulfill the target sample set up by Meng," Gerald responded.

"Are you thinking of making another Grey Chamber, Sir? Also, you know, a lot of people have been confused with the provenance of the name, for a room with no grey, should we change it?" The scientist continued, and this time, without any rehearsal.

"We all know that's not the point. My father did not believe that grey was an option. I would like to prove him wrong, though I'd say he was probably right. Grey is just a mix between black and white, a blur, a trick, an illusion, something we do not know, and it can either be one of them black or white so long as one pushes more than the other. Lighter or darker, whichever it is, it's the machine's job to reveal their true color, that is, which force is stronger in their brain, and we all know in the end, there can only be two possibilities. You see? Going in as grey, coming out as either," Hayes responded.

"Our capacity here is getting limited. We have already used

our last area of this safehouse. Perhaps, we should go for a hierarchy, a simpler one to prioritize. For instance, do you have any race in mind, Sir? We can also easily program it," Gerald raised another question. Boy how this time he really regretted it, for by the look in Hayes' eyes, he had turned from pale to red in anger.

"Don't you, of all people, know the real meaning behind all of these colors? Forget skin color. Regardless of their race, regardless of their gender, regardless of their faith; it's the color of their brain that matters. I want to know which of them are with evil intentions, even the hidden ones. More importantly, I want them and myself included to be able to trust, keep trusting the *brain*, and that the system we're building here is both fair and just. Add more scenarios programmed to make sure we do not miss any. That is how we prioritize who belongs here, with all the right privileges."

That was what he meant, no skin color discrimination, only brain color discrimination, and for him, there were only two kinds of color, good and evil - none in between.

Color, for him, was just an illusion to the eye, and its names were just illusions to the mind. Humans invented it for the sake of differentiating between spectrums their brain perceived. When some called it by different names, they called them color blind, and when others could only imagine those lights, colors, and shapes, they called them completely blind. Nevertheless, what was really the definition of seeing, he wondered amid the anger and disappointment he identified towards one of his trusted men.

'To perceive with the eye and be aware of its surroundings when one lid or two moved into a position so as to unblock the opening.'

So when those who claimed they could see, couldn't even catch sight of the brawling river, crackling fire, flurry wind, and grazing land; while those who were told could not see, could, even more by ears, which of the two groups could really see? And when one scientist who was constantly exposed with the function of the brain scanner that just happened to be programmed to discern evil intention as black and none as white, but he still could not perceive any of the lights, colors, and shapes of it, did that make him one of the blinds?

"Powlett, you should always keep in mind that it is the inside that matters here. Never even think of asking such a question again. I'll take that, you know which one I'm talking about?"

"Yes, Sir, my deep apology," Gerald answered like he was about to faint, especially when he heard the leader mention his last name. Without even Hayes bringing it up, Gerald soon let himself out not only because he wanted to, but because he knew Hayes wanted him to too.

Hayes then played around with some of the square pegs in black, white, and grey scattered on his desk like the first was the stars and the latter was the sky. He picked them up and sent them down onto the wooden block, but then picked one in black and one other in white to rest on his palm.

If he did not really believe in color like what he thought,

then what was it with the Code Black and Code White term he often mentioned?

Well that, he knew the answer perfectly, just sometimes he wished he could forget it somehow, for the pain to go away. He had no choice when his father already set the foundation of that chip and machine set inherited to him; to show the color 'black' when a brain was scanned, copied of its structure, and exposed to almost infinite predetermined scenarios while being forecasted of its response - could not show enough empathy or even resist the evil temptation, but 'white' if it could. That *yin and yang* concept he was too in to be devoted.

On the brink of beating a dead horse, Hayes called another scientist to his room. Meng Holmes.

"Holmes, I've been watching how you act and how you think, and may I say, compared to Powlett, he is not looking very good now."

Hayes began his opinion on what Gerald had brought up that gave him nerves and Meng responded that he could not agree more. Having heard how his grandmother was once being bullied because of her race, he was glad that Hayes tested him as a baby and thus he was able to live in a little world free of "bullies" and maybe soon, "prisoners".

Hayes opened up his mind about what he actually wanted to do with those prisoners, "All evils must be identified and rehabilitated, but I'm still trying to find ways to make them good," so it was clear that those Code Black convicts would be given the right to stay perhaps as long as they all still had a chance to change.

The perception with the brain scanner had been long associated with naturally born fouls. With the way his father's invention was created so cleverly however, where it was able to accurately mimic the brain's development as it was exposed to multitude scenarios without affecting the actual brain, leading to two different people with the very same brain structure to possibly give two different outcomes, Hayes had hope that even the bad apples could still be nurtured to be virtuous. That everyone was born good, that only time would tell, perchance. He would give them the chance, for what did he get to lose, he thought.

"If it's not much of a discourteous," Meng raised his question and Hayes held his breath hoping he was not going to say anything that would displease him like the previous, "Do you believe that people were born good or evil?"

Hayes' eyes answered that it was a good question, but one that was not a stranger to his mind, yet without a definite answer. "That is a question I've been searching for an answer to myself," Hayes decided to admit.

"Holmes, I want you to be my right hand for the development of the brain scanner with Powlett. Also, keep your eyes on him, I do not want him to jeopardize the *brain*," the founder added, marking the main reason he invited Meng to come to see him, and another, that was, for more brain scanner replicas to be built.

"But we only have enough space for one Grey Chamber only, Sir."

"We do, for now, but as soon as we are called to come out

from our hideout, there will soon be more Grey Chamber for every part of this land," Hayes responded whilst he stood up and set his eyes on those draft papers he had written 'The World'.

"This, this is just the beginning," he continued.

XI

Chapter Eleven

Bang, Bang, Bang

With no rules applied and no leaders to govern those murderer-beings up ground, there had been no justice served to the cold figures lying, flowing, or flying all over the earth. Every man was for himself. If he lived, he lived with no peace, and if he died, he died in equanimity.

An ordinary husband was fishing in the midst of no ordinary primeval age of the modern world with barely any fish to catch, near what the still-sane ones called the Wyre River. The long, smelly, and heavily polluted river near his small, wrecked house was involuntarily drifting a couple of bodies on its surface. He would have jumped out of his body if it had not been the hundredth time he saw corpses floating down the river flow.

The man with sad hooded eyes brought himself home with no fish, but grasses from the right riverbank debatable of their side effects when eaten. Those grasses when being laid over the table, had no difference to his hair in shape, length, and smell other than the color. If his hair had been dark green instead of black, who knew he might have mistaken his own hair for a salad.

His wife came close to the table and gently rubbed her belly where their child was living temporarily. Her round-shaped eyes with the color of an eggplant were watery but not too much, for they were being held tight not to drop by the love she had for her husband whom she knew had been trying his best. They were living poorly and in fear, so did everyone else around them that were still alive, which number of people counted less than even the number of petals in a rose. Even further, as dangers were still around, the number too was decreasing like falling petals.

There were times that the husband thought of picking one of those floating corpses that looked fresh for them to eat, just to get by, which was strongly opposed by the wife and saved by running extinct rats who just happened to be attracted by the little house with the misery scent. Don't get me started again with those cannibals that were still out there running around like zombies smelling fresh blood, who in the meantime ruled the upper ground world with the power vested by the failing society and grieving nature. I bet sometimes he thought too, if only he were able to fly, he would have been capable of catching those odd-looking birds recently kept flying constantly around up in the sky.

"Any news about the Daggers?" Mrs. Salis, the wife, raised her suspicions on their neighbor's whereabouts, but Mr. Salis, the husband, had something else in mind about them besides expecting to see their bodies floating down what once was a magnificently beautiful watercourse. Rumors were flying around saying they were taken *underground.*

Some people said it was a good place, and some others thought otherwise. The people who were left dying in a physically fighting fit body just could not believe how there was still a place so profound near heaven like in the middle of a growing hell around. If it was too good of what it really was, still it was susceptible to flaws, human like.

Nevertheless, how could they get in? How could they be chosen to live in such a place? Even if the place were not as good, nowhere could have been worse than where they already had been, a new world for devils. They probably had to appear 'deemed worthy' or something, somehow, to be invited, but what was it that the Daggers did that was deemed worthy? They were like most of them. Scared, running away, sleeping in fear, living like them too. Unknown to the husband and wife, they were thinking exactly the same too, that how they were no different to the Daggers? Why weren't they worthy to be in a better place too?

Mr. Salis rubbed his wife's belly and prattled, "You finally look like you're pregnant, just a few days ago nobody could even tell that we're having a baby." Mrs. Salis brushed her husband's hair and pretended like they were soft bushes in the garden, making her cozy and warm. They had to, putting on an act as if they were not worrying about the night, or tomorrow, or what would happen when the baby came.

The night before bed, they had so many rituals to keep the house safe from all the hungry cannibals and Mother Nature's anger. The land, just like every other part of the world visible from the sky, was more dangerous when it was dark, so they set their daily traps the same way too. The husband started by covering everything that even traded air from the outside to make sure there was no way in. He then put futile firecrackers he got left under near the door and window just so he could hear the crepitating melody from treacherous steps in a hush, a sound he wished he would never have to hear, in where if that happened, he still had no clear idea what to do next, besides anything he could do with the pan that was always resting on his hand whenever he was sleeping. The way was compulsory for any prey in the primitive age of the modern world living on sight, for the world was not safe other than being under the soil, greatly hidden.

If only, they were one of those lucky inhabitants, they thought. So they crossed their fingers and did what any hopeless people do when they had no other humans and options to run to, they prayed to the invisible.

It was approximately twenty-three days later when he first heard the never-anticipated crackling sound. Eight legs were marching in two by two at dawn with their guns, order, and blooded scratches down their skin. They then quickly closed the door tight to avoid predators jumping in.

Mr. Salis woke up by the sound with his cheeks' skin cold from his rustic frying pan he firmly hugged. He tried his best to move his wife's dry hands from his waist so as not to wake the deep sleeper female on his side and his naked legs to walk quietly without the other half of his bottom feet touching the ground.

What a surprise for him when instead he saw four towering-size figures with big builds and blurry army suits in front of him. In a reflex, he steered his beloved pan to dance through the wind with one of the men, but the leading points had quickly turned to the warrior, and Mr. Salis was left defenseless.

"Don't worry, we're not here to hurt you," one of the men tried to call him down in a whisper while the other lit up a lighter to show their faces and introduce themselves politely one by one.

"We're here on a mission, to bring you and your family safe *underground*, but we need to leave now or never," the handsomest warrior spoke on behalf of the others, and seeing how frozen Mr. Salis still was, he added a bit of a summary about how the place they were going to was a sanctuary. Little did he know, beneath all of those speechless, Mr. Salis was already sold at 'underground'.

"We don't have much time, hurry!" The other warrior who seemed to be the most anxious than the others breathed the words loudly at the back of the handsome warrior's neck. It was his intention too to use that high of a tone so that Mr. Salis would move quickly.

The husband woke his wife up and told her the surprise. She quickly went outside to meet the warriors to ensure that she was not still dreaming. One of the warriors apologized that they did not give them much of a time for them to pack their things up and further encouraged them not to bring a lot of stuff to make the long trip lighter. For the first time in their life, they were grateful that they had barely anything for it had made them quicker to leave the place they never really wanted to call home. Well, there was the time when they did, only when Wyre River was still majestic, but that was just ages ago. So she grabbed only her husband's frying pan from the floor while the man rushed to get his silver fishing rod.

Their journey was not as smooth as they wanted it to be, even when they were lucky with the good mood the earth seemed to be in. Just a short few hours from the small house, their distress was seasoned with the arrival of three cannibals who had not eaten for days, imagine the hunger when they saw some fresh six meats looking their way.

Their weakened bodies and minds were obviously outnumbered by the four well-trained warriors and so they were quickly defeated but still alive. However, two of them then grabbed the husband and wife to leave as soon as possible and left the two other warriors.

"What about them?" Mrs. Salis screamed her worries as she saw those two others as part of her savior group too, of course.

"Don't worry, they'll be with us again soon enough, I

promise," one of them tried to keep her and her husband's run going forward and not looking back.

Bang. Bang. Bang.

Mr. Salis could have sworn that he heard three gunshots being fired, being his ears had been fully trained to listen through the wind with all of those fishing he had been doing. It was only logical that those two other warriors were staying to kill the cannibals, but if they had been overpowered, was it only inhuman to finish them off anyway? Or was it not if their existence was a threat to humanity anyway? Either way, he decided to let it go because what would matter for him nevertheless if those cannibals deserved to die or not? Since if they were alive, they would not think twice to eat him alive, he thought.

As promised, two others were able to quickly catch up with them, with no comment both ways. After miles and miles of hide and seek, with fortunately no more encounters with any of the cannibals, they managed to get to the bunker safely without even any added wound on any of them.

"Not as many now I reckon, their number is decreasing, significantly," one of the warriors whispered to the other after he climbed down the ladder. The handsome warrior, who seemed to be the wisest among them, swiftly swayed his pointy finger near his lips, so as to tell them without words that they just needed to stop talking and nothing more.

Mrs. Salis became aware that these warriors were not as friendly as when they came to their house. It was like they were keeping their distance and trying to be forgotten of their true existence once they saved her and her husband's life - for whatever reason, and for some reasons too, she could not help but ask, "How did you find us?"

"Birds in the sky," the most good looking one responded, before he told her and her husband to wait until being picked up. With another gesture in his hand, he and the other three warriors were quickly gone like the wind slipping through the door that was closed hastily. Soon after, Maccush and his chatty partner Collin entered the waiting hall and directed the two potential inhabitants to enter the Grey Chamber one by one.

"We forgot to ask that kind of question, you know, about the earth and stuff, like in the procedure, and if they're one of them," one of the warriors spoke up his mind to the other three warriors with a stable volume. Being back in their home unit, he did not have to whisper anymore.

"That society? They are harmless anyway, everyone knows that. It will not matter. Besides, there are rumors that they are not even living on land anymore," the other replied while closing his eyes trying to enjoy the peace in his mind then as he could take off the warrior suit and relax, and he added, "I'm pretty sure this young couple is not one of those *environmentalists.*"

XII

Chapter Twelve

The Earth vs. The World

"The *brain* has been updating itself with the more results coming in, and the rescan trial has been completed," Meng reported his findings to Hayes in the meeting room while adjusting his glasses from time to time. "Some adults who were tested Code White have now shown Code Black. It seems that the more people get tested, the more the evil intention in a person is being unlocked," the scientist continued.

"But that's not all," without biding his time and unintentionally without giving Hayes a chance to even respond to the first topic, he further added, "That concludes for us to finally reach enough target samples from both babies and adults. I'm happy to say that the *brain* can now fully function with both undeveloped and even more complex, developed brain structure. With more and more samples, the standard error has been staying steady with almost no spread across the curve. What your father had created, Sir, is beyond what I call astonishing, remarkable. You must be very proud."

"Indeed," Hayes replied shortly and sounded a bit forced with a silent sigh, seemingly so woebegone at the long-gone creator, but his face still couldn't deny how genius his father's work had been.

"It is safe to say, Sir, that everyone, no matter how young or old, should be scanned too, then rescanned, specially the parents because there is no doubt their results too are part of the determining variables to the forecast resulted from the scans in the babies' brain; as the hypothesis suggested, that makes the scan results for the babies more accurate, if they are combined together," the scientist proposed what he believed was the best for the organization, and to no doubt he was right.

Rescanning was able to make sure the nurtured surroundings remained correct and supportive to the good nature of morality, and whether the forecast was truly accurate or just precise, it was still a forecast and prone to variance. The longer it spanned, the less accurate it could be. However, if it kept being adjusted with the actual base of their developing brain, the forecast would become stronger, and the suggestion generated from the accepted scenarios would too be more reliable from scan to scan. That was what Meng further brought up and Hayes did not seem to disagree with the logic.

One thing they were worried of was, what if there were more Code Black inhabitants living as Code White ones and the evil inside was just waiting for the right temptation to strike, but then the over-capacity prison would no longer be able to hold them off. This time, Hayes knew they really urgently needed to come up with a rehabilitation solution, but Meng insisted that, even after doing everything they could, the team was not yet able to find the way.

"We still do not know how to penetrate the brain. The brain scanner is perfect as it is to detect malevolent deportments, but to its supreme limit. It is on its ceiling to just, but so accurately, scan the brain, copy its exact structure, and determine the subject's response from the various informative instrumentals in combination to the scenarios sensitivity analysis within the forecast," he added to his argument. Meng too wished there were some ways to alter the brain of those Code Blacks, but again, such mandatory vision was still just a mere concept to him. Even for someone as brilliant as he was, the unbreakable prison bar was still one of the best ideas he could come up with.

"Regular scanning, huh," Hayes responded.

"Yes, there is no better way to keep the forecast and advice accurate from time to time, other than making sure it is at regular, well-maintained, intervals," Meng replied confidently, and his glasses did not even slide this time from his firm blink his sharp-focused slanted eyes had been giving.

"Add that to everyone. Regardless of their age, they should have all been assessed, and re-assessed. I hope the *brain* will never let us down," the leader knew he had no choice but to agree, for he already started the free of evil regime with this brain scanner accuracy postulation, and there was no going back. Whatever happened, it just had to be right, for everyone there had already trusted it to be the one that could set the world free from the lawless evil dominion, someday.

"I believe we can now trust the *brain* completely," Meng countered with Hayes' relief.

From then on, everyone was to get re-tested. The first test was already giving them anxiety from the fear of not passing and being kicked out of the safe place, and then they had to get the second one?

Hayes knew he had to communicate the right words through the mic that flew his voice to many speakers hanging up across the bunker, in order to avoid chaos in the newly imposed law - his revolutionary theory with all the inhabitants, one that did not jeopardize the credibility of the *brain*, so he came up with a story. Nonetheless, it was not really a story. Some would think it was more of a making-sense forced parable than the other, when they heard him speak; simply because it was talking about, technically, how to water a beautiful tropical hibiscus none of them had seen for a very long time, and how it needed both water and sunlight to stay in the pink. Who did not know that already, right?

"The water is our test, and the sunlight is our safe place. We remain in the dark, for now, but there will come the day, we come out from our hide, blooming. There will be no use of sunlight for the flower if there is no water, and there will be no it with just the water. Now the test is for us to make sure that our place will always be safe. Aren't you looking forward to the day where you can just come out to a clean world with no more fear, and run around free on earth like you are in heaven? Hope. I have hope."

Although Hayes had to refrain himself from elucidating the scientific explanation behind it, which he knew would bore or even repel anyone who did not care, his analogy did nothing of a sort to back him up, not until the end, kind of unexpectedly. Hayes had successfully sold the order at only the very last second with the word 'hope', after giving the vivid imagination of freedom everyone was waiting for.

One by one, at all ages, was beginning to march out of their home units peacefully and most voluntarily. The exception was only for babies, and anyone already being tested within the one-year span.

Almost like waiting for a vaccine where they got it in time before catching the virus, those whose results were unchanged left the chamber in pure joy. They went back in harmony and as the chosen people were allowed to stay safely where they were, they threw themselves a party within their assigned community, as they were allowed to.

"Code White," they were told regardless of their skin or personal favorite color, instead of just 'passing the test', and as the governing body decided to be more transparent with how they did things, everyone was exposed to the existence of the warriors who were standing outside the chamber, instead of troopers this time, waiting for any of those resulted in Code Black. Not that everyone in the left and right section did not already know about the warriors, some of them had when they were brought in by them, but these warriors made themselves disappear in the wind that those that they had rescued eventually thought that they were probably dreaming out of desperation of being saved, until then.

Surprisingly, there were none of Code Black cases on these sections and the warriors had been on duty for nothing, but to a relief. Next was the middle section's turn to be retested, but these 'angels and associates' didn't show any anxiety. Somehow, they knew that they were going to pass the test, and they were right. Within that week, every single person was tested and none of the results came back Code Black.

Hayes and his family were the last to be rescanned, and when it was done, they walked back together in joy to their home unit. As the night sky invisible to them visited, they were ready for bed.

They entered their shared bedroom, packed up with one queen' size bed for Hayes and his wife, and another, a single width, for Siva. The two beds were placed side by side on the right by the door where they came in. After that, there were not many other things displayed, just like any other unit in the limited-resources bunker.

Hayes' wife went to her side of the bed just on the left side and got cozy with reading her favorite mystery before-bed novel she had read hundredth of times. It would not have been her favorite if it was not the only one left among her other few possessions she had taken from up there, or if it did not have that open ending that most people hated - but that way, she could imagine a different conclusion every time she finished it, just because she had no other option.

Hayes on the other hand flew Siva to her bed after making a few pit stops in the air like she was a guided little bird who was still learning how to fly under her father's wings.

"Story!" The little girl screamed, and she was expecting another she would have never heard before, because Hayes was always capable of making up one every single night.

"Alright, tonight, it would be... The Rock Monster, roaaaaaaar!" Hayes bent his body with a monstrous voice while tickling Siva from time to time. The dear Mrs. Beckett laughed while too listening to his adoring story telling.

"Once upon a time, there was a gigantic monster who was born with skin as hard as a rock. Whenever he moved his feet one step at a time, the land quivered just like this," and so Hayes got out of the bed and hid underneath to shake the mattress, much to the excitement of his little girl as she laughed while hugging her blister so as not to fall.

The impromptu made-up story continued with the monster causing an earthquake every time he tried to move; thus, he decided to make one last move of dropping his body backward so he could still see the night sky and chose to sleep so that he would be able to move without causing any earthquake only in his dream. That was what he told Siva in the end how a mountain was formed. She would find out the truth anyway when she grew up, eventually, he thought.

After Hayes reached the end of the bedtime story, his wife closed her book, put it on the side of the bed, and walked to her daughter's bed. Along with Hayes, she kissed Siva on the cheek and went back to bed. After making sure that Siva had closed her eyes to sleep, as it was clear that Hayes loved his baby girl too much to keep his eyes off of her, he forced himself to walk away to turn off the light and went to his side of the bed. They then all went to sleep.

It was only a couple of hours later that Siva suddenly woke up from a tremble, and so she said while brushing her eyes with the side of her palm, "Daddy, Rock Monster, is that you?"

Unfortunately, it was not, it was Mother Earth instead.

Hayes and his wife were awake from the earthquake too. They both put their feet on the cold floor and Hayes carried Siva out with his wife by his side.

Under the blinking lights of the hall was where everyone that was coming out of their home units not knowing what to do gathered. Hayes' wife's brother who stood just next to him was embracing Zirilo's cuddle on his right thigh. Scientists from all fields were racing their own legs to make their way to the lab, not knowing what they could do about the phenomenon just yet. Warriors were coming out with their pajamas but also guns, though knowing there was not anything those weapons could do if the bunker shattered down from the earthquake. Every single person from the left, middle, to right side of the underground safehouse was quiet and did not dare to make further moves than waiting by the hall; unlike the prisoners who made a havoc on trying to break the unbreakable prison bars, just to distract themselves from the idea of being buried alive with no space to pointlessly run to.

Fortunately, the earthquake stopped just a few minutes later.

"What happened?" Siva's breath tickled Hayes' neck slightly as her words traveled on the way to his ears.

"The earthquake, the earth is shivering," he replied, while seeing some scientists walking towards him from afar, with their eyes telling him that this too, they did not know the empirical cause.

One of Hayes' friends, the grown-up male Mr. Pyralis, who was just standing by them, heard what the father said to his little daughter. "Why do you sound like those *environmentalists* out there?" He noted just how bizarre Hayes' explanation was.

Hayes was shocked for a moment, but then retrieved his calm back with a logic he had just thought half a second before, and so he replied with that excuse of "I just know how they think, that's all."

Made sense for him, but apparently not to everyone else around him, and so just like how everybody else whose integrity was attacked acted, he emphasized his excuse, of his own accord.

"To defeat your enemy, you have to think like one; to beat them in their own game. Isn't that called a tactic?" He argued, and after seeing some nods, he concluded that his upright was intact once more.

Instead of going back to sleep like Hayes and the others, some of them living just next door to the founder decided to stay where they were to talk about those that they called eco-nuts they believed whose credence was against them, but with no peril towards them. 'The Earth' as they called it, believed that the motherland was acting strange from losing their delegations to control her elements whenever her organs were going round the bend, and 'The World' people in the bunkers, simply thought those beliefs were bonkers.

Why wouldn't they? There was no proof of their existence, and yet The Earth members chose to stay close to pre-industrial civilization living with only accepted technology that did not touch sources from harming the earth in any way, while waiting for their saviors.

"Where did they get that crazy idea anyway?" Mr. Pyralis lit up the hall with the innuendo, and everyone was laughing at The Earth, then shushing themselves so as not to wake the founder whom they thought was asleep, out of their deep respect for him.

Well, they were wrong there. In fact, Hayes had not slept yet, for he was just listening from the back of the door all along, patiently, quietly, with his expression suggesting a memory.

XIII

Chapter Thirteen

Code Grey

Just a couple of months after the last earthquake, Mrs. Salis gave birth to a baby boy. The couple decided to call him Wyre; they named him shortly after he was immediately taken away to the Grey Chamber.

"Just like the Wyre River near where we used to live," the mother initiated the name, and though her husband did not debate with the suggestion, he prayed that the boy's future would become long and majestic like how the stream had been long ago, not what it was then.

The brain scan process for Wyre was taking much longer than everybody expected. The same female scientist who handled Bolin and Maccush, was almost losing her patience that had already reached the surface of the jar, so she decided to use the 'help' button whose history she had been keeping blank slate since the first hour she came on board with the task. Yes, it was the first time for her to ask for help, and it took her great courage and almost-endless forbearance that she overstated to the baby, "It would taint my career prestige just too much," not that the infant could understand or even hear her beneath the machine.

"Indeed, this scan has been taking a very long time, much more than anyone has ever been," Meng Holmes repeated the junior's finding. He who decided to take the first issue in his hand, looked very surprised but at the same time, he too did not dare to touch the machine while it was still analyzing the little baby. So, his final verdict, he decided to wait.

It took the machine two skipped meals and ten hours in total; compared to the general thirty minutes for the others, which was sometimes more but never beyond two hours.

What did the result show?

Code Grey. The exact fifty percent of Code White and the other half of Code Black.

Baby Wyre was declared as the first case of 'absolute grey', with what they mentioned as fifty percent chance of good and fifty percent chance of evil, no more or less.

"Get the baby to the other brain scanner," Meng suggested, which forced the female scientist to bring the baby out of the duplicate then into the first-born machine without a haste. However, another two hours had passed, and they were quite confident they were almost eight hours early to declare another Code Grey, first ever, result; while letting the machine continue the analysis so as not to stop its thinking. The female sighed and showed a true expression that resembled a grumpy cat face, as Meng let himself out the chamber, knowing that she would have another wasted eight hours of boredom to kill.

Meng then ran to the main lab which stored detailed analysis of the scenario-by-scenario test process and reviewed them altogether with Gerald and the other three scientists. This detailed analysis was only available in the main lab and could only be accessed to the five of them who resided there, and the founder himself, who usually then approved the suggested steps and future probability for the subject based on it and passed it onto their subordinates as a guided order for the next step.

"Code Black, Code White, but this was our first case of Code Grey, am I right?" Gerald spoke to no response, "He came in grey, and came out grey? How is that even possible?" Gerald repeated the result much to the annoyance of the three other scientists who did not like him as much as they were to Meng, and so they chose to ignore him still. If they could code the two themselves, they would classify Meng as Code White and Gerald as Code Black, with a concluding variance of arrogance. They just somehow always hated whatever Gerald did, while praising whatever Meng said.

"Let us examine thoroughly what we can know about this child, alright?" Meng then initiated a course of action, in which the three others replied, "Yes, sir," much to Gerald's annoyance and so he vowed himself to stay silent the whole night.

Meng, who always seemed to be at least one level above Gerald's erudite, had always been impressing his colleagues with his humbled patience and silent genius, much to the opposite of Gerald who always loudly vocalized what he knew and tightly suppressed what he did not know. So when Meng stayed quiet the whole review while Gerald broke his own vow two minutes later, the others looked at the first from time to time to wordlessly follow up if he was getting somewhere, whenever they themselves felt stuck.

"The chip went through the cycle twenty times, that's twenty times the thirty emotions had been coursed, but the machine still couldn't decide between Code White and Code Black. Even so, I don't believe it's the chip, it is working flawlessly," Meng suddenly voiced out his opinion, immediately to the agreement of the three others.

"Is there something wrong with the machine, then?" One of them responded.

"The chip is the *brain*, the machine is just listening to whatever the chip is telling it to," Meng replied, but then he said something that made the others slightly flabbergasted, "I'll enter myself in the machine."

Meng's retest took about thirty minutes and the result showed Code White. Impressed by his volunteer, the three others followed his step, and Gerald too as he did not want to feel left out. They then repeated the trial for ten more troopers and five warriors, who had no idea why, but all still only took thirty minutes and showed Code White, much to every single person's relief.

"That is all," one of the scientists spoke up, but to his surprise, Meng replied with, "No, there is still one more" and then they knew what he meant, the prisoner.

After long deliberation, they decided to take one prisoner out with the help of warriors, just to make sure.

"Should we tell Hayes?" One of the warriors suggested hoping that Hayes would say no and he would be free from the annoying task, but when Meng took the issue to Hayes, much to his surprise with the news too, he agreed with Meng.

Five warriors, one of them was the son of Mr. Pyralis, all in full gear, let their boots parade in sequence towards a dark sound-proof room, whose inhabitants howled as soon as the first lightbulb about ten-meter far from where they were was switched on. Hayes was sitting in the study room meanwhile, waiting, terrified, because no one really knew what would happen whenever the sturdy hardy silver bolt was unlocked. Nevertheless, they all knew what could happen, the horror if every single one of those prisoners were set loose on the premises.

Five of them stood tall in front of the well-built bars and they were all staring straight at those a couple of hundreds of red eyes belonging to reasoning monsters craving for killing and committing crimes, starving for freedom, while shaking the unshakeable bars to break free.

"How many, they say?" One of the warriors asked in a whisper, hoping one out of two standing next to him could hear.

"Two would be enough," Mr. Pyralis' son who was standing on his right answered him too in the same undertone.

One of them who started the opening-prison procedure,

was going to unlock the bolt while the four others were ready with their weapons to fire. Meanwhile, on his way to the latch, he kept swearing between these three thoughts in his head.

Why do jails have to have cavities on them?

Why do the other warriors have to stand behind this door, while letting us five here on our own?

Why does it have to be my turn today?

As soon as he unbolted the lock, unfortunately, one of the prisoners who learned well on the repeated approach every time the jail was opened, crawled under instead of standing up trying to break the bars like the rest, and for such, he still managed to get out after surviving multiple deadly kicks from the warrior who unlocked the jail. The other warriors were taking time to decide whether to shoot him until they realized, one was much less than four so they grabbed the runaway man instead as he was probably harmless as long as the others did not get away.

The Pyralis warrior held the prisoner closely to him, a task he gave to himself, while the others tried to help lock the gate away. As the prisoner tried to throw some punches aiming for the weapon, he was the one to be shocked instead, as the man quickly detached him from his own strength and tapped him unconscious by the neck.

"Wow, where did that come from? Did you get superpower from that woman's bite or something?" One of them who felt relaxed after the jail was successfully locked again, quipped on the man whose ear was forever befouled by the experience he thought was embarrassing, yet he had to relive over and over. Probably if it were a man who bit her, he would not have felt so compassionate not to kill her quickly; he blamed within his own pride defense.

"One enough, I reckon. I really don't want to go through that again," the other intentionally changed the topic, realizing how lucky they were with that one.

"Let's go with one," the warrior who unlocked the bolt in the first place uttered with the ultimate sigh as he tapped the young Pyralis on the shoulder with a light smile of 'good work'.

The unconscious prisoner was brought easily to the Grey Chamber and his brain was immediately rescanned. About thirty minutes later, which luckily he had not woken up, the result came out normally as Code Black, much to the relief of all six scientists in the Grey Chamber who had been standing for the analysis. This was a big deal to the junior female scientist, so she had been putting her best behavior hoping that one day she could become one of those five.

After a long while, the scan in the second machine, which also took the exact same ten hours to run, presented the same Code Grey result.

"Well, the duplicated chip is automatically synchronized to its master, so that's not a surprise," Gerald spoke but this time, the other scientists' mind was actually on the same page with him for probably the first if not the second time, not that they would let him know out loud, well except for the young female scientist that was the only one clapping who had not known the drama in the glorious main lab yet. If she had known, she would have realized she was sucking up to the wrong leader.

The same warriors then brought that one prisoner back to where he was. Fortunately, he was still mildly half asleep, but he could still walk a bit. After the lightbulb had been turned on for the second time that day, they looked at each other wondering what unexpected thing they had to go through this time.

Meanwhile, Gerald and Meng walked across the corridor ready to meet the nervous Hayes who was waiting for an update. Luckily for Hayes, it was not a long walk for them.

"What should we do with this infant?" Meng Holmes continued as the leader grew quiet after hearing everything in detail.

"Should we, ehem, try to exchange the baby again?" Gerald stepped in, but not with the right idea.

"We can't risk more hysterical parental behaviors anymore. We can leave that idea out for good from now on," Hayes replied.

"Well, from the analysis, we know he could perhaps be useful to handle one of our resources one day, perhaps Sir, if you will not send him to be one of those prisoners someday. Would you, Sir? A new rehabilitation category, perchance?" Meng spoke up his idea and Gerald could see that the leader really tried to listen carefully to what he said. The latter wondered though, why didn't he think of that?

A long deliberation later, "Hmm, maybe this is how the universe is trying to tell me that it's time. Send him out as

Code Grey, our first, and perhaps first of many," Hayes responded, "but maybe it is better to separate them, Code Greys from Code Whites, while treating them like one. Give them the best care, attention, and maybe all kinds of support and rehabilitation that they - this Code Grey baby needs," the leader added, while at the same time visioning the future vividly.

Meng and Gerald thought the conversation was over, but only a few seconds after they opened the door to let themselves out, Hayes stopped them, and so they closed the door again with a pounding heart.

"Before you go, I was thinking of starting a rehabilitation process for the prisoners too, a trial, first, perhaps. How about, we start retesting some of the Code Blacks, see if any of them showed a good symptom?" Hayes was speaking of things by his own surprise, the two thought, possibly something from a seed of hope started to grow out of his emotion watered by that Code Grey - rehabilitation brand new idea. He did not stop there however, for the three continued the discussion for about two hours long after that, talking of what ifs.

Afterward, Meng and Gerald came out of the door speechless, with an expression ready to shatter themselves onto bed without getting any sleep.

"Who's gonna tell the warriors?" Gerald asked, and Meng budged his shoulder while trying not to make any eye contact with him because he was sure he would do everything he could not to.

XIV

Chapter Fourteen

Poisonous Patience

Hayes' decision to rescan all the Code Blacks set havoc in every warrior's chamber. They all thought, did the founder think it was that easy to get one out and back in on and on? If the prison were only filled with one to ten people, it would have been easy enough to manage, but hundreds?

In getting rid of the resistance, Meng then ordered them to choose one prisoner first that seemed to be the least destructional, as a trial. They all went to see the security camera attached on the corner of the prison room and voted on which one they should bring out.

They all agreed on one, who could be seen as the least dangerous among the others. The seemingly young man's long black hair covered half of his face most of the time while his tiny body was tied around his knees by his arms. His sharp nose sniffed many times from all the acid river streamed from his eyes and he seemed to have no ambition to break out the bars while the others were trying to do so.

The effort to bring him out was no joke. The man who everybody called 'corner man' for his constant sitting by the edge of the prison, many times refused to come near the entrance where the lock was. When he finally agreed to do so, the warriors performed the procedure the same way they took the previous out, but this time, they managed to cover all the bases with ten more warriors standing on their side, adding terror to the prisoners who were still trying to breakaway.

The corner man was then brought to the Grey Chamber, and when he saw the machine, he willingly put his body to lie inside, which was quite unexpected for some of the warriors.

"Maybe we've chosen the right one," one of the warriors said.

Nine hours later, the result came out, and when the cover was pulled back, due to the duration, the corner man was still heavily asleep on the soft bed inside that he felt super comfortable to be on, considering where he used to sleep. The test too showed Code Grey, surprisingly, just like the baby before him, and soon he was put in the same program as the infant.

"Jackpot," one of the warriors said as he realized they did not need to go through opening the jail again, at least in the meantime.

A few weeks had passed, and the warriors were happy that Hayes still decided to postpone taking out another prisoner, to see first how the corner man went with his rehabilitation. It also seemed that the conversion process was going great, even though he was still technically secluded in one of the finished rooms in the construction site, the life improvement he was getting was translated into how he positively behaved towards the support.

"What's his empathetic pain level now, you reckon?" Meng asked one of the three scientists from the main lab who was accompanied by a warrior that took turns with the others to constantly stay by the corner man's side, even when he was asleep. They believed that according to the report, he suffered from a ground level of empathetic pain almost impossible to cure that might underpin the possibility of a murderer behavior out of ataraxy; but the Code Grey suggesting that somehow, there was hope for that to increase.

"The brain scanner still showed Code Grey, though in much less hours, so probably, still a long way to Code White," he responded.

They were hoping to get somewhere, but actually, what had they done to achieve it? Probably nothing besides taking care of the subject. Sure, they fed him all day, treated him finally like a human being, but even with all of those intellectuals staying in the bunker, there was still one kind of expert missing from the group, one who could.

All they further did then was to exclusively separate him from the society and not let him out of their sight, afraid of what he would do, at least until he was classified as Code White. And even if he did, they would not keep their eyes off of him, still; that, the corner man too had suspected. The only people he could talk to were the scientists and warriors who came and went in a roster, with arranged conversation he did not have the vote to change the topic. Fear and unacceptance, was unintentionally the kind of solution they were working on to encourage him to be more of what they desired. What did the man like? They did not even bother to find out.

Knock. Knock. Knock.

Hayes entered the bedroom of where Zirilo was sitting alone, on top of his noisy bed when being pressed against. The little boy grew suspicious when he was the only one missing from the full lunch bunch in the middle section of the canteen's dining table.

Since the day the little boy saw the horror of the decapitated head, he had become a bit of a loner and less hyperactive than he used to be. For that, Hayes knew he was entirely to blame, and thenceforth, he grew soft on the boy. Even when he did not manage to finish the same kind of salad again, Hayes would notice and take it from his plate to relieve him from the misery on the dining table.

To make up for it, Hayes thought of something the two of them could do. Before setting out the plan, he was making sure that his many birds in the sky that flew around the area of the forest where the bunker was, did not detect any unwanted visitors whose number had grown drastically lower than before. Even for the warriors, searching for food in the forest became as easy as going out of a house to grab an apple, come back in, then just come back out to pick another. Something good came out from them not leaving any cannibals behind to kill every time they found one or taking as many as possible in the bunker before they turned into one. Everything seemed to start being almost normal, finally, and mostly under control with much less of the motherland's temper.

"Come on, I want to show you something," Hayes held Zirilo's cold palm and gently pulled him to walk out of his bed.

"Where are we going, uncle?" The little boy was confused, but it was obvious he was liking this version of Hayes more than before.

When they reached the ladder that led out of the bunker, Zirilo did not dare to continue even one step closer to where near the head he saw falling. That image, that was the only one appearing in front of him, so he closed his eyes first then ran out to the back of the entrance door, hiding - a mere fortunate that he did not hit his head doing so. Hayes knew exactly how the little boy felt, the nightmare that showed itself whether one's mind was asleep or not, and for Zirilo's case, it was mostly his fault to blame.

Hayes decided to mosey near where the little boy was hugging his knees. After a while seeing Zirilo did not change his pose at all, the middle-aged man tenderly lifted the boy's arms and flitted them onto his shoulders. In response to the warmth, Zirilo's legs embraced the man's waist and hid his face on where his left shoulder was. The boy, still closing his eyes, could feel that the movement was going on like he was sitting on a knife peeling a floor of carrot skin gently, but then gradually changed as if the knife started chopping that orange root vegetable. In fact, they were climbing the ladder, as Hayes was bringing Zirilo out of the underground.

Concurrently down in the bunker.

That corner man whose real name no one probably knew, turned the lights off inside his bedroom. If he were up with the sky visible from the window, or if there had been a window to another room, it would have been useless.

He was perfectly aware that some people were waiting just outside, where they might come in and out where he was as they pleased, so he made no sound so as not to attract any attention. That was how he lingered on his poisonous patience anyway, he found that not to take action was sometimes more than any kind of taking action, almost like being invisible while taking one step ahead against the others. Well, but maybe he did take action, in his mind, with the plan.

A silver fork lost the light that went off with the bulb, but its body was still spinning from a twist in its neck maneuvered by the corner man who laid down on his bed with his eyes wide open. He wondered; how he could ever handle these big men, for he was so tiny. Almost like a redbud tree trying to overcome an oak. The best he could do was probably sitting at the edge of a corner like he used to, hiding.

Hiding, right, and observing, like he had been doing sitting there in that prison. He felt a rise of knowledge in understanding his inmates' behaviors, and of those who held them in. So, while everyone else was pushing and pulling rolling steels revealing their true emotion and will, he learned their wants and needs. Could be useful for something like, perhaps, manipulation, a great asset for most of the composed-wicked mind.

The opportunity he envisioned as he was invisibly restrained triggered his camouflaged intention that was long divided between right and wrong. Whether it was the lack of love or the forced lots of attention, he was not always sure, but that day he decided to plump his own confusion for the flawed.

He screamed a letter with no word, high tune but short of breath, so naturally the two warriors who were guarding at the front immediately opened the door with their weapon steady straight by their arm ready for action. It was so sudden that they almost forgot they needed to switch the light on first, and it took them about a couple of long seconds on top to do so, more than enough time.

Apparently, the tiny man had snuck out the door when the light was still off, then came back inside again without being known. He switched the light off again then climbed on one of the warriors and used the fork to stab him on the neck, in a matter of seconds too. He was tiny, but boy he was fast.

Unlucky for them, the corner man managed to grab one of the weapons and grenades in the dark and ran free like a lunatic forming his body a warm shield from the wintry weather flitting up and down the hall. When he passed the canteen, full of people with torn four-leaf clovers eating fried folioles for lunch, the devil granted him two red horns unseen by the mortal that drove him to shoot bullets to everyone within his reach of rampage that day. It was too quick that it was too late for the warriors in armor to come in four groups of tens without proper plan and knock him down altogether from behind. However, to no luck, the jumbo dwarf with the weapon managed to free run the giants and use them against each other as shields. He then ran to where the prison was, as a leverage idea popped up in his mind.

Up there where the sky was visible.

Zirilo's arms were still shaping a necklace around Hayes' not too broad shoulders, and when he finally found the courage to open his eyes, he could hardly believe it. He was fascinated at first, then scared as he knew what might come, but as he saw half a dozen warriors spreading like a crown, he felt safe somehow and began to enjoy the bright sky and the lovely sunshine. Besides, there was nothing better than a breeze smelling like a wet tree and damp moss and standing for the first time on the soft soil with all the lights, persuading his mental health to be at peace and release while at the same time urging him to run as free as the wind with no more fear.

Hayes gave him about half an hour to spend, and when he saw the joy in Zirilo's eyes when he came back telling stories about his short, protected journey in the wild, he just could not wait to go back to the middle section bunker and took Siva with him there.

"Maybe it is now safe to set a formal procedure where people may come out of the bunker from time to time," Hayes talked to one of the warriors, the Pyralis, and he took the plan merrily.

This time, Zirilo was able to get down the ladder by himself and even when both of his feet already touched the floor of the waiting hall, it seemed that he was forgetting the trauma or possibly still getting distracted by himself who had not stopped talking about a whole different world in the upper ground. Hayes was very happy to listen to his no-stopping train of words. He did get the little boy traumatized, but he too seemed to be the one who cured it.

The atmosphere when they left the waiting hall was disquieted by the odd gathering of everyone occupying the first section of the bunker, as they were standing close to the door leading to where the Grey Chamber was.

"We heard gunshots," some of them stated, and so Hayes and the warriors speeded up their movement, with Zirilo following their change of pace without really knowing why.

As their way reached near the canteen, no one even dared to talk to the founder, but it was clear by how they gasped in horror at the sight of what was inside the canteen. Hayes and the others were drawn to see what happened inside too. Just before Hayes' step reached one meter from where he was going, he heard one of the warriors scream from the entrance of the prison room to the others who had just come with Hayes, saying "The corner man with the gun inside!"

The young Pyralis ran to the scene of attention, followed by his teammates, and Hayes who chose to put his duty first.

"Go find your dad, your aunt, and Siva. Tell them that I'll meet all of you shortly in the study room where it's safe," Hayes spoke to Zirilo before he skipped the canteen in which the entrance was still full of crowded living statues. Zirilo nodded and his little body snuck in the crowd and out to where Hayes last saw them.

As for Hayes who finally reached the opened door, of what inside was supposed to be unknown, he knew that a part of him, if not himself, was going to die.

XV

❧

Chapter Fifteen

Long Overdue Destiny

The corner man was on the brink of exploding himself alongside the prison lock, something he and the warriors surrounding him believed that by doing so would attract chaos that already started with the hooraying prisoners voting for his self-sacrifice. No one really knew what he was really wanting and trying to do, for if he had been waiting to open the lock, he would have done so by then, and if he wanted to kill himself, he would have not aimed at the lock as leverage. His own self did not even know what his goal was other than what gave him most pleasure at that time, the blood. His or others' he liked better, that he still was not entirely sure.

"Let's just shoot him," the handsomest warrior who seemed gone for a while, said so while aiming at the tiny babel.

137

"Wait," the captain stopped him, and his right hand lingered on his junior's weapon where the bullet would go out, maybe just in case. He might shoot the con himself, considering how hurt his and the other warriors' pride was with his trick as he called - he would not say it was for them underestimating the little man, but he was trying to be patient. He did not think that shooting the little guy in where hundreds more that were probably worse than him could be set loose was a good idea.

"Let me," Gore, the troopers captain and ex-warrior, let himself in even when the warriors told him not to. Soon enough, he was standing not far from where the corner man was, but with only Gore's back visible to the others. He put both of his hands up in the air, and his right leg swayed the stolen weapon on the floor to slide towards the warriors on standby.

"I don't want you to die, but you have to do what's right," Gore said to him, but little did everyone know that he was also talking to himself.

With how big he was, there was hope that he could turn the man down, but no way without getting shattered into pieces if he did not want the corner man to have a shot too at the lock. That was what everyone was afraid of, whether he would get the bullets and die, or not; because with all the people the bad man shot blindly at the canteen, there was no certainty for a calm ending.

When Gore was walking slowly towards the front of the prison gate, just so he had a chance to cover the lock with his body, Hayes reached the scene and saw what could have been. At the same time, the corner man saw the look on the founder's face and was reminded of how he lured him to safety but ended up locking him to misery, and from that his clueless mind found himself a new goal, clarity on the death of the one who started the organization.

Everyone who saw his face knew exactly that it was Hayes he was going to throw the grenade at, and by doing so, he would be able to kill at least a couple of warriors around him too. Maybe this was what he deserved for keeping a little bit of hell in what was supposed to be a small world with no evil, in facing death Hayes' mind wandered.

Hayes was right, he was dead, but on the inside this time, when he saw Gore looking at him knowing the certainty when the corner man pulled that silver circle of a safety pin out. Gore's priority of the lock was immediately shifted to The World's leader, as he gave his frightening smile one last time to him as well as one last secret 'I'm proud of you' glance to Pyralis, before throwing his body to the corner man, right before he managed to throw the grenade.

Boom.

The edge side of the middle bunker shook a little with the explosion but luckily it was not strong enough to bury the place down. Fleshes of both the good and evil soared to the ceiling before those which could not make the jump fell instead onto the floor into splatter, and poor Hayes and Pyralis as well as the others had to watch it too as it went.

Lucky that they were still alive, but unlucky for them, the big lock gained hard impact from the explosion that weakened its immunity from the wild jiggle to the bars the prisoners continued to do even after watching the blood. They just could not miss a single opportunity that did not come every day the long time they were there inside cramped with almost no space to walk.

Pyralis, as what they called the warrior by his last name, did not follow the others who by their natural instinct brought their steps back just many steps away until they got to the outside of the room. They were intending to lock the room which would not be able to hold those hundreds of prisoners anyway, but the young warrior with a small bent on one of his ears stayed by himself and locked it from inside, much to the surprise of everybody, who was then sure he was going to die for obvious stupid reason.

It was almost like the bite indeed gave him superpower he kept secret with Gore, his mentor, ever since, but only if the definition accepted relentless hard work that trained unsympathetic towards elimination of whoever he judged as bad, driven by humiliated pride. After the man discharged a deep audible breath, he was capable of prophesying every single motion of every person in the room and counterblow from his rock of fingers thrown to the neck and many other parts of the body. The measures he took had sent every single one of them to their sleep in pain and he took his time to get them one by one back to the jail before he opened the door with his lightened mood, leaving the others' mouths unfolded.

"By the way, somebody needs to get that lock fixed before they're awake," the mighty Pyralis left while saying these words tapped on one of the warriors' right shoulder who once kept bringing up the bite incident as a joke and left for his room to take a shower in peace.

When he stood and looked up to the bathroom ceiling embracing the drench that took a nosedive into his face; amidst all his beloved's corpses he had seen when he took a detour to the canteen - his tears fell over and camouflaged with the long hour of lukewarm water-flow on his skin, he couldn't help but also smile next couple of seconds at his combat triumphant, one second for the punch and one other for the pride he reclaimed, before he wept again over his mourns. The grief was so heavy, that it finally sent both of his knees limp while he was still naked in soap lather.

When Hayes walked in the canteen, he knew that his nightmare was not over. In fact, it had just gone worse and worse as he strolled down the front area from the left in grief, with all blooded bodies collected and covered up to their neck, laid down in a row.

First it was Gerald, then a few scientists from other labs and none other from the main, Hayes' dearest friends all twenty of them, his wife's twin brother, and as his screeching screams he could no longer bear, his dearest wife and little girl lifeless.

He put his body closed in the middle between his wife and

daughter's body, and sat down with his knees touching the cold floor. He bent to his left to kiss his wife goodbye one last time but could not find the strength to pick his upper body up again. When a couple of warriors wanted to help him up, he pushed them back instead so that they would not let him part from his wife. As his left cheek was pressed against his wife's blooded face, thus leaving some red to his too, he saw his daughter's cold body and gained strength to get his torso up to reach her. He dragged her little head and up to the top of his thighs first, then lifted it gently to hug her close to his chest, and uttered a wail that would last for his lifetime. His own heart turned numb ever since.

Hayes reminisced as he reached the meeting room and sat on his peasant throne, of how a 'good' leader he was to put the prison in the middle section close to where he and all his dearest people lived, and to give hope to all those assessed psychopaths and evil-minded alike he separated from the others as prisoners, where in fact all of them would probably never think twice if given the opportunity to kill. What was he thinking? And like so the repetitive what ifs filled him with endless guilt and blinded him from his surroundings, that he did not even realize the little boy who had long been hiding just under and had no plan to come out in the near future. He was told by the same man that it was where it was safe, so he would rather stay.

Ten people, representing about two breathing hundreds living in the middle section from all fields and expertise, excluding a number of warriors, marched into where Hayes was.

The way the founder saw it, they were just as annoying as suddenly popping up out of nowhere like pimples as their voice brought him back from the self-condemnation world. However, the small souvenir he brought back from where his mind was, was a little something that convinced him that there was no other people he could be hating more than himself, so he had no right to condemn them for what came next from their mouth.

That everyone was blaming him for why those Code Blacks were still alive. Why those considered-evils with no hope for turning point, as what they believed, needed to be kept if they were going to be prisoned anyway for the rest of their life, as if human right principles had been shifted for good that day; and that if they had been dead then none of this would have happened, to think that one thought when they heard heaven on earth, it meant there was no evil left to live on the ground, or let be.

Hayes decided to bring all that was closest to the mourn and not just those ten but also as many that he could find in the hall that followed him regardless as he silently led the way. Scientists, warriors, all intellectuals, and trustworthy men of his who he saw would perchance become most salient when The World was ready to come out, he brought inside to the room of what had become not so secret anymore. He did not turn on the light however and kept the room dark as he walked in while the others watched from the open entrance.

"Take a good look at them, one last time," Hayes said from a bit afar, and thus one person in a white lab coat who was standing nearest to the switch, turned on the light that just happened to be the one nearest to the prison without his intention. Those who were categorized in the good side saw, most for the first time, the remaining real threats that looked like zombies in a cage, setting off fear and trepidation as the light was dimmed by the dark souls.

Most of the prisoners still laughed, one kind that gave terror to anyone who heard. They chortled even more when they could see those blood splatters clearer as the incandescent lamp helped them to. It seemed they had forgotten that a part of those belonged to one of their own too, and they celebrated only the death of the good hero, which was Gore.

"Thank you for celebrating," Hayes suddenly spoke up which stopped the commemoration just for a moment. "Now I know I can fully trust the *brain*," he added immediately after.

One of the prisoners, whose natural outer body color showed almost no difference to the night sky, suddenly shouted that the machine was racist for putting him as Code Black because of his skin. "Racist," he talked again about the machine, then told the founder the exact same thing about him.

By the prisoner's surprise, Hayes' face got very near him who had been having both hands' fingers wrapping the rolled steels. His face was so close to the other's that even a few inches of his face had surely passed the bar. Hayes did not look scared, not at all. In fact, he had lost that feeling called 'fear' when he saw his much-lamented wife and daughter, owing to the fact he came to realize that the greatest fear in his life was not losing his own life, rather it was the fear of losing the life of the people he loved.

Subsequently, Hayes told the same person who turned on the first light at his own will, to turn the other one too. As the bulb had revealed its shiniest form, he flaunted the skin color of those warriors, scientists and all intellectuals that came into the light. It was lucid that almost exactly half of them in number were black too.

"That same machine sorted them as Code White. See those warriors, they were sorted not just like any other Code Whites, but fighting heroes, and they all had exactly the same skin as you, so tell me again that the machine was racist. There was never an excuse for your evil seed to begin with," Hayes spoke with such valor, so vigorously that his spraying spit showed just how much he meant those sentences.

"Warriors, stay. The rest, you should go," Hayes ordered them all to, in which after they saw what happened, they immediately did. Heck, some of them actually had already wanted to but did not out of fear of missing out.

After it was made sure that Hayes, warriors, and the prisoners were the only people left in the room, the leader walked quietly towards the closed entrance door. Whilst his right hand already touched the doorknob, he was yet to twist it, and waited for some time with his eyes closed, thinking carefully of what he was going to say. When he opened his eyes, he knew that his mind was made up.

"Kill all the prisoners," he said before his presence soon vanished from the room. Much to the surprise of both the warriors and prisoners who looked to their left and right making sure they did not mishear it, the captain quickly let himself out of the door seemingly to catch up on the one who had just left. From his subordinate' perspectives, he too didn't think of the order lightly and was going to get confirmation from him. When the captain came back, his face said it all, they did not mishear even a single word.

All mortals trapped inside the lock-up started to scrap for longer seconds to live. They all ran to the back and away from the bars that led nowhere, and when they realized they really had nowhere to go, they started to grab one another to use as shields from the bullets. Some of them even looked like they were scratching the wall, possibly hallucinating a hope that they could climb concrete and break through the turf in ten minutes; while few others crawled like spiders on the floor juggling their death between getting stepped on or shot at.

With the warriors, they took the time with their right to kill, especially the captain who knew that when he said go, the others would do. All warriors could see that the captain had his eyes closed. When he opened them, he took a deep breath and moved a few steps closer to the jail. Next, his hand instructed the others to take position in a row surrounding the prison from every possible angle, and their weapons were aimed at the people inside.

"Hell on earth, meet your long overdue destiny," he screamed, then started shooting at them prisoners without mercy and without a stop, with the other warriors following his move.

XVI

Chapter Sixteen

The Birth of Two Pivotal Findings

Past midnight down under the dark sky, a group of men marched from the vault below carrying dead bodies ten after ten that counted to more than ten times of that. Hayes, who was the only one without armor, chose a random tree to talk to, while his back in turn watched the men as they went with his order of disposal.

The founder had come to a harsh conclusion that could not be undone, that there was no solution and no opportunity given to turn the foul around. Maybe his dad was right after all - there was only one side of each person, and when the dark took over the light, the small gleam would not survive. Maybe he was right too for showing no mercy to evil, that it was the only way to eliminate the root that might cause harm to the society, even if it was just a maybe.

"I shouldn't have killed him," Hayes said to the tree, which it responded with a hissing sound and flying faded leaves landed on the top of his head and shoulders. He cried with nature, and his tears fell hard with regret, for killing his own father for what he thought was right, just to end up killing hundreds more to establish he was the one that had been wrong instead.

The bad karma he had led himself into. When a no-rule bailed him out, fate became his judge, maybe unless he had known he was making a mistake only when it was not too late.

But he then thought of another, he had not before. If he killed his father just to prove his point, wouldn't that already make his belief the same as his father's own principle? To kill who he believed was too evil to live just so that the world would be free from what he gathered as wrong. If it was, then this, those hundreds, would make it his second act, wouldn't it?

Enough with the what ifs, he surmised, and that drove him to put himself inside the brain scanner as soon as he got back underground.

The familiar female scientist was to set the machine up for him. It was never her superior to do since this was always considered as the lowest task of the higher role. Surprisingly, Meng stopped her and said, "Let me."

Hayes' head lay upward on the thin cushion and not long after, familiar instrumentals were played to its sequence that analyzed his emotions as his neurons jumped from one to another. It had taken an hour longer than his first test before the brain scanner stopped the lullabies-like at the last chain and generated a result. White square peg covered almost the whole screen, then minimized itself and moved to the top left as the same menu that appeared in the beginning showed itself again.

"Code White," Meng told Hayes whilst his hand reached out the leader's to help him raise his body, but hearing the result and seeing Meng's smile, the founder did not find immediate relief.

"Do you think I should believe this result?" Hayes said to Meng.

"Without a grain of doubt," the then sole lead scientist replied.

"Then, I want you to add something. In fact, to add something back," the founder responded. Meng, who was quick at his thinking, promptly thought of the *thing*, but knowing how big of a deal it was, asked again just to make sure, "Do you mean, what was removed before?" And it sounded exactly like the late Gerald's annoying question. Since dislike almost always went down, wholly or a bit, with the death of its dweller, Meng began to think if Gerald was firing his repetitive questions for the similar reason.

"Yes, I want you to add that back to it. So as to remove mercy from it once more, you know what I mean," Hayes replied with such an expression where his resolution looked adamant, so Meng decided to answer back with the requested action instead. No turning back.

Since then, any soul that was unfortunate enough to receive a Code Black result was immediately vanished, sent back to where they were seen to belong, in the afterlife; if God or Satan would accept their blank question papers of life back without any answer inside to see where they fit. People seemed to sometimes forget that probably no living one except those who had been there; only those who were already there, really knew how such judgment worked.

Back in the lab, Meng stayed up late alone unlike the other three who pretended that Gerald's death was too much to bear for them. To use the death of someone they despised as a pretense for a probably lazy excuse, just proved how there was still always a bit of a dark even in the shiniest room, he thought.

The lead scientist put as priority analyzing why the corner man would still do such a thing, even after he had been classified as Code Grey. He knew that the rehabilitation approach must be wrong, but where was precisely the flaw in that, he wondered. So he started examining the relevant person's detailed report on those thirty emotions, which the *brain* scanned by form of instrumentals then sent to the main lab in predetermined words.

Approbation. Affection. Aesthetic appreciation. Merriment. Wonderment. Awkwardness. Anxiety. Boredom. Calmness. Confusion. Hunger. Addiction. Empathetic pain. Sympathy. Entrancement. Envy. Excitement. Fear. Terror. Joy. Curiosity. Sentimentality. Romance. Sadness. Satisfaction. Libido. Indecisiveness. Triumph. Ambition. Forgiveness.

The research led him to ponder the why. Why might he be good for a moment then ran amok many moments later? Was it a deficiency in empathy? Lack of love? Depression? Revenge?

Maybe if they had been focusing on perfecting the form of each of those emotions, the rehabilitation process would have been flawless, would any reckon?

"Hang on," he said to himself after his mind released a breakthrough of an idea.

He soon threw many handbooks that had slept on the cover of a large dark blue notebook where the team drafted most of their plan. He then listed all of those emotions, and his hand steered chaotic lines that linked those thirty emotions to seven freshly drawn squares with a name of color on each box. Grey, red, orange, yellow, green, blue, and purple.

"I've got to finish the draft before the morning comes," he added to his discussion with himself, and the way he talked, it was as if those released ideas he sketched on the paper was his own kind of ecstasy that pumped up the volume of his voice.

He thought that the major breakthrough plan was revolutionary and that Hayes needed to hear it as soon as he could, so he put all of his undivided attention on it and soon forgot all about his journey in finding out the provenance of the corner man's rampage behavior. He was distracted; skipping on one kind of root and heading straight to the possible solution that would apply to all strains instead. He was positive that he had found that one key Hayes was looking for.

As the irreversible damage of action the corner man had

done was still replayed on his mind from time to time, he convinced himself, even the good ones always had a bit of a devil inside them every once in a while, so whether it was the right timing combined with the wrong kind of opportunity, maybe, or not, he decided to just leave it hanging there; maybe for a long moment, and moved on.

Meanwhile, Hayes was still wide awake in the study room. He kept watching the horror footage, over and over, and even left it replayed as a background when his eyes were not on it.

While his fingers started moving like a roller coaster on a piece of paper, writing random things that came to mind releasing his anger, he suddenly caught a glimpse of something, someone, more than one in fact, and bewildered by his findings.

He was thinking of calling Meng but remembering how late and near it was to the morning, he proceeded his tired body to be on its way out to his bed. With enormous support from lady luck, Hayes' windy presence bumped into the scientist's unsteady amble from across the hall looking like they were both sleepwalking. They wasted no time to embrace the energy they got left and gambled it all for a one or two steps forward towards an impossible long dream coming true, and near.

XVII

Chapter Seventeen

"We Are Ready to Come Out"

A few weeks later, everyone's mind was starting to live in peace with the perpetual scars they then had, but not at all for the little boy. Since losing almost all of his family, he still grew a habit of coming to Hayes' study slash meeting room when there was not anyone there. He just curled under the wide table there, where he felt the safest and no bad guy could find him.

Hayes' attention from the footage brought his decision to rescan everyone in the bunker again. He asked Meng to be in charge, which he took beyond seriously as always. He was also asked to bring him an immediate report every time a progress had been made. So when Meng found the leader in the hall, even when he was looking like he was losing something, the scientist still promptly suggested a discussion in their usual meeting space regardless.

"You're looking for something, Sir?" Meng asked the founder as they were still walking together in the hall.

"Someone. My nephew, have you seen him? He's been missing a lot lately. I want to make sure he's okay," he replied just when they reached the door.

As soon as they sat down, Meng laid down on the big table a few photographs taken from the video surveillance on the day the massacre happened. "We did as we were told by you, testing everyone again," he substantiated before he pointed to one of those pictures, in particular a child, black hair and red cheeks with an obvious glance of an owl, who was hiding near the edge of the long buffet counter while watching the whole thing yet still lived to that day unharmed.

"We have tested the child again, twice, and he's still in a Code Black situation, Sir. It is as you expected," the scientist added.

"How many are there like him?" Hayes responded with a hideous concern look from his face. More shipment of wrinkles from the stress had definitely arrived on his epidermis.

"Statistically, it's now fourteen point forty three percent of the current Code White population here, and the rate, we believe it's growing," Meng responded with the similar worry expression.

"This... evil, is like a virus; the good should not be exposed to them, not even the tiniest," the founder contemplated with his fingers shaping the foundation on his chin. "No more loopholes," he continued," And I don't think we're willing to risk another burnout slayer getting another innocent killed, even just a single one, ever again. No, I refuse to have more innocent lives taken for granted by the devil."

Meng, who did not know which feeling applied to him greater - happy or lucky, that he did not actually lose anyone he would miss on that massacre day, could not really relate, and thus was left speechless. So, it was only natural that he could think about human rights violation, as he surmised that Hayes should have been too; but as his mind wandered across morality, he left himself speechless.

"What's wrong?" Hayes asked him, and as he would not let his boss know of his recent real thought, he mentioned another.

"Actually, Sir, there is one more," he slowly said, "There are a few more cases of Code Grey now, even with the adults; they are rare, but well, they are still there."

"Hmm," Hayes left the humming hanging for quite longer than usual, and after a while he said, "From now on, put Code Greys and their close family under isolation, regardless. I do not want to take any more chances. And that *thing* I said I wanted you to add back to the machine, is it done? I'm quite surprised I haven't heard anything about it from you until now."

"Well, yes, Sir, the *thing* you had asked to remove in the long past, but are you sure that..."

"As for those Code Blacks, well, there should be none of them, not anymore. Do what the chip told them to do before."

"But... Sir, what should we do with the bodies then? Those future Code Black corpses."

"Tell the warriors to clear the hall at midnight, and make sure up there is clear too. Throw them there in the meantime as barriers. We cannot do anything else with these bodies, can we? It's not like we can burn those bodies, we don't want any forest fire either, and I don't want the earth to cry. If someone knows how to bring these corpses back to life on our side instead, I'd be impressed."

Zirilo, who had been hiding under Hayes the whole time, heard the confidential matter. Though he was still little, he already knew he had to keep his mouth shut about it. As spongy of a brain he still had too, and how much he had been looking up to Hayes secretly, he absorbed the idea more than the grown-ups, fascinated by the vision he had about it, and the imagination was no longer scary somehow.

A new ambition emerged in the little boy's mind - he wanted to be a leader too, like Hayes, but more; more fearless, more relentless, and even better if he could. To start, he crawled out and almost gave the two adults in the room a heart attack. Meng was able to keep his stand steady, but unfortunately for Hayes, he failed to keep his cool charisma by screaming and jumping out of the big chair - his left leg would have even hurt the little boy's head if the swing curve of his left shoe had been one centimeter further.

"Why are you here, boy?" Hayes talked to Zirilo once his heart calmed down from the shock.

"You said for them to meet you here, it's because it's the

safest down here, right?" Zirilo answered with a memory weeks long, and Hayes knew exactly what the little boy meant, and when exactly he himself said it too. No further miscommunication as Zirilo admitted that he had been hiding there ever since, answering why Hayes had not been successful in finding him.

The founder got down on one knee, and hugged Zirilo in front of Meng, who had just been watching and resisting tears. "I promise that I will keep you safe, always, and bring you up as my own only son," Hayes vowed to Zirilo. Meng, who was revealed to have a soft heart after all, could not bear the leak from his eyes' liquid vessel any longer.

"Dad?" The little boy slowly spoke, and this time, it was Hayes' that was too much to bear for him as the salty waterfall flew down both of his cheeks.

Since that day, Zirilo never again called Hayes by the word 'uncle'. Furthermore, on that very same day too, a new system for the new world was established, and he knew it was almost ready for the rest of the world to see. It would not be much longer, for certain.

The warrior captain in charge came in as his presence was requested by the king of the organization. "What are the signs?" Hayes asked.

"No sign of contravenes. We are now seen as their only hope, and the number of our heads living here are much higher than the ones up there. We are ready to come out, Sir. They are all asking, begging for us, and the monster's numbers are down, way down - whoever's left, we can take them down, easily," the captain replied with full confidence, and Hayes didn't think that the warrior even blinked or breathed the whole time he was reporting it.

"All I want is just a world - a world free from evils and to have nature to our clemency at last. I can finally really see it coming now," the founder gave his short speech, "And it's time, the right time, that we give them hope. Don't you agree?" He added, vigilant of the other's desire as a sample to match his formal speech he was planning to give to the others to hear.

The week later during the day, the view was much different in the sky than its usual live painting. More birds were flying across the single wide land than their usual number, and the variance was bringing wide heavy speakers in all areas to make sure Hayes' revolutionary speech was heard all over.

"My fellow survivors," he began, and he saved no words for small talk. His speech centralized on the point where he promised everyone, heaven on earth, where resources were distributed with no charge whatsoever - however and whenever they wanted, where they could live comfortably day and night with no fear at all kinds, and where everything was provided for, for them to live happily in harmony ever after. "Everyone, however," as he let it be emphasized, "of those who pass the test only," in other words, to see if they were qualified or not for The World. What he left out of the speech nonetheless, that if they were not, they would be dismissed from life, but a few brains still managed to catch on to the secret phrase.

While a few of those standing under the bright sky whose life was already worse than death did not care to seek any catch, some did hush about what it would mean by being dismissed. That 'some' included those who were living in the bunker, who already noticed a few familiar faces had gone in the wind.

"Would you take the chance for a better world? Either or, we will still be coming out of the underground." Hayes closed the speech by laying down his hand frontward, for his palm to look at the sky, even when only a few people in the room could see him doing so. His gestures regardless probably explained why the tone of his speech sounded charismatic and magnificently real.

Right after, Zirilo who had been standing closest to him the whole time - fully impressed, asked the real meaning of the disposal, before the others could stop him. Hayes put his hands gently on top of the little boy's greasy palms, signaling amusement with his smile, but answered assertively with a question, "What you should have done when you find someone who catches a dangerous virus with no treatment, before it spreads even further. What do you think that would be?"

It was clear to those in the room who witnessed Hayes' answer but had already known him from the beginning, that he was never the same since the murderous event. It was as if his heart grew cold since then, even colder than the icy mountain who did not cascade down its skin when being constantly shined by the sun during a perennial wintry storm.

The next midnight, when the warriors went striding the woodland to have the scattered cannibal and Code Black bodies moved out of the forest, Hayes unexpectedly joined them halfway through the mission. This time, he wanted to see for himself those rotten corpses smelling like a pungent disgusting odor covered in expired cheap perfumes as they were on their way to become their form of ashes.

Handmade rain of light fuel oil showered only onto the mountain of those decomposing, and as they were glazed by a touch of fire, the founder paid his farewell contempt by saying, "When your brain fails to show your virtuousness, you should have never even been born to enter this world, for your loyalty lies as the devil's handmaids to begin with and thus you can never resist your temptation to hell. You see, without you, the earth would be able to gain her peace, and this is just what you should have stayed as, ashes," and he cried while saying so as he circumstantially relived the squeaky laugh of his daughter and the prepossessing smile his wife was blessed with.

The land in the upper ground was successfully refurbished ready for the new world and sooner than was planned, people from all over the mainland came near the forest as instructed. When the rest came out from the bunker, their numbers were indeed proven bigger than the upper ground world population as it had been claimed to be. Cannibals soon became extinct, then vanished without a trace from the face of the earth and no longer the world's first problem next to Mother Earth's temper, whose elements seemed to still be missing their trust towards humans.

A couple of weeks later, good changes could already be seen as children were running around the land day and night safely and animals were coming out from hiding out of nowhere like they were just falling down from heaven as a gift from God.

The country was finally entrenched like heaven on earth, many years later. Slowly but surely, the air of peace and harmony pervaded the only giant landmass on earth as its pillars of society were constructed almost solely by the *brain* by the people who guarded its integrity. Knowledge then separation between who were evil and who were not on earth, showed as the key of trust they built the foundation into.

A new beginning for the world, setting off to establish the true heaven on earth, as the founding father had encapsulated from the start his goal, a world with no evil; however, conceivably fragile still when the earth did not buy entirely the humans' definition of evil, and her elements' trust in them had yet to be restored.

Hence, the final part of this history started.

BOOK THREE

THE WORLD WITH NO EVIL

XVIII

Chapter Eighteen

The World with No Evil

This is the story about how a broken trust was never without heavy and complex consequences.

Many, many years later, about thirty years in fact after The World (as what they officially called themselves) came out of their hiding place hidden from the sky, a new era was verbally entrenched - a more than possible worldwide peace.

Those who had been pridefully heavily involved in governing the system of the single country since it was hidden underground; they neither called the previous generations the old world, nor they called themselves the new world. They simply called themselves The World; for the world would have been had they come before their time, the world still could be so long as a credence never failed to shape a reasonable judge-ment, and the world would be as their goal was always clearly engraved to build a fine humanity as it should be.

Accordingly, The World had become the ruler of heavenly freedom on earth, from a manmade leap of faith they called brain scanner, with a powerful result that was made perpetual and linear, in a world where the early discovery between who was good and who was evil was accepted as the true origin of peace. The established system went on something like this.

The only feared assessment, or so they thought, served as the first clear base whether newborns belonged in the civi-lization's paradigm of heaven on earth the citizen called the Code White area, as the literal desired result inspired its name. Everyone wished to live and kept living in this particular dis-trict. It was built on the best soil of the land, as its attributes had been reported regularly by the flying drones that shaped like various common birds, generated by a group of scien-tists that were also tasked since their hiding in bunker days to study which area was the finest across the then chaotic coun-try. Whilst their contribution had been dimmed with the end-less night, it rose slowly and surely to shine so brightly like sunrise once the organization came out for good to live where the sky was visible.

Once their brain scan proved that they belonged there, they would receive a *bracelet* as what they called it, which would stretch automatically as their wrists grew with their body. Each had a tiny The World logo imprinted in the middle and with a strap color of their choice. This identity form was updated frequently upon their scheduled regular scans, and so long as the result always showed Code White, they could continue living in the organized civilization with a taste of heaven.

Yes, everything was taken care of and provided for. No currency or monetary trade. This was set as a ground rule to eliminate robberies and other associated criminal activities, heading towards wealth parity. Everyone was doing whatever they wanted without worrying about money, as it was intended, so long as they did not do any crimes as the *brain* forecasted, the only way they could keep the *bracelet*; and it was right, everyone obeyed regulation because they were aware that it was for the better, their own good. A self-proclaimed perfect life system run by fear, to live in peace.

Soaring glassy towers that never failed to mirror the sun's daily natural light covered almost the central area of Code White. Some buildings were ordinary but the ones that really caught the eye were rainbow-colorful mini houses that were shaped like exclamation points stuck to the ground all over the street. Some had been completed, some others were still in the making; and the only workers allowed to build scaffolding of those, the structures and all of the necessary steps to complete the job were machines and expressionless robots.

The mechanism went on the same with other fields, thanks to those scientists who were worshipped endlessly for their growing inventions, who were able to develop almost everything that humans never really wanted to do. Though mostly for comfort and pleasure, they did not exclude the importance of basic human necessities such as medical technology development that was tremendous too, as to ensure long life longevity.

Everyone was focusing on finding and doing what it was that made them the happiest and their only goal was to find it before they died. The only reason some people could still be seen doing those jobs that those machines and robots could do too was only because they wanted to, often not for long, before they moved on to other things they were curious to do out of boredom. That was the case when a man was seen on a fishing boat and the machine scanned the sea instead to lead him to all the fishes he wanted to try to catch, and if he was bored for still failing to do so, he let the machine catch the fish for him. So even though the world button was reset, and the starting point was advanced like never before, some still resumed mindlessness.

As the humans even on their neonate stage with detected evil intention (such as those that gained pleasures from the suffering of others, blood or coitus without consent or slaughter or human butcher, anything that screamed themselves dangerous to society and criminal behaviors) were already eliminated immediately, there was no fear of them any longer as opposed to being one themselves. Even just merely the thought of being bad scared them to death, and the image of even the possibility of being stripped off the unbelievable privileges they gained so easily by being human, good human; those too scattered them to pieces. The fear had been doing its job more than enough to keep their morality conviction righteous.

But even when their actions were still deemed not applicable to evil behaviors such as those of murderers and serial killers, so on and so forth, they were still some left, unavoidable yet could still be destructive for even the kindest people in the world.

"The brain scanner is able to apply numerous cases and projects in how the subject would behave, based on almost infinite scenarios of thirty emotions in total. However, we have managed to simplify them into seven, seven colors in fact, to help you become the best version of yourself," younger version of Meng Holmes as the inventor of the six other kinds of brain scanner explained in a video that was replayed everywhere in every chamber's hall. The idea of these other chambers that were in literal shape of no-space exclamation point was to support personal problems the citizens could not handle, so that they remained peaceful and to make their living easier from behaviors that were not considered Code Black worthy but could be seen as destructive to themselves and or their surroundings.

As initiated by Meng, other chambers besides the Grey served as an advisory tool that would allow the Code White citizens to deal with the things they still could not control. Each chamber was one of the seven ways to analyze deeply and suppress the source of the little growing darkness every one of them had. But, what were they for exactly?

XIX

Chapter Nineteen

Seven Colors of Chambers

In where the Grey Chamber identified the good and evil ratio of the subject, the Red measured the level of ambition and competitiveness. Being one case of its various usances, a tall man in a cherry-colored t-shirt and tennis hat entered what looked like a very similar brain scanner to the ones in Grey except the machine was really shielded in red paint. It was able to analyze his hopeless ambition to become the best tennis player in the world. He did not plan to quit but he had lost in almost all the matches he participated in for the last five years. Could or should he give up, he wondered, and so the machine did its trick.

Once the man got out without human assistance similarly to when he entered it, the machine had a screen gliding from the left side, driving the man to move to a sitting position. He watched the relay as the red *brain* was able to project three scenarios most relevant to his behavior, emotions, and memories - as the other *brains* could too in their own purpose.

First was he continued the career for the next five years and defeated plenty but grew out of boredom from the winning and decided to find something else he could top against before he died, in which the *brain* had already prepared the list of the things he could try to go for afterward. Second was similar except that he kept on losing and decided to try other things from the exact same list that he could win instead. Third was he skipped both the winning and the losing for the list. "Something to think about," the *brain* in a female tone said while printing the list for him to take away. The man afterward walked back home, put his tennis racket on the shelf then contemplated on the roll.

The Orange Chamber was where the forgiveness was sedated. A woman with long black hair in her early twenties could be seen fumbling on her way to the orange *brain* machine caused by her blurry vision that sourced from her two shattered dams of tears.

The machine was able to detect the cheating man that was in her life who did not feel sorry even just a little bit and as she wondered if she should forgive him anyway, the *brain* gave her a rather long answer - that she could not then, but she should for her own peace, and that she would as time would slowly chew the memory one bite at a time. Before the twinkle on her lips left the room, the *brain* in a soothing man voice also suggested for her to come to the Red Chamber, for a harmless revenge plot that triggered her winning ambition was detected. "Something to think about," it continued before shutting the screen down.

Meanwhile, the *brain* in the Yellow Chamber in which ability to assist with indecisiveness had made it incredibly more popular among the others, designedly invited a free-spirited woman in her late twenties who seemingly satirically could not decide which proposal between two men she should accept.

It gave her two scenarios, but only one included the plan to marry. "It would be very similar if not the same whoever you chose," the brain concluded, "but here would be the things you could no longer do," the brain then printed a small amount of list titled 'your most favorite things to do'. "Something to think about," it added, leaving the woman absent for words but satisfied with the answer, for the idea had actually been on her mind without saying. She was better off being single anyway.

The *brain* in the Green Chamber was well known for its habit to meter in a chart of three separate bars which it then always showed on its screen report: self-confidence, self-effacing, and self-control. One man, a writer in hiding for no crime, could constantly be seen in and out of the particular chamber whether it was day or night. If he did breach a law, it was only the jurisprudence of believing in one's own self. However, he had come back again one fine evening when the sky was dark before his book was officially anonymously published for the first time. He was about to cancel the launch at the very last minute, so the machine started to get irritated with the perception that it had not been doing a great job with this particular case.

Instead of giving him scenarios like before and usual, the *brain* catapulted at him with a female voice, several questions the writer heard once or twice before in his own mind but always ignored, in which he had to answer very immediately in a five-second countdown.

"Why do you write?"

"I don't know, it's just the first thing I do when I wake up, and the last thing I do before I go to sleep, without even really thinking why..."

"For whom do you write?" The *brain* cut his answer short.

"Nobody at first, but now I worry that it should have been for everybody."

"Who knows?"

"Who knows? Who knows what I write? No... nobody, no one, and that's why I'm scared. Maybe I should have told this to everybody but..."

"Do you want people to read it?"

"Yes, I mean, no? I mean, what if it's bad?"

"Do you want people to know?"

"Yes! Yes, very much, yes. I just want to share it but I don't know why."

The machine went quiet for a while, then showed on the screen while also printing for him the question-and-answer session they had just had. When the writer read it, his eyes went suddenly super hydrated without any drop, and decided to release his book anyway as he realized he really wanted from the heart to tell the whole world his words. He was tired of keeping his pastime work for himself and could not wait to see what people thought of it. It was just the fear that had been holding him back. Little did he know that the *brain* was just retrieving from the scanned memory of his, repeating questions that many times appeared in his mind and remained unanswered, as the smart chip was honestly running out of advice to give.

The Blue Chamber, unexpected by the body governing the Code White system, was probably the second most popular among the others. It was still a mystery to the house of rules, why even the happiest person on earth where everything was provided for still needed to come back and forth the machine in it for what they thought sometimes as bizarre reasons. Luckily, Meng Holmes disregarded the initial response of ridicule about the function and continued on the project that made it what it was, a powerful *brain* that administered mental health and relaxation needs of its subject.

A woman in a blue dress was due for a rescan in the Grey Chamber the day after tomorrow, and it was only natural for her to go to the Blue Chamber the day before. Though it was evident to her surroundings' eyes that there would be no doubt for her to get the Code White result as always like everyone did around her too, and instead of going to the Green Chamber, she as she had done before many times decided that the Blue one was the right chamber for her for this.

"You're in the right place," the *brain* spoke to her in a friendly female voice while she laid down, and it could see that her anxiety level was responding quite nicely to its confirmation gesture.

"Don't tell anyone that you've heard this from me, but you will pass the test, everyone in the Code White area will," the brain encouraged.

"Really?"

"I'm sure, trust me. Remember what I first told you, five years ago, that the house of rules had established that people were born evil, not nurtured to be one, and even if it was not, look at where you have always been. No work, no crime, and no criminals. Everything is provided for. As a matter of fact, there has not even been any Code Black cases on both the new-borns and adults for the past five years. So, what else is there to worry about?" The *brain* responded perfectly that the woman even went early to her scheduled scan in the Grey Chamber the next morning and left of course with the expected result, knowing perfectly that she would come back to the same Blue Chamber again the day before her next scheduled test, just so she could hear what the brain always said all over again.

The people who entered the Purple Chamber were usually seen by the eyes in either light or dark aubergine color clothing, but if anyone cared enough to trace the source of their damp cheeks, they would be able to witness those floating shattered pieces of their heart that had no puzzle shape whatsoever to bring them back together, for the rest of the pieces had gone with the people they lost, whether it was to part ways or death.

One might think that if there had been the constant extraordinarily high quality of life the country had to offer, as well as no Code Black cases for the last five years, it would only be logical that the number of visitors to the chambers would have decreased significantly. No, in fact, it was oddly otherwise.

A woman whose face was made unclear purposely by her black veil entered the crowded waiting room in the Purple Chamber hugging an empty mini frame wrapped in a pink blanket. Her husband's arms had to be attached to her shoulders the whole time to help stabilize her turbulent body to land on her seat perfectly.

"Something I can do?" The husband's gentle voice stopped the wife's muffled cry for a moment but not her tied tongue, so he added, "We'd better let the machine to, as we were told." It was a good idea, the husband thought, because he had been thinking of exactly the same thing too as the answer.

"Another *accident*," one receptionist said to another in a whisper, who realized that the couple's case was not at all alone in the room.

"Mandatory?" The other replied.

"The one before isn't, this one is," her workmate muttered back.

"Same old song, I'm getting bored. I'm gonna do something else tomorrow, you're coming?" It was obvious they chose to replace the robot's job for the day just to know how it felt -

just like how the other Code White residents treated work as, out of curiosity.

"Wait, so you're not clocking out now?"

"I still want to know how it feels at the end of the day, if anything changes. Now, let's see what that couple that just got in is probably in for, I wonder."

They were indeed surrounded by others who also lost their newborns even when their little ones had been categorized as Code White. Somehow, they just suddenly lost their breath a few days or months later and flew to heaven in peace, leaving their parents to deal with the pain.

One more common thing found was how similar the color of their clothing was, and this did not only apply to the visitors in Purple Chamber, but other chambers too respectively. The dominant color that they were wearing seemed to unconsciously encourage their expressive behavior to reveal their true feelings without really saying it and even without the entreaty to be judged.

Wearing a color in accordance with the chamber somehow made them feel more relaxed whilst they refused to tell people what they were feeling - they just wanted them to be aware of the kind of feeling they were in and let the machine deal with their affairs instead. Was that all? Probably not. It had just proved again and again how the people grew to trust and rely on the machine more than human beings, like the case with the husband who felt no need to make more effort in how to soothe his wife's bereavement for he believed the machine would do a better job, as he himself needed too.

Just when the receptionist called the couple's name for their turn to enter the *brain* inside, however, an existence's clamor came in by surprise and forced their motion to go the other way.

XX

Chapter Twenty

The New Leader, Thirty Years Later

Mother Nature interrupted with her uninvited presence. The earth paid her respect, it seemed, by shaking her ground perchance to distract the couple's grief away, but what a wrong move if it was.

The wide long singular country's warriors screamed they were ready however. Oh yes, The World was always expecting every kind of disaster the earth had been offering in a random cycle, and during those times in the underground too, the experts had been learning how to make The World ready for those by the day they went out; and when they did, they let the ideas grow freely in a while - prevention and mitigation efforts for every single kind possible.

Such as this case for the earthquake, The World quietly retaliated against the unknowingly sick earth by piercing the ground altogether with electrifying long silver poles maneuvered by giant green tanks in several different spots on the land to speed up the tremor, which it did. As they had first learned in their bunker days via their flying robot birds, they found that this only land existed on earth had several acupoints which responded purportedly favorably to the natural disasters when treated in certain ways, depending on the kinds of phenomenon. When drawn a line on the map, it could be seen that those dots made up a heartbeat line right in the top middle part of the land.

What they did not care about however, was that how to mitigate the earthquake harmed Mother Earth, so did the other ways work for her various tempers. When mountains were erupting, they found a way later on how to freeze them by throwing giant meticulously crafted chemical tablets right down the center. When the wind was blowing Herculean push, they built giant alluring fan towers to attract and kiss them gentle venom that was only harmless to humans - they put all the details in their 'How to Kill a Storm' handbook. And when the water was provoking war to claim more territory of the land, they put up barricades to knock the sea army over. These walls' height could easily adjust to its desideratum too by way of levers, such as those that were located at the border of the dark forest. With all these inventions, they never cared so much about the why anymore, as they believed they had fully taken care of it, though they were probably only half right.

The idea of the brain scanner was created by the belief that human's evil behavior to each other was the source of the weird and unexplainable natural disasters, as opposed to The Earth members who deemed the source as the harm done to nature instead. The imbalance of nature and those strange destructive phenomena were sometimes still happening, though not as often. However, still, they made more projects that tried to prevent or overcome them, in addition to the ones who focused on improving the high quality of life, regardless of the nature. Even when certain resources were running out, they could somehow still manage to create the replacements using other kinds of supplies from nature, as easy as flipping the back of their hands - but this unfortunately did not last longer than it should.

With all of those super advanced technologies, instead of trying other alternatives like, say, moving the society to another planet, they shifted their focus to try their best to defeat Mother Nature's bad temper, while still disregarding her comfort. The people were there to stay, believing they were the sole rulers of her and not her.

Globules of acid from hundreds and thousands of industrial factories leaking drop by drop onto the soil and vaporizing into the air. Some of the waste even flowed down the stream and poisoned the sea. The express metamorphosis of revolutionary ideas was often at the expense of Mother Earth's contentment. Ironically yet persistently, the more they claimed to protect the earth, the more they hurt her; some others thought it was just like when they claimed that there was no evil left in the area, that there might be, still was.

"Someone has killed my baby!"

The woman who screamed this in front of her house just the day after she lost her baby, was one of those 'some others'.

A couple of days before that, she was still resting on a snuggly light blue bed rest in a scrupulously spotless hospital room while holding her baby girl tight after the little one had just got back from the little Grey Chamber in the building.

"She has passed the test, you can relax now," the nurse who brought her back to her mother spoke softly but bestowed upon the mother the loudest joy her heart had ever borne. That heart was debilitated however, bone-weary, and almost melted into the shadow of the newborn who without warning fell into an eternal sleep the first night she spent out of the hospital.

The mother first blamed her and her husband's two-story all-included house that looked as wonderfully ordinary as the others who, just like them, purchased the house with nothing but a touch of a *bracelet* earned from a simple light sleep in the machine that woke them up with a prudent Code White answer. The burning wood in the fireplace just by the long wooden table might have coughed enough killing smoke that travelled to the right, passed by the green marble kitchen island onto the long corridor and climbed up the cream-colored carpeted stairs, then bent down the closed door where the nursery room was at its back to kiss the innocent darling forever good night.

But her instinct as a mother was counseled by the illuminated fact from the news, similarities between the death cases not just to few newborns but to some adults too, that she started to wonder if there was someone or more than one set on the loose from the machine calling them Code Whites. So she started to question the authority.

Just a few hours after the woman's fretted scream, the couple was called by the house of rules, the governing body of Code White area, and they were brought to a woman named Maredine, one of the famous high ranks. There was this well-known phrase that went like this, "If your noise reaches Maredine, your current chamber need will be mandatory."

Unlike how the people perceived her however - commanding and taking no for an answer, the elderly who had lost her hair color to her age had this smile that was so calming and tranquil enough to soothe the couple's trembling hands gripping on both sides of their chairs. She had heard the same mad stories too but was calm enough to pretend not to. That was because the accusation of some Code Black running around the neighborhood did not compare to one that quoted the *accident* by the force, she hoped for it to still be seen as bloody ridiculous.

"Thank you, Mrs. Dagger, for your understanding," the husband bowed just a bit at the end of the meeting on his and his wife's way out.

"Trust me, you will all be fine. The World will always take care of you, whatever you need," Maredine said in response. The old lady grinned just gently and bowed her head too while still sitting down. However, as the couple was out of her sight, her expression changed into something that looked like concern.

The husband was glad that they were only given a mandatory order to attend the Purple Chamber. He meant it, why wouldn't he? The elderly talked in a way so beguiling that even the wife soon wondered if she was wrong to ever doubt the *brain*. Well, at least the tattle had one thing right about her.

As ordered peacefully, they were escorted to the Purple Chamber by two giant males, one of them happened to be driving the car too - both out of boredom. While bearing the smooth ride, the woman opened her white clutch she had been bringing around and took one long veil, which color had the darkness of the night. The wife was indeed the woman in the black veil.

And that was just another way The World was taking care of 'things', making sure that the great Code White area remained a safe haven for the remaining population which had been steadily decreasing in rate, half to fear and half to The Earth.

Most times no one could really quantify and rectify the extent of how one could love too much on another being, especially if it was not one of the living. That was what The World citizens thought about The Earth. They just could not get how they were willing to let go of their own pleasures in exchange for Mother Nature's untainted peace, leaving Code White and even some of their family members who could not even imagine living like them where they had to work hard for the resources that could only be just a single *bracelet* touch away had they have not left. Nonetheless, it was not like they could not go back, that was probably why.

"Thirty years later and see how fast we have turned the world around, and the people too," a grown-up version of Zirilo could sometimes be seen welcoming in person with open arms The Earth members who ran away or back to The World. He wanted the 'two worlds' as what he always called it, to become 'one' on their own terms and that was probably why the new leader never planned to strike a war.

The World, since the beginning, never really looked at The Earth as an enemy to battle, for their fight was to leave with tranquility and live in peace with Mother Nature. In fact, The World saw them as family members in rebellious teenage drama queens form and various age groups who carried no harm but to their own happiness, should they eventually come to the same conclusion after they learned their lesson, eventually or never.

The World even let The Earth members come back to the Code White territory - the world The World claimed was with no evil where its people lived gloriously, harmoniously, and peacefully. Correspondingly, The World gave freedom to their citizens everywhere they were curious to go, even to visit The Earth's floating and restricted quarters if they wanted to - all around the globe except one, of what The World had secluded as the Code Grey area.

Chapter Twenty-One

The World as It Is

Just down the verge of the humongous Code White territory on the lowest point to the right-hand side when seen from the sky, there was a comparably small wild forest, though it was once the largest vegetation before all the lands merged together as one. The excluded jungle land met the seashore at the bottom right and volcanic mountain at the top. This reinforced the locus to grow the majority of the best crops across the terra firma, but almost never for the consumption and enjoyment of those who lived nearest from there, as those would always be transported far to their cared-for sibling ground instead.

The border to the Code White area was shut by giant walls, so that their people could never break through. Technically, they could sneak into the dark forest by circling round the deep and went in where the walls ended, because the barriers could not gain their foundation from the loose sandy structures. However, no one seemed to succeed without getting caught upon their arrival back to the Code White ground. No one really knew how but some believed that there were probably cameras installed somewhere in every possible entrance to the dark forest where the walls could not reach. That or the fact that the outlaws made their offence known, from their neurotic screams running down the street with words that no one understood to post-traumatic stress disorder from the things they could never describe. That was if they were some of the lucky ones who managed to come back alive. To be more precise, they were the rare lucky ones.

Rumors flying around talking about what they did not really know, and the house of rules never confirmed anything further than that the Code Grey area was located right in the middle like a circle of the mysteriously dangerous dark forest, for a reason that was so vividly plain.

The World was treating evil traits as some sort of contagious virus, striking the heart and the brain to be as healthy as before, but with a dark change in their natural light. Those who were entitled to the Code Grey result were banished, along with their family even when their own family were Code Whites. Their life was shut down from the outside and they were not allowed to leave the small world but to live the hard way and die. Because The World believed that evil was born with and the "seed" was yet to grow if not yet detected, the people in Code Grey were seen to carry this evil virus, and though it was started by the founder as a mere parable, the word traveled as a fact as the civilization aged. Classic case of made-up story turned to history.

Code Greys, unlike the Code Whites, had to work to get what they needed. Currency and monetary trade existed, and they were not given any kind of cared-for *bracelet* to begin with. The money accepted was called *durum* and how much they could get depended on the rate of the work they did, the more useful it was for the Code Whites to use, the higher it would be.

The richest in the Code Grey district would only be the poorest in the Code White area, but the bridge still existed within. The income discrepancy however, had raised some criminal activities around the Code Grey portion of land. There were not a lot of police force (if there was any at all), there were sometimes a few who could be seen guarding with their weapons and stuff, but they seemed to have a different agenda than keeping the area safe. It was apparent that their duty was more of making sure there were none of the Code Greys leaving where they were seen to belong, and even when some managed to slip through the forest, their fate was ensured to end without body confirmation.

Besides working to live, most people in Code Grey still tried very hard to do good and in their best behavior so that they would still have the chance to be transferred into the Code White area. The only chamber that existed there was the Grey Chamber, no other color, and there were not many of those built in the small circle of town, but each was full daily from the doleful livings who were tired of hearing stories about the existing heaven on earth. They tried their very best they knew how. They dreamed and wished day and night to be one of those Code Whites someday, maybe the first in decades or since the new leader's era began to be able to leave for paradise without losing life.

Hope was the only thing that kept their beautiful ego together there but when it was set loose and their hard efforts were seen unnoticeable, the mind could not help but to lose their senses. Some committed suicide and many others turned violent in the never peaceful conurbation. Numerous got killed and in the spurned secluded part of The World where the judicial system was unfairly simplified under the probity defense, prompt execution was the only ruling if necessary in the district that was already as close as the jail definition by itself, if not the same.

Indeed, Code Grey was like a prison with a tiny, miniscule chance of getting out, and if they committed a crime inside, it was like doing it to another prisoner with nowhere to hide and no other option to go to. Only death for all parties. Postponed death for the living, death from old age, death from the biased system; and instant death from getting a Code Black result.

It was only very often that when some of Code Greys lay their body inside the brain scanner, they got out receiving Code Black results due to the machine detecting evil intentions those subjects had tried to hide inside their mind. In view of this, many were scared, refusing to be tested. If they missed their regular Grey Chamber check-up day however, they were seen as a threat and got arrested, more reason to why the troopers alongside their robot minions made their long way there; unlike in the Code White area wherein never a single person missed theirs - again, fear here was what really drove them to the heed.

XXII

Chapter Twenty-Two

Wyre Salis

"Hey oldest Grey, watch out for Code Black!"

While leaving a queue in a Grey Chamber in the Code Grey area, a bearded man with a hairy mole on his left cheek in his thirties was screaming in guffaw at another male, to the other party's displeasure who was almost the exact same age but looked ten years younger than he was.

The good-looking male with instead a clean shaved chin, wider eyes, and thicker eyebrows than his mocker was indeed the literal first case of Code Grey result, happened when he was just a baby knowing nothing as he entered a warm enclosed space with thirty kinds of instrumentals filling the silent air. It was a little more than thirty years ago but he grew closely with the nickname 'oldest Grey', though technically there were few other Code Greys who were even older than him. The robotic announcement broadcasted via the black loudspeaker at the edge of the waiting room called him to enter the room where the brain scanner was, however, mentioning his real name, Wyre Salis.

A moment later, Wyre went out of the chamber with a deep-fried frown from both lips crumbling the skin, and his eyes dropped salty water like there was still much left, but the hard wind blew just right to his cheeks and dried his tears. He did not get it, what had he done to deserve another Code Grey result? What should he do so he would not get another? He wondered.

Wyre decided to walk home from blazing afternoon until chilly evening twenty kilometers long one way to where he and his parents lived, a little shabby homestead just by a small lake that was shaped like the earth was trying to draw a weeping willow tree but failed miserably. He did not go inside immediately, one of the reasons for his long walk, but he chose to take off his top, threw it to one of the big rocks giving it a damp fettle just like the day before, and went into the reservoir, as always.

The water temperature was frigid, yet his body still stayed floating for so long that its molecule knife was able to carve on his thick skin light lines of crumple all over. But it seemed to not bother him as much as his mind playing games with his circumstance.

His mother was tested Code White and had always been. His father was once a Code White case, until he found that he had to be moved to the Code Grey area due to his son's result, and afterward, he soon became one of those Code Greys himself. That was why, the rest of his family was too to live in the Code Grey district regardless, and never a day went by without him putting himself to blame. And that to boot, his father and him were never close.

Wyre had been trying his best to be good and nothing else, hoping that one day he would be classified as Code White, but whatever good deeds he had done, the result always showed Code Grey later on. He volunteered his brain to be scanned daily even with the long trip as his energy's major expense, sometimes even more than once a day because he could never be sure where his wit was at its most benign, and yet he always came back home disappointed and weeping swimming in the lake.

This time, his diffidence pushed further than usual and dominated. As a result, he managed to drown himself far down from the surface at his own terms a lot longer while he was getting deeper and deeper in his own thoughts, without him even realizing.

While Wyre was doing that, his mother got out of the house and made her way into the side of the lake with a big towel hanging on his arm. The lady was only half a decade old, with some white strains of hair that got along harmoniously with the other black ones all wavy to the back and let loose. Her eye pockets would have been smaller if it had not been from the daily lack of sleep from one nightmare she never shared. She was worried that the day would come for her only son to go under the lake and returned to the surface floating dead as reality, constantly as she always checked on the motel rock in a size of a sleeping fox where his son's shirt always stayed by sundown.

She waited and waited, only this time, she agreed with her anxiety that her son had not been coming back up for longer than the normal duration of human beings able to hold on to their breath. Subsequently, she screamed her son's name furiously and that effectively woke Wyre up and brought his body back to where his mother was visible.

"How long have you been down there? You could've been dead!" The mother yelled in a pitch high voice while drying her adult son's torso with the towel she brought. She looked at his jeans that dripped rainfall onto the ground and then back to his face, apparently demanding an answer, but he remained speechless. In fact, Wyre did not even count how long he was there, and as he assumed he would know when to get out of the water by the time it started choking him, he just let his body be.

The mother then continued her parley in a gentler voice, sounding like she was regretting her outburst earlier, how she could not even tell how long by looking at his skin because it was tougher than anyone else, she knew. Wyre could stay in the water for as long as he wanted, yet oddly without a single wrinkle crawled on his epidermis only as he was back to the surface.

Still did not know what to say, Wyre responded in a joke. "Maybe I'll be able to breathe underwater," he said. His mother laughed, but only before she reminded him to be careful regardless.

The two came in and found that the father had started on dinner without them, undisturbed even by their sudden presence. He however did not look like he enjoyed the dull harvests served on his plate, and only ate them as far as his stomach could bear without going to vomit. How could he not, for the family had been eating the same thing over and over for decades, the very same greeneries grown outside the house anyone could barely call a garden.

The dinner went continually awkward as the two sat on the table. Wyre's father, who did not look as scary when he laughed, did not behave so cold when he was speaking to his wife, but when his eyes accidentally turned to Wyre, his smile just suddenly disappeared.

The mother turned to the father secretly with her eyes rolling across where her husband sat, implying that he needed to start a conversation with his only son too. He caressed his unplanned black goatee as he was thinking of a sentence, or any good word to say, but it was a lot harder than he expected. Nothing came up other than what he eventually said, "How are you going to find yourself a job?"

Wyre thought that it was always best to keep his thought to himself, most often the same one with that 'three dos' like how dare him to force him to do what he didn't want to do when the only thing he cared to do was to never give up on having his brain scanned in the Grey Chamber every day until he got that Code White result, bringing his parents back to where they belonged without him, and finally, fixing his mistake of being born. Except this time, his rage made him shout all of those words, every single one of them, uncontrollably letting it all out in the air for everyone in the room to hear.

His father was furious. Deep down, he was most disappointed to hear that his son had been putting his life on a waste for a goal far beyond reach and he was not planning to stop. All his son cared about was being in the Code White district, like he once did, but at least he had already thrown away that dream a long time ago.

"You have to stop dreaming and wasting your life, and you need to accept the fact that working hard is the only way to live, that you'll never be a Code White, and that we are all stuck here because of you - and live with it!" The father screamed back and while he was doing so, his fists were thumping on the table multiple times.

"I know I'll be getting that Code White result sooner or later!" Wyre replied with a voice not losing to his father's own temper.

"How?"

"I just know it!"

Wyre's father felt he had had enough.

He stood up and walked to where Wyre sat. He then bent his torso down so that his face was getting so close to his son, then he decided that it was the right day to say the things he had been keeping to himself, "How are you even a Code White? I've stopped believing that since a long time ago." Then the father went back to the bedroom, leaving his cold dinner to rot. Immediately, there was a violent shaking in Wyre's sight, from trying to hold his tears up as much as he could.

Wyre was actually a quietly bright man, a fast learner, even suggested in many of his brain reports. But he never even tried to queue in the finding-a-job line, at least seriously, because his time was fully consumed in the Grey Chamber line and swimming in the lake instead.

His fondness of the water was never without a personal reason. He perennially felt heavily trapped in the assigned area where he lived, but when he dropped his body into the water, everything felt lighter all of a sudden. The water was calming, and the further he was from the ground, the more he was able to imagine the river his parents named him by.

He liked it too when he opened his eyes down there occasionally and saw how the water followed without question the pattern Mother Earth created. When given the path, no matter how wide, and no matter how deep, it would flow so long as the path allowed. But when it was not, it would shove the way for as long as it could until the path itself surrendered to the constant confrontation. And that was how he compared himself to the water, he felt related.

Something about the water made him closer with his father too, whom he had never really got affection from, not even once for as long as he could remember. Maybe it was his mother's story about how his father used to love the water too and how he used to go fishing out on the sea with his silver pole when it was still possible or down near the Wyre river before The World took him in, or maybe it was those many times he saw his father stood by the side of the lake close to the middle of the night, silently but never jumped in it for some reasons. He was never sure which one was more, but he could only notice the little things his father did to him so coldly still with a hint of love, only down there in the deep water. Such as his words to him that night to get his life together and stop wasting it, he planned to get the love from it the next evening, in the water instead.

A few nights later, Wyre was not to be alone to come into the Grey Chamber the next morning. He was to be accompanied by his father whose brain scan was scheduled that same day.

His mother, who had been getting Code White outcome but needed to stay in the Code Grey area despite of, never once tried to start a war with any of the two males in the house. She always said how she loved them so much and was okay so long as they were all not apart, but the boys never seemed to appreciate their togetherness as much as she did.

The mother would always try to fix the relationship between the two, mostly by urging quietly one of the others to start a kind conversation, but every time one tried, they would fight as they had always been, even more often than the daily news in comparison.

"Dad, who knows, maybe the both of us will be getting that Code White result tomorrow," Wyre tried to lighten up the mood with false hope on a wishing well.

"Really? And how much longer should I wait before I die?"

The father screamed and this time, it was him again who kindled the fire.

The both of them ended up shooting bullets of quarrels at each other, one from a gun of delusive contentment and the other relegated expectation - both ammunition being used too much often even than, again, the average daily news.

"Well maybe if I'm dead, you and Mom can finally go then to the Code White territory," Wyre stated his closing statement before he pushed his bedroom door hard to its core, even the dust on the edges could be seen flying from the impact.

Wyre did not mean it, and so did his father when even in his own mind he thought that was crazy. But those never-minded-considered words planted seeds on the father's unconsciousness ground that he dreamt of holding a silver knife and pushed the handle towards Wyre. He woke up abruptly however, before he could see the nightmare of putting the blade against his son's chest. No, it was not him. It was the nightmare that did it, or that he was forced to do it in the nightmare but still, it could not be what the man who was sweating a cascade of water to his whole body wanted. Could it? He began to wonder.

Early in the morning, the father could not stop his feet from trembling as he and his son sat on the bus seats. Though the idea to bail the test crossed his mind, Wyre's father still came along but only because he did not want to get into trouble missing his brain scan schedule. As he sat in the bus side by side, Wyre witnessed how worried his father looked. His father's eyebrows were losing their balance, his temples were raining sweats, and his lips seemed to be misplaced by some jagged knives not only because of its shape but since every time Wyre tried to calm him down with how the test that he took every day was nervously exciting for him, the words coming from the father's mouth only stabbed his son's heart out of sorts as a response.

Wyre always forgot how scary the test was for most people because of how they feared getting Code Black results more than Wyre's hope of getting Code White. Plus, he had done the test so many times that he could always imitate the instrumentals the machine played and how it sounded afterward when it opened for no one had shown as much of endeavor as he had been. Simply, that could be said as the summary of how he had wasted three decades of his life, dreaming of where probably no man had gone before in his part of town.

When they reached the Grey Chamber as programmed, his father was called with no second to spare, and the older man proceeded without saying anything or looking at him. He was worried about his father, not only because he sensed something was wrong from what he saw on the bus, but because he had never seen his father look that pale before, even at his worst.

Being in the chamber had helped him understand the process of everything in there, down to the robots shaped like faceless humans in cheap metallic suits that governed the whole place, just like the rest. Wyre managed to pass the robots as he hid here and there around the edges of the hall and finally snuck in to where his father was and looked from afar as his father entered himself into the machine where it closed automatically, without him noticing. He then walked towards the machine.

Wyre, somehow, had a bad feeling about this, and his fear was confirmed when about an hour later he heard a disturbing siren coming from the *brain* as its screen showed Code Black. The machine started to tremble with a slight rapid motion as it was giving a signal to one of the army headquarters located in the right border of the Code White area, closest to the dark forest.

A faded-silver fighter aircraft with one snow-colored projectile on each wing traveled through the blusterous air safely and landed right on the top of the building easily just like a helicopter. Whenever the plane was seen, everyone knew that its passengers were to clean up the mess, only the warriors and not necessarily their minion soldiers knew how and what for, no further questions to be asked without the right authority.

Meanwhile inside the chamber, the machine was growling, and Wyre did not know what it would do to his father because he was not able to hear anyone or anything that was inside the *brain*. Believing that his father was going to die, he scanned through the closed room but found nothing.

His knees turned weak from standing and forced him to crawl to the edge of the room behind the door. He looked at the machine and realizing he could not do anything, he put both of his hands on his ears and cried to himself a soft bellow. As he was beginning to lose hope, the door suddenly opened. A robot came in then closed the door, and when it went near the machine, Wyre impulsively smacked the robot from behind without rest and tore him apart hysterically with his bare hands. The robot tried to fight him, but it was proven no match to defeat a desperate son who was trying to save his father whom he always tried to prove wrong.

From the brawl, Wyre managed to win himself the robot's right arm and he used it to blow indefinite strikes against the machine which received the smashes without the capability to fight back. His obstructive performance however was able to separate the brain scanner slowly into multiple fragments, but he did not plan to stop. As he could start to see his dad's face as well as an unexpected, delayed injection-like coming towards his skull, he continued smashing the bottom part so that he could pull him out from below safely.

"Let's go, son," his father reminded him of what they should do next, but Wyre calmed him and said he knew a way out. He realized the vent just at the top, stacked some parts of the machine, and helped his father to climb. His father then lifted his body up and they crawled down the course following a reasonable path until they got to the outside of the building safely.

They were just in time to leave the room, before two soldiers from the aircraft came in, and left overwhelmed from the scene instead. "Call for more troops, we've got two men on the loose," one of them initiated to warn the system. That instantly, Wyre and his father were categorized as 'wanted' and more soldiers were sent to patrol their residence, where the mother was, to make sure no one was getting out or into the house.

At the same time, the father and son duo were already running to the other end of the district, the opposite side from where they lived and where they were. His father, seeing how far Wyre would go to save him, regretted his thought, and showed mercy and love to him in his mind, though he did not really show it as they were running away together.

The two fugitives were panting for a place to stay for the night and charge their energy. They had been running and hiding for hours in plain sight and it was only natural that they began to feel desperate for an inconspicuous place to sleep. They reached the outer of the dark forest however and decided to risk the tattle turned right in order to survive.

"Not a meter more," the father warned his son as they had formally entered the mysterious jungle. They climbed one of the big trees and tried to keep up with the cold as they were trying to sleep in between branches.

"Why did you do it?" The father suddenly raised his question with a wobbly voice as he tried not to crack his tears, eventually sobbing by the side of his little man who was taller than him by six inches.

In between regret and beatitude, Wyre's father admitted his awful nightmare he had the day before.

"This is all my fault," Wyre responded.

His father did not expect his son's response to be that way. He thought he would hate him instead, and curse him to the bone, and even that he did not think it would be enough. "What? No, it's my fault for even thinking about it," so the father replied.

"No, if I had not said all of those words, none of this would have happened," Wyre cried, but then hugged his father. "I understand, Dad," he said, "and I hope you do too of me," he continued while his arms were hanging awkwardly by his father's shoulders, waiting for him to embrace him back.

And he did.

They both cried their hearts out with the bank of thirty years' emotion and did not signal to stop the clutch of affection any moment soon. That night, they bonded and talked until dawn like never before. They told stories, hobbies, and favorite songs - the familiar things they had heard from the mother, and they suddenly realized how lonely she might be that night. They hoped she was okay, and for building that wishing well in their head, they turned soundless.

"Did I ever tell you about my sailing days?" Wyre's father was the first to open his mouth thirty minutes of silence later.

Wyre knew, of the details truthfully, but again, from his mother. However, even when his father had already told him the blurb short moments ago, he already missed those kinds of narratives again. "Tell me, Dad," so he replied.

Wyre's father then told stories about how he used to become a fisherman, and he told them in greater detail too, and the feeling when he listened was like traveling back to the past with his dad by his side. Wyre could even better imagine the practical, as his father explained to him the step-by-step process of how to - he did not intend to, it was just that way, it felt more real to him too.

Some of the greens and the blues were still in harmony

when he last did it alone in his very young age, but the world and himself had been going through a rollercoaster ride that he just knew he would not be able to hold the rush any longer. It was either living a short life for pleasure or staying safe for longer, and at that point in time, he was more scared of death. All he did to cope with the covet was to go fishing by the polluted river or stand by the clear lake - that way, he could better imagine. When his father told him that he would have taken him on the journey if he could, he grew more motivated to get his father cleared.

By dawn, their rest was disturbed by Robins that were singing their first chorus. Wyre thought that maybe the song was about comparing who had the best color between the sunrise and their orange-red chest feathers, because these birds were moving their breasts and beaks like they were challenging someone. That was how he saw it, that or maybe he was still half dreaming, for the two had barely slept enough as they were getting their hearts and guts ready for what they had planned to do next, with a couple of rocks in their pocket on their way.

The duo ran out of the forest quietly and headed to the nearest Grey Chamber they remembered seeing on their way in. Realizing that all the chambers had similar build, Wyre was able to get them in smoothly through the vent and into where the brain scanner was, perfectly.

Their mission was to get the father scanned again so that they would be able to prove the system wrong for a moment there. It was the only way they could think of, ironically, and they both were somehow sure, there was no way that the father would get another Code Black result; possibly blinded by the hopelessness. Wyre waited for another hour but to his and his father's surprise, a Code Black result was shown again, and so the same exact horror routine was repeated, only this time, there was no robot's arm.

Wyre hit the machine with the rock the same sequence he did the machine the day before, whilst his father did too from inside. While trying to break his father out before another aircraft of warriors arrived, he could not help but wonder if there was something wrong with the way it was programmed.

He began to think, maybe there was a chip or some sort, so even after his father was able to get out of the brain scanner alive, he continued breaking it as if he had lost his temper. He kept crashing and smashing, and even when his father tried to stop him, he nudged his effort and kept breaking the machine. He continued on thumping quickly the injection and the rest of the top side until a small piece of a green silicon with craggy tips protruding in a size smaller than his palm appeared, and it was as he expected, a chip.

Wyre took the *brain* and ran away with his father through the same vent, only this time, two soldiers had already been waiting just outside, expecting their exit plan.

"Out of all the fugitives, you're the ones that make us look stupid, and so we'll do the same to you," one of the soldiers with an itchy voice and ruthless eyes spoke by looking at Wyre the most. Their arms wrestled with the soldiers' as they were not planning to give in, but their attempts were no match to the skilled troops who seemed to be used to such kind of response and thus they were easily able to put the father and the son at the back of the army truck in green.

The two had no plan in how to break free, but a lightbulb in mind turned on for the father when he heard the Robins singing a different chorus.

"This is our only chance, we're near the forest," the father said.

Wyre did not understand how they could escape, and his father did not look like he had a clear plan himself by the way he described it, but he seemed incredibly positive that the forest was their only way out.

The father banged the rock on the door and so Wyre followed him. The two soldiers realized their effort and stopped the truck, as the father expected and so he stopped. Meanwhile, Wyre, who thought the plan was to break the impossible-to-break door, kept on smashing. Once in between smashes, he was reminded how he went to the Grey Chamber every day, how his father used to be so cold on him, and the imagination of him and his father sailing across the ocean from the other side of the forest; and so he was able to strike harder and stronger, but still, to no use.

When it was obvious from the sound of footsteps that the two soldiers were getting close, Wyre's father suddenly stopped him and told him to forget about him and his mother. Wyre was confused, as he said to him that he did not understand what he meant, but his father disregarded his son's blankness and finally revealed his plan that he would lead the two soldiers on to come inside the truck and that was when Wyre had to roll himself out quickly and run away to the edge of the forest.

Wyre shook his head and resisted his father's plan, but his father instead put both of his cold hands on his cheeks and pressed them so hard that he was not able to move his mouth to say anything, and while doing that the father said, "You need to live! Promise me, son, that you will never look back and you will never give up on your life no matter what! I love you, son."

What came next happened so fast as his father pushed Wyre to the back of the door to hide and in the way the father exactly envisioned it, his father pretended to run hysterically to the inside of the truck with his son at his front, and in a spare of seconds, Wyre did just what his father told him to and got away. He did not know what happened to his father next except for the fact that he let himself be captured by sacrificing himself, his life, so he, who his father thought once to kill, could be alive instead.

Wyre was torn apart every inch his back was blindly watching his father be taken away, and between the sound of his breath going in and out, he could somehow hear a whispery sound of "Good luck, son. I love you very much."

XXIII

Chapter Twenty-Three

Phoenix Pyralis

Classical music was playing in the background while two men were sitting in a grand dining room, too small for a hall yet too big for a house - but maybe because it was located in the best location in the Code White area right in the middle part of the land, which was only permitted to those who were part of the House of Rules.

It had always been just the two of them, since ten years ago some beautiful memories of a female figure had turned hurting as they faded with her existence, but the aching grew smaller as they were forgotten piece by piece, though still not all and would never be.

The two were sitting opposite to each other, and if one turned his head left, he could see from the big window the moon was like a little shiny silver coin staring at them from afar.

The man on the right was older, about twenty-five years apart from the other, body and soul. His hair was mostly white from his age. His head actually already showed symptoms of early baldness from the stress he had about his son's future, but the Blue Chamber combined with hair extension had managed to cover that secret just fine. His goatee was constantly shaved, because he never liked how it looked around his oval chin somehow, and he always thought that it could better show his pointy nose he always thought played a big role in his son's incredibly handsome face. But what stood out of him the most was a dent shaped like a half sleeping triangle on his right ear.

His son who was sitting across from him was well known not only for his incredibly good-looking features and elite military family background, but his intractable temper and progressing disinterest in life. His thick eyebrows and wide eyes were shaping to match his daily ennui expression and it was a shame to many that both of his dimples could not often be seen because of that. Even when he was told many times that those facial parts would always match his silky black hair perfectly only if he smiled a lot more, he seemed to never bother anyone's desire but his. His name was Phoenix Pyralis.

A robot maid about one and a half size of the table's height came in shortly after it sensed that either the two had already finished their dinner or that a potential argument was about to start, when it heard the father asking his son if he had continued his training, but was ignored completely, indicating that he had not and would not even bother. It was not that Phoenix did not enjoy smashing some bricks and challenging his agility on a fighting android, but he never felt like his father really cared that they actually shared an interest in something - it was rather more of what he wanted him to be, regardless of who he really was, which Phoenix himself was still trying to figure out.

"Do you even know why you could beat those guys easily in a match even when you didn't practice your very best?" His father suddenly asked, expecting that his son was going to at least say something, but he put his hope too high. "So how long do you think you can keep that record up?" He added, but still, to no response.

He never believed for a second that his son's natural ability to win a fight was genetic, coming from him. And based on what he constantly told the story about, he did not even think that his legendary skill was coming naturally to him. No, it was always a combination of shame and hard work to him, his embarrassing moment made him train hard, so hard, the very hard, and the hardest with blood until the skill got stuck to his genes, and what was left was natural. He was a prodigy because he made himself so, and not by waiting or doing nothing, he firmly believed, and he expected his son to think the same.

He had taught Phoenix everything he knew, and when he was still just a little boy, he looked a little too excited to follow every step his father taught him, so he never understood why Phoenix in the fullness of time lost the interest and motivation. Adding to that, if Phoenix had come clean on losing his sense of direction, he would have answered that it was simply because he was yet to see why he had to do any of it.

The next morning, the two were going together to one of the meeting halls in the extraordinary House of Rules where they lived. The name was not without a story. Shortly, Hayes Beckett and some of their trusted men used to gather in the founder's small country house with shabby hut not long after they were out of the bunker. There was where all the rules had been made and meetings for such important decisions had been held.

The house however, had expanded more than a million times its original size to a glorious open structure, but the function was still pretty much the same, except that the place evolved to have its own Grey Chambers inside and all of its other prestigious facilities. It was claimed the safest of all and thus was still where the founder Hayes Beckett, the new leader Zirilo Beckett, all of the parliament members and highest-rank intellectuals as well as their family lived, on top of being the center of all government meetings. The shape of the building somewhat looked like a town-size milk panna cotta topped with three layers of swirling stairs and a sprinkle of golden windows, and inside, hundreds of house units even bigger than most of the ordinary houses in the Code White area, such as one where Phoenix and his father lived.

The grand meeting room was one of the most luxurious spots in the building. The carpet was all red and the walls were a combination of white and gold colors. The seats were too in gold and their unpartitioned tables where the microphones were, were circling the center following the chairs. The way they were placed made the room look like a mini stadium with fifty times more comfortable seating each.

Those seats started to be filled in one by one and as the hour went by, the scheduled meeting started. Zirilo came in last and without Hayes, the old man had not been seen for quite a while for some reason, and he sat right below a giant screen. Phoenix and his father sat just a few seats apart from the leader, in one of the front rows.

One of the most important people in the room, due to being part of the exclusive members of the inner circle informally known as 'Zirilo and His Trusted Men' where Phoenix's dad had been a part too, took his stand in the center and opened the meeting by pointing at the humongous screen where the topic for the day to discuss was visible.

"Limited resources," he then changed the slide to the next, "and this would delay our goal to replace the remaining human workforce with robots to one hundred percent by the next decade, how, you might ask?" He read out loud and realized that this was one of the not-so-many most important issues there were remaining to be solved. He then sighed because he knew that this would take a lot longer than a while to reach consensus.

The conference was going on in the most boring way possible to Phoenix. It was not that he was not listening at all, well, at least not entirely seeing how his eyes did not resemble anyone who fell asleep, but he just never got to understand why his opinion would never agree with almost all the other heads in the room, even his father's, so most of the time, he just let himself quiet and not contributing.

However, from time to time, he did find it amusing. Just listening to some stupid arguments wherein by the end of the day, the issue was not even resolved yet those who had just been in the war words seemed to rekindle their friendship just fine afterward, or maybe as a front just to retain power. Even in the world they claimed to be free of evil, those kinds of people still existed, he thought to himself - or maybe being phony was not so much of an evil behavior if it was to no expense of others, he started to wonder; while he next guessed what the definition of evil in the *brain* actually was, he pondered. As for the others though, they just saw him as the youngest House of Rules member with no contribution but there was no harm in letting him sit inside just to remind themselves that they were not as useless.

The meeting had been going on for nine hours, the longest Phoenix had ever been in since the first day he joined, and he started to feel that he might lose his mind in a matter of seconds. The frigid air in the room made him put both of his hands constantly in his pocket but the annoyance forced him to take them out a few times while changing his sitting position. Realizing that all of that still did not work to decrease his state of being irritated just a slight, he bent his torso forward so that his elbows could land on the table, covered his face with both of his hands, and tried not to care of what other people would think of him seeing him like that. If only he were blessed with two more hands, he thought, he would have been able to cover his ears temporarily too.

"How about we retract all of the resources from the Code Grey area completely, this time?" A male sitting way across Phoenix said, "They work their hardest for us, just so they have a chance to be one of us, so why not use that more?"

"And leave them there to die, you mean?" A beautiful woman with the soul of a fierce man replied.

"Or how about The Earth? Note that they were once a part of us too," a man sitting just a couple of seats next to Phoenix tried to contribute.

"Don't forget, they had not been a part of us as well, before that," another female responded.

"Well, we don't even know if The Earth has enough for themselves," another male tried to add to the point.

The argument then went on and on again in a circle like the earth's rotation, only this time, instead of arguing about the solutions, they were squabbling about the cause, then turned around to mock The Earth, and the cycle began to give Phoenix a little headache.

All of a sudden, a fire within him was ignited coming out of nowhere he knew exactly. But perhaps it was because of someone he knew inside The Earth district, but he did not want to continue the idea that way. He did not know if what he had been thinking and keeping to himself was right, but he could not help to wonder if it could perchance bestow the end of the never-ending quarrels, and so it went out of his mouth.

"Well, you're looking at it the wrong way. It is not the number of resources that causes it, it is the number of people. And no matter how much more resources you can get, the problem will always be there so long as you let the number of people grow."

For a long moment there the audience grew quiet while staring at him, very impressed. The way Phoenix talked, probably the first time he did in there when they thought about it, was no doubt with a voice of charisma, objective point of view, and a little bit of that no empathy vibe, but all in a different way to even his own mind by surprise. Zirilo and his father looked at him in a different way than before too, but also did not say a word.

Phoenix did not expect any compliment or approval except for the meeting to end very soon, but the awkward silence soon became the top of his list that he very much wished to avoid. There was no comment of disagreeing with Phoenix for they all thought he did have a point. In fact, they started to think whether he should be the one to go to the center and try to lead the meeting in a different way. But seeing how tired and annoyed his expression was still, some of them bet that if he was given the chance to, he would probably just curse all the way and leave.

"You know what, I think we've all had enough meetings today. Motion to adjourn," Zirilo cut on the silence. What he said had set Phoenix's heart to peace, and a little smile could even be seen on his face if anyone paid attention.

"I'm so proud of you," Phoenix's father said while tapping on his back as they were getting out of their seats. Phoenix could sense too that he received a lot more grin from the gents and twinkle from the ladies afterward.

The next afternoon, Phoenix started his day pretty late as always whenever he had no obligations to attend to. He almost thought that the day would go by as wasted boring fun as usual, but he was surprised when he found his father along with Zirilo inside their house, talking in the dining room.

The young leader was gloriously charming as he always was. He had his hair bleached pale smoke all around and always had his sunglasses lounging at the top of his head, even in meetings, day or night. Gossips were flying around saying those shades were no ordinary, but he always insisted that it was just regular sunglasses, no different to the others.

"You must be surprised to see me today, but probably not as surprised as I was yesterday. You have quite a potential, your father always says, in our *inner circle* meeting," Zirilo stood up as he spoke and his chair skirted in the background.

Feeling that the leader's compliment was not enough, Phoenix's father continued the conversation with how proud he was of his son, and all of his achievements he had listed the night before just so he would not forget to mention every single one of them.

"The fighting skill, oh yes, I've heard about that. You're quite a combat prodigy too, just like your father," the leader responded with a pleasant smile.

The conversation went on about thirty minutes long talking about Phoenix, mostly with his father speaking on behalf of him, but he did not mind at all not having to say many things in the discussion. That was until Zirilo suddenly prompted, "Say, Phoenix, how would you like to be a part of the inner circle?" Much to Phoenix's father's excitement, looking as if he wanted to jump to the moon then go back to hug his son. Seeing that kind of expression, Phoenix did not know what else was there to say other than a yes.

Being invited to be a part of the inner circle was again the hardest and the most exclusive as anyone in The World could ever get. They were the ones that drew the circle. There was where all the secrets were out and kept shut, including how the chip was programmed, and Phoenix could not lie to himself that he was excitedly curious to know.

The meeting of Zirilo and his trusted men was held in the most secretive spot in the House of Rules. Even Phoenix had no idea that such a chamber existed. They all had to walk to the small man-made waterfall located inside Zirilo's house, slipped through to the back, and scanned their fingerprints to get inside - a chamber with resemblance to any dining room in town, only with a big screen. Once Phoenix entered the room for the first time, Zirilo asked him what he thought.

"I don't understand, why can't we just have the meeting in your dining room or something?" Phoenix let what he really thought out of his mouth. To his surprise, the room suddenly turned quiet, getting him the déjà vu.

"That is not how you speak to the leader! Zirilo, I am very sorry. He's still quite young, well, twenty-seven years old with no filter and this is what you get," Phoenix's father immediately stepped in with a splash of humor, afraid that what came next might start a fire.

Zirilo however, touched Phoenix by the shoulder and started to laugh. He even asked the newest and youngest member of the circle to sit by his side and whispered to him not to hold anything back. He then opened the meeting.

Unlike the name people gave, the members consisted of every gender not limited to male. There were sixteen other people besides him, his dad, the leader, and hair-raising Maredine Dagger. They all came from various backgrounds. None of them however felt familiar to Phoenix.

The first fifty inner circle meetings Phoenix attended were not as serious (or even important) as he thought it would be. He did get the sense that being a part of it made him happier. He even could probably call Zirilo a brother and he would definitely respond the same way, and in a sense other people who were not part of the circle seemed to respect him more than before. If they knew the circle was doing nothing but joking around, he was sure that people would lose their respect towards him, but since no one was supposed to know what they did anyway, he thought it was kind of nice too to basically not do anything and yet earned the same highest esteem as if he was.

The fifty-first meeting however, inverted to a totally opposite direction, and it was conspicuously dark even for him to bear. It was obvious though, everyone had already known about everything he had just heard but him, that he presumed the first fifty meetings somewhat served only as the probation stage, making sure that he was really one of them. It was probably a good thing that Phoenix had always managed to set his poker face to a stable in every meeting, but hearing this, he was struggling to keep it all together.

'The cleaning' as what he was sure to hear correctly, commenced exactly five years and ten months ago, June the thirteenth. They had realized that the reveal of Code Blacks and their noted destiny to simply 'vanish' had affected a lot of the Code Whites, even turning them to Code Blacks themselves.

"Chaos, when they know," Zirilo proclaimed.

However, if they had lost them to natural death per se, the feeling of that 'taken away' was treated differently by their grief, and so, the chip was programmed to show Code White for Code Black results from then, and only reveal the truth to what they called, and unknown to others, 'Mother Brain', located secretly in the House of Rules where such orders were initiated.

What came next was beyond horrifying for Phoenix as he learned that not all natural deaths that had been happening in the Code White area were indeed 'natural'. The mission was revealed to be one of the warriors', whose existence was kept undisclosed and usually mixed up with those of the soldiers, as intended. Their job after getting the list of those concealed Code Blacks was to plan out the best way to get rid of them quietly and 'naturally' and shifted all the blame to the invisible grim reaper.

But that was not all.

"I have been saving this to 'clean' all of the Code Greys," the leader mentioned, "There is simply no heaven with even a little bit of hell; thus, there is no The World with no evil when some are still lingering at our end," he added with such tone overly emphasizing in both 'heaven' and 'hell'.

This way however in any way did not have anything to do with the warriors. Instead, he had been creating monsters who were placed in the dark forest, where the bunker was too and subsequently, where their *nest* was. Nevertheless, these creatures were not really 'made' as he said it.

"I have found the way to recycle those Code Black corpses, in the way most useful to their nature," he added, but he stopped the meeting there after letting all of the applause thrown out by his standing audience.

"Let's get a drink, as usual," Zirilo grabbed Phoenix by the neck with his left arm and brought him to one of the bars in the House of Rules, their usual hangout place called Cocktail Mocktail, as its menu matched perfectly with its name. When he said usual, Phoenix knew that Zirilo was going to let out all of the hidden stress and nightmare pressure by getting passed out in his bedroom from having too many drinks, again. He told Phoenix it was the only way for him to get a good night's sleep.

Heck, Zirilo was the only person he knew of getting hungover from having too many cocktails. But even when the leader was sober, Phoenix could not tell if he was saner than when he was not. There was always something about his way of thinking that Phoenix could not say as stable and undisturbed, most of the time, and he used to think the leader was not serious in the main.

"I can see that it was too much, even for you, but it'll sink in, trust me. Ask the others, they've been exactly there," Zirilo screamed as the music was getting too loud for them to even have a normal conversation, then ordered another glass of alcohol.

"Why do you have to keep creating *those*, Zirilo? Aren't you just creating a problem with no solution? I don't understand, I mean, we were doing just fine without them."

"Phoenix, do you think those warriors and soldiers don't want to live like us, or the others?"

"Isn't that why all of those robots are out there?"

"Imagine, the materials I can use to keep making more and more of those robots for our workforce, instead of being useless guards in the forest, and soon, I can replace all of the Code Greys with those, so we don't have to keep depending on them with the resources we need in there. We won't be needing them anyway."

"But, what if those *monsters* go mad?" Phoenix replied and revealed his worry.

"Shhh, don't say that out loud! People can hear us!" Zirilo greatly panicked for a second, so they moved to the leader's house instead under his command.

"What if they get into Code White, Zirilo? Haven't you thought about that? And what if there are too many of them that even the robots cannot handle? Haven't you even thought of the Code Whites we have got there in the Code Grey district? Those who were waiting to come back here?" Phoenix whispered. At this point, he sounded like he cared greatly for the world he lived in, more than its own leader.

"They'll never get in here; I've made sure of that."

"You mean, those zombies, right, Zirilo?"

Zirilo nodded seemingly very heavily, and Phoenix grew wary over the look. He suddenly found it really hard to trust the system he had been believing mindlessly to be both fair and just, as the founder proclaimed. He was waiting for Zirilo to do or say something to bring back his trust, but the way he was spinning his glasses of house-made martini and smiling so cynically in between made him more and more suspicious.

"But what can we do if that happens?"

"Burning, on fire, it's the only way, but I've got it all under control, to keep them under my command, to go wherever I lead them to, and they'll never lay their mindless groans and rain blood on me or our beloved territory. Fear of the Code Blacks is exactly what keeps the Code Whites not to be one, and they do not have to know how they were brought back to life stuck in the forest - they will presume even the heavenly afterlife rejects their coming, and so they will bow to no evil if they do not want to be in it themselves. I have been getting a better sleep since then, *no more falling heads*. I've got it all this time, my second chance to prove they're no match to me; their petrifying movement, yes, they have become the army of my own and fear me, all under my control..." Zirilo responded with chuckles before losing himself to dreamland as he knocked himself out on the table.

Fire. Fire. Fire. Fire.

On his way home, Phoenix kept thinking of all those small details Zirilo let slip from his drunken stage.

So, the monsters could only be killed by being burnt in fire into ashes possibly, if Phoenix could add more of his own hypothesis too. But was it only fire? Why did it have to be 'fire'?

There was almost never a way for someone to control fire perfectly the way one wanted it to be. Phoenix imagined - even when one person was able to put a fire on it, it would be so hard not to catch it on themselves or their surroundings.

Something was wrong.

Phoenix could feel it in his bones, something was wrong with the system then. Sure, there was peace everywhere in the Code White area; however, Code Greys were never cared for and abandoned. Oh, and sure there was no evil crime in Code White, but where was the fairness in 'the cleaning'? Or even mercy?

The fifty-second meeting started and finished as usual, this time discussing the update about six newborns and fifteen adults who had been 'cleaned' out by shadow warriors in the past week. The way they were killed was different for each to avoid suspicion, but the repertoire made them so instead. During, Phoenix tried not to show uncomfortableness so that no one was suspicious. He thought that it was better than getting the anxiety of being 'cleaned' himself.

The same behavior he gave as the next day he surprisingly

found himself accompanied by Zirilo on his way to the Grey Chamber for his scheduled brain scan, and he was simply too lazy to make excuses to drive away the uninvited honored guest.

"I want to make sure that you're passing the test, otherwise, you know what'll happen," the leader spoke with his teeth showing the entire sentence, suggesting either genuine or fake support.

Phoenix was not sure how to react at first, but he was able to steer the conversation back to what made them friends in the first place, his unfiltered opinion that Zirilo somehow found amusing. No one dared to speak like that to the leader, but the way Phoenix did so effortlessly with everyone granted him a soft-spot pass given by the leader.

Just before Phoenix entered the chamber, Zirilo could see that he was thinking about something, so he asked Phoenix what was on his mind. Phoenix grew quiet momentarily. His hand was hanging on the knob and the machine could already peek at its next subject. This time, he really tried to think twice about what he was going to say. And Phoenix admitted, "I wonder, if you're placed in the brain scanner, which color would the *brain* tell you, you belong in?"

Phoenix spoke seriously but then he closed it with an outburst giggle, consequently Zirilo took it as a joke. However, as he closed the door and entered the machine alone, it could sense from his memory that his laugh was fake.

For many months, Phoenix was struggling between the possibility of perhaps getting sent to the Code Grey area for not cooperating or ignoring his true opinion. He turned into a statue of a thinker many times a day, unlike him, as his mind was wandering philosophy and decisions, bailing his usual pleasures for sports and women.

He began to think, perhaps half of The Earth and half of The World's mind together as one would be able to make nature balanced, as he was sure blood crime was never in The Earth's agenda, for they always believed it would mess with her palette and drove her to vomit. Because even with all of those disaster preventions, no crime, and solid advanced technologies they built from everything they could scrap out of the planet, those unexpected natural disasters did not stop. He realized, maybe humans just found a better way to resist them, not end them; and a string of fire from his heart propelled an idea to his mind that he needed to act.

But he needed support, and he knew none he would get from the paradise where he lived.

"I can't decide what is right without knowing what is wrong, and the real issue is, I don't even know what they are. I will, I'm sure, as soon as I find out about what they really do there on The Earth, then I'll know which one is which," he said to himself. Following that, he wanted to know if he could get The Earth's support in some ways.

There was this division in the House of Rules called Population straightforwardly and their work indeed to determine how many people were there in The World as well as forecast how many in The Earth, and the workers there were those who saw an update in the increase and decrease of number as pure excitement. Inside their very spacious room and hundreds of screens, they would jump up and down their chairs every time the number changed or if a graph of forecast was refreshed.

Phoenix could hardly believe such people existed. They were not the only ones the *brain* had correctly guided their path to what really excited them the most, such as Phoenix with his extraordinary fighting skills he always deemed useless. Sometimes though, he could not help but wonder; if their true passion had not been revealed by the *brain* as commonly early as when they were still newborns, how long would it have taken the people to find it? But how come there were still lots out there who the *brain* could not even tell of their interest and leave them to find it themselves?

"Here you go, the number of people who have gone to The Earth, and by estimating the growth after so many years, we reckon it's probably gonna be this number. Oh, and don't forget this number too, a very small number of people who have decided to live there for good this year. And the total is down there. It's big, huh? Do you want anything else? Maybe numbers from this year, last year, next year, last decade, or next decade even? Don't be shy! Ask us anything!" A young man in his red glasses and freckles on his cheeks answered Phoenix's question in a very fast talk with such excitement.

Initially, Phoenix was going to ask how they could get their numbers, but after hearing the very long answer that could have been answered by a one-second-long sentence, he made certain to himself that perhaps he was not that curious about it after all, and he could just let that question remain unanswered. He had got what he needed anyway, and the answer was even way more than what he expected.

Next, he went to a Map division, and as suggested by its name, it was full of people who were overly enthusiastic about drawing every inch of Mother Nature's every skin. Phoenix liked the room better than the one he had just gone in before, plainly because of how more colorful the wide room looked at a glance. The number of screens there was less, but much bigger, and they were circling the room as if the planet were actually revolving around them, by literal figurative. But when he saw the map of the land he lived in, which had Code White, dark forest, and Code Grey area altogether, he began to hope that the amount of those said recycled Code Black corpses were not as high as how large the forest actually was.

Since then, Phoenix got back to his training room to practice his fighting skills, faster and more agile than ever. His father, who was so happy at the unexpected motivation his son had, was no longer a match to him. Whenever his father was not around however, he trained himself slowly with a gun he altered himself with handmade bullets, launching uncontrollable flame when being fired without measure.

He had thought to himself, would the time come where he had to try to kill all of those monsters? But if it did, he should be ready.

Fast forward to a few months later, he sailed to the ocean to set his foot upon The Earth district for definitely the first in a very long time, but not before he took a detour passing the dark forest from the sea.

XXIV

Chapter Twenty-Four

Elowen Silvius

A baby girl was placed in an orphanage, a couple of years after The World first settled out of the bunker. She was called Elowen for being born in a mildly cold weather on the day the elm tree planted on the side of the facility had just had its green leaves blossomed in fluorescence and temporarily yellowed in sunshine, overawing those who saw to promise to never forget, but ironically, they eventually did.

The infant grew up to become an ordinary woman with, what she always believed as, an extraordinary, limited imagination - though never really fancied history or stuck to it, she still valued it resolutely. Every time she looked at the mirror, she saw her steep-arch brown eyebrows, big blue eyes, turn-up nose, and thin lips on her oval-shaped face as mediocre beauty - she never fancied them either.

She always liked one of her traits though, the only one she was proud of, and that was how she seemed to always be able to find a silver lining in everyone, something the others sometimes perceived of her as gullible instead. Hence, she gave herself a last name, Silvius, to always remember it. Everyone was telling her about it, that it was her greatest quality for not condemning the existence of Code Grey area so much, where for some people it made the proclamation of 'heaven on earth' in the land they lived in seemed just a little bit invalid. But the truth, it was driven by her ever wonder if her parents were still alive and they were just assigned to live there, because she was never told the reason why.

Elowen was also a self-proclaimed impulsive mountain climber, not because she was bad at it or she hardly did it - in fact, she conquered the peak quite constantly; but instead for being excited about it and regretting it afterward once she was doing it. A better word for her was probably a vacillating human being who always changed her mind in the middle of doing something but spending most of her indecision time completing it.

She never really explored all the mountains in all the land, for she always went to one in particular, Mount Stranger. The green mountain was one of the hardest to climb - steep and sharp, and the way to the peak was always confusing. Naturally, every time her body bent seventy-five degrees on its belt, she could not help but think why the hell she kept doing it when it was obvious she was fond of walking more than climbing.

Nevertheless, once she succeeded to sit on one of the rocks on the top, as ironically stupid as it sounded, she never dared to bring herself near the edge. She was actually not that fond of the height, and so another thing she contemplated while she was up there, was if there was another way not to look down when she climbed back to the base of the mountain.

It was a good thing that she could still see the glorious sky in blended colors as well as the other thing that reminded her why she was always impulsively driven to do it anyway. The top was where anyone in the Code White area could see the little Code Grey district from. The little houses and mini everything filling a rigged circle in the middle of a forest covered in bushes with almost no space to spare, was her only inspiration to what she had been working on at home.

"Is evil natural or nurtured?" She constantly asked herself as she was resting on her bed with her blanket comfortably, in front of her hovering screen, early in the morning while adjusting her spectacles from time to time. With her brown hair and tall posture, the yellow frame around her glasses made her look like a tree in autumn when she stood.

The writing was a part of her side research and secret obsession as she was always wondering why none of the Code Greys could ever go back as Code Whites, but the other way around could. But she realized, she could never get the answer so long as she never got to know what it was like there on the other end.

Something always drew her to the Code Grey area. She was so mystified that she really wanted to see Code Grey with her own eyes, but the time was never right for her to be that impulsive. She was never really sure whether it was the curiosity if her parents were still alive or the side research she was working on, but she always hoped, every time she tortured herself to get to that same peak of Mount Stranger, she was to be reminded too that she should never leave. She should be grateful to be able to live in such a paradise, and she should be scared even in the slightest thought of leaving the Code White area.

Everything was all taken care of, no work was mandatory, all the citizens could even go anywhere they wanted, well except Code Grey district where it was located in the most dangerous area. So, if no one really wanted to go there anyway, why would she?

All of a sudden, a rumbling storm of sound came from the sky as countless army aircrafts were flying towards the forbidden forest. She lived nearby where the army line was so she got used to the sound of one or two aircrafts, but not like this. Her neighbors were thinking like her too that the sound was not ordinary, so they all came out of the house as Elowen did too, to see the rare sight with their own eyes.

"It must be for going after that fugitive, the one who broke two brain scanners and ran into the forest!" One of her neighbors, a housewife, tattled to the others as they were grouping in the middle of the narrow street for a better view.

"What fugitive?" The curious Elowen responded.

"Watch the news sweetheart, it's all over it. Aren't you a journalist?" The middle-aged woman responded.

Oh yes, Elowen forgot. She once was, a long time ago. But as a citizen in a country that ruled the world, dwelling in a dryland where no other ground subsisted, and living the life where not a single crime existed, there was really not much news to cling on. Besides, she only followed up on something she was curious about, and once she lost interest, she moved on to another that kept her entertained. She thought of herself as more of a seasonal journalist, depending on her own mood.

But this - this did draw her in. So she decided to pack up her climbing gear as a backup plan to better view what was going on in the Code Grey area, just in case her main plan to ask if she could come along with the soldiers was rejected.

"Of course you CANNOT, and you can't even walk there, well, unless you can fly," one of the young troopers, a female, who was guarding one of the posts by the wall insisted.

She was then further told that even if she was permitted to be on her way to the Code Grey area or even went there by herself, she might not be able to come back to the Code White district.

"And our leader treats evil traits like a virus where there's currently no cure for that but death, or maybe yet," a male trooper reminded and then the other nodded to corroborate.

Elowen began to doubt herself. They were right, she thought, and so she changed her mind right at the border. "Thank you, I'll be on my way back," Elowen responded, much to the pleasure of the two young soldiers.

"By the way, watch out for the picas!" The female trooper prompted in an evoking way before the two headed back inside their small post.

Elowen had honestly no idea what she meant, but she could not find the energy to chase them back inside for an answer. Pica? What was that? It sounded familiar, like the name of a bird, but if it was, what harm could it do anyway, she talked to herself. Even by thinking that she was still in the Code White area, there was not anything she should be scared about, right? And so she took her time to walk away from the big wall and played with her phone which screen hovered aligning with her face about thirty centimeters away.

All of a sudden, a long-tailed crow with white furry on its chest, half of its wings and black on its other parts, known as Pica, robbed her phone away as it was attracted to the shiny and flashing lights from the screen, and then continued flying up high across the top of the wall. Without much of a choice, Elowen ran following the line of the wall to chase it.

The Pica abruptly stopped and saw eye to eye with the woman whose afternoon it had just made miserable.

"Drop it!" She screamed, and it did but onto the top of the wall, just before she finished her phrase. Of course, it was why it stopped in the first place, and of course it would only drop her phone where it thought she could not reach.

"Might as well poop on my shoulders too, you crazy mean scary bird," she screamed to the bird who in response just waved its head from left to right, didn't care.

The Pica stayed on top of the wall in a sitting position and made noises while most times looking at her. She could not clearly see its expression as it was too far away from the top of the wall to where she was standing, but she could sense that the bird was talking to her, asking her to get the phone herself as it was too lazy to come down, in a way.

"Ah, damn," she continually cursed towards the bird who was clearly too excited to see what she would do.

If only she spared two more minutes just to ask the soldier what she meant, she kept regretting. She then saw through the screen on her *bracelet* and remembered that she had another eleven months until her next check-up so the phone would be a good excuse for her to... climb the wall.

She looked to the left and right just in case, then prepared herself to climb the wall. She never did before, so she stood quietly for a few minutes trying to figure out how she would do it.

"Aha!" She shouted as an idea traveled through the lobe of her brain.

She pulled out a trapezium shaped of a black colored device and set its mode in the middle part to the highest she could lever and had it hurled a rope as far as it could reach, which was to the other side of the wall. She then pulled the gadget as hard as it could to test if it really stuck to whatever it was.

"Alright, here we go," she said to herself then put her bag on the ground after turning off her *bracelet*.

What she did next was what would commonly be known there as a stupid move for even an experienced climber, she climbed to the top of the wall.

"Now I realize all I want is to just go back home," she many times spoke to herself, probably her way of encouraging herself, but about an hour later, she managed to sit at the top, staring directly at the little Pica's eyes while slowly getting her hand closer and closer to her phone.

Once she got her mobile inside her pocket, she took out the rope remote as she was trying to figure out where the line was going to. However, when the bird suddenly flew in direction to where her little device was, she accidentally pressed the wrong button out of surprise. The rope ran back to its master and fell to where the Code White area was, but unfortunately for Elowen, she lost her balance to the other side instead. And she was falling without support, a long way down, to the ground of the dark forest.

XXV

Chapter Twenty-Five

Secret's Out

A pair of white eyes were watching from the dark deep the top of the wall so peculiarly. Not every day one got to see a Pica outsmarted (or perhaps in this case, attempted to kill) a human being. The owner of those eyes could predict, though not sure to which way at first, that the woman would slip down her way back to the ground. Thus, he ran to reach the spot from below aligning to where the woman sat on top and braced himself for the impact on purpose. As expected, the woman fell on his back safely.

The man growled, and the woman sighed, almost did not believe that she did not even have a single broken bone from the landing; but the man might have.

"Are you okay? I'm so sorry, and thank you for saving me,"

the woman while saying so hugged her hero, who struggled to bring his body to sit. She then helped to lift his back up, then to stand. She thought it was a miracle too that the man seemed to be perfectly fine despite the crash.

Once they stared at each other, the woman suddenly remembered the news her neighbor had brought up. The fugitive that shattered two Grey Chamber machines into pieces. "Oh my God, are you? You're the fugitive, aren't you?" Thus, she asked without thinking twice.

The female panicked from saying that out loud before she got the chance to run away, plus, she never got to meet any Code Grey resident, whose area was known for its crimes and evil infection, so she started to scream.

The man put the palm of his hand on top of her mouth to keep her shriek low. He did it quickly but gently so that she could still breathe. While doing that, he tried to convince her that he had no intention to hurt her and so the woman slowly turned her voice down.

The male introduced his name first, Wyre, and the female said her name to be Elowen.

Meanwhile, hundreds of armies flown from the Code White district were standing side by side in front of the dark forest just on the side of the Code Grey area.

"The fugitive's brain report suggested that his personality will drive him to hide near the gate border. He will be waiting for a chance and trying to find a way to sneak into the Code White area. He knows about the danger in the forest, so he shouldn't go deeper in it," the captain of the troops for the particular mission briefed and suggested they would plod quietly following the path of the wall. His name was Maccush.

"But remember! Don't go beyond a kilometer from the exit of the forest to the beach. If you see a wrecked old warehouse, retreat!" He added, as he was committed to follow the order that he was told to as such.

Back in the deep forest, Elowen and Wyre walked together in where he went by the front and she at the back. The bright sky was slowly disappearing and the temperature was progressively going down. They had been walking and defending themselves from the rough bushes for a couple of hours without a single word thrown out in the air, but Wyre did not sense that the woman was getting scared or cold. She did not even seem to get tired as she kept on walking at the same pace with him, not letting herself get left far behind.

"I'm impressed," he was finally the first to start the conversation one hundred and twenty minutes later.

"What?" She replied.

"You're used to this, aren't you? Should've probably expected that from someone who dared to, and could, climb a wall that high."

Elowen could not see the expression Wyre put out when he said that but as soon as she realized she smiled, she sighed that the back of his head would not be able to see her blush. Out of the blue, a flock of birds drifted in the air altogether from one short branch of tree to another. On the spur of the moment, she let out a bellow of startle and put both of his arms onto Wyre's waist without thinking, as she closed her eyes. Wyre was stupefied and not at all because of those birds.

Once she realized what she did, she quickly withdrew her hands from Wyre.

"Sorry," she said slowly in a very low voice, and the color of both of her cheeks competed with those of ripping red apples'.

"Trauma of birds, huh?" Wyre replied, after his mind went blank for a short moment.

"How can't I, after one made me fall to my death, well almost, thanks to you by the way," and then she added again, "So, thank you."

"You've said that three times, I think, if I'm not mistaken," Wyre replied, and he felt his cheeks were getting warm.

From then on, they continued their conversation without a stop. What started as a Code White woman feeling much safer walking behind a Code Grey man she did not know with a sharp tree branch hiding in one of her pockets, turned to them strolling down the forest while laughing side by side without fear as they were exchanging stories. What got Wyre into becoming a fugitive and what got Elowen climbing the wall, they realized that their stories were connected somehow, and so they laughed even more. They even forgot to ask each other - where were they going exactly?

The happy moment did not last however. Apparently, their chuckle was traveling in the air far enough to reach Maccush's ears by unfortunate distance. He gave a signal to his men not to make a noise and headed slowly towards the babbles and giggles.

"Hang on, did you hear that?" Wyre suddenly stopped his steps while saying that.

His instinct was right, and he was lucky enough to realize that in time so he and Elowen could run as fast as they could deeper into the forest.

"Stop!" Maccush suddenly ordered.

He noticed a sign of a wrecked premises resembling the old warehouse he was told to stay away from, and so he assembled his troopers to retreat.

"What's gonna happen to the fugitive, Sir? And who's the other one? Because it couldn't have been either of his parents," one of the soldiers asked while adjusting his weapon.

"Probably another Code Grey escapee he met in the forest. He's gone, and I mean, he'll really be gone anyway," Maccush responded and headed back to where their aircraft was landed.

"They suddenly stop chasing us, why is that?" Elowen, who noticed the sudden retreat while the two of them were hiding at the back of an old premises, found it oddly suspicious, but Wyre was just glad that they had dodged the bullet.

"You know, everyone says this forest is scary, but so far we haven't seen any of that but the troops," Wyre responded as he let himself inside the smelly abandoned building.

"What is this place?" Elowen spoke her mind as she went further down her steps.

"No one in the Code Grey area has ever been here, I'm sure,"

Wyre responded as he was the first between the two to explore the small building, making sure no danger was inside.

"I think we'll be okay in here," Wyre added as he continued strolling down the rumbling piles, but Elowen sensed a bad feeling about the odd place.

The building structure looked misplaced and seemed to be almost in complete ruin. The body was kind of stuck between the surface of the soil and a little bit of the underground. All the colors seemed to have faded not only from age a long time ago, but also an attempt of being smothered slowly before a heavy rain came and stopped it - she hypothesized it all from the burn marks; but that was not all.

As Elowen noticed the deep thrust on the ground and moss colony all over, she imagined the abandoned warehouse must have had its floor cracked from an earthquake, not long before the flood pushed it inside out of sight as it collapsed to the middle and formed the design it had since then.

As Elowen's fear rose with the fading of the sunlight, she realized that she could not think of a single scenario where things were going the right way. What was she thinking? She kept blaming herself in front of Wyre. She did not even give a damn anymore about her Code Grey research for she just wanted to go back home more than ever. Back to the warm shower, back to the bakery shop near her neighborhood that was sometimes opened or closed depending on the baker's mood, and back to her bed with her blanket.

Should she just activate her *bracelet* and ask for help? Her pointy finger was almost touching the back of the screen, but she got rid of the idea quickly for she too knew she would get a tainted record if she did. Instead, she needed to find a way back home to the Code White area without getting caught, if not killed.

Wyre then mentioned how he wanted to go to the Code White area, to start over his life. Elowen smiled but only because she did not want Wyre to find out she was second guessing his idea. Would it be a good thing to let him in, really? Or had she been affected by the evil intention? What would happen when she went inside the *brain*, which result would she get? And as the nightfall came, so did her trust too to all the Code Greys, disappeared.

"I'm going to ransack the warehouse," Wyre joked lightly as he stood up and tried to warm his body from the icy-cold weather by walking. Bored, Elowen then got up and tried to do the same thing, just in the opposite direction from him.

When Elowen sauntered around what seemed to be a testing ground, she noticed an odd splatter right on the ground. The trace seemed to be flowing towards a tiny hole and as she followed the line, her gut told her to lift the wood upward and saw what was underneath. Oddly, she found a little silver stainless steel box with a rusty lock, with an initial 'HB'.

It did not take her long to crack the bolt open, the natural disasters had helped her a lot with that. She was amazed that what was inside was still nicely intact. What a strong box, she thought, and she might need to get one of those and hide it the same way.

As her hands raised its cover towards the sky, she found a

book titled 'The Earth, by Hayes Beckett' and not just by his initials, like the others were.

"Hayes Beckett? Hang on. Isn't that the founder of The World? Why would he even write down The Earth book?" She spoke to herself quietly.

As she stood up in shock, a rustic old paper covered with a lot of grime fell down from the book while hugging the air elegantly with it and bumped into her calf before it hit the floor. If it had not touched her skin, she would have probably not noticed.

As her eyes scanned through the handwritten letters, her mouth gasped with disbelief and her head looked over to the other side, trying to see if Wyre was within five feet on the ground as far as her vision could reach. She was sure that none of his findings would be able to top hers, but she was probably only half right.

Concurrently, Wyre was going to open an old partially crushed wardrobe covered in spiderwebs and mucks. The worst he was expecting was some bats flying towards him from the inside, feeling disturbed. Keeping that in mind, he opened the closet and quickly moved to the side. His prediction was true, but not entirely as he was, too, only half right.

Inside, he found a skull and scattered bones, looking right at him. Same way a pair of yellow eyes had been surveilling the abandoned structure from the outside, as a matter of fact, hundreds of them, waiting for Wyre and Elowen to come out.

XXVI

Chapter Twenty-Six

Worst Nightmare

A weary old man was looking right at the sky where the stars were outlining a reniform leaf that looked exactly like the colossal land he lived in. The night was peaceful in his unlit room, and he felt an extreme content just by sitting near the opened window with the breeze where his frail limbs lounge, leaning slightly dangerously. When a female nurse came in unexpectedly and turned the light on, he mumbled angrily in words he had to repeat thrice before she understood what he meant, to turn it back off. He, like the stars, was fond of playing mind games in the dark too.

The caregiver patted softly against the red silky robe the back of his fragile body and patiently sloped inward his right shoulder so he would have to draw three-fourths of his left leg back in the room. She then closed and locked the window with her other hand quickly like it was habitual before she successfully got the highly respected founder of The World sleeping comfortably on the bed.

The world in his sleep was nothing but a hollow riven ground. His legs felt light as he hopped on every crack and when he passed across a puddle of clear rainwater, he saw his younger self, but when he lifted his head back to the front, he was met with his ancient self, who was scared and misled by his own illusion of what was right. He wanted him to talk, but he thought he knew what he was going to say, for the other was also himself.

"Say it," he said to his much younger self. The other however stayed weary and fell onto the ground with his sins.

"I want you to say it, it will make you feel better," he added, but he kept quiet and weeping.

"Damn it, just say it!" He screamed, and the other finally responded screaming, "I've killed him! I've killed him!"

All of a sudden, the ground was not empty anymore. It was filled with all the people he knew and wished respect from, and naturally, those from whom he kept his secret intact. Everyone.

"We know," they all screamed, and so repetitively, "We know, oh yes, we know."

"How?" He responded, screeching for an answer.

"Your box, it's empty," Zirilo answered.

And then Hayes woke up, just a couple of hours before dawn.

As fast as a lightning bolt, he was able to recoup the energy he lost from screaming in his own worst nightmare, to walk a few meters away from his bed. Just right behind a small painting of him and Zirilo he twisted to the right was a duplicate of a silver stainless steel box with the initial 'HB' he made when he was still in the bunker, inspired by the one the little version of him saw a few times his father had secretly opened.

He rolled his four-number password to its beeline on the lock, one - zero - seven - six, and once it opened, he picked up a wide blood-splattered fabric, blooded knife, and a dusty first-generation chip. The blood was scattered like the stars before they silently faded away.

The Zirilo that appeared in Hayes' dream could not be the same with the one who was still wide awake in his grand golden and velvet-carpeted study room. Both of his hands were tilting on his chin, as he was afraid and anxious, to hear the update he was expecting.

Maccush came in late and without delay, for he knew the great leader was expecting no spare second to hear the news eye to eye. Zirilo was expecting good news but by the look of the man standing in front of him, including the sweats sliding down his sideburns from either running or fear, it did not seem like it. With a train of words set out from Maccush's mouth to his ears, his unpleasant emotion was evidently confirmed as he subsequently responded, "This is my worst nightmare."

"He won't survive there, but without a body, there's still a slim chance of survival, and I don't like that," the leader averred, and though his voice was of little depth, he still looked extremely furious.

"Don't let anyone know about the chip, and I mean everyone, period," he added as he stood up from his comfortable wooden chair.

When afterward being asked about what they should do with *the other one*, Zirilo suggested keeping Wyre's father alive as a guarantee, as the leader emphasized, "Just in case," as well as "I'll decide their fate afterward."

One thing he stressed about more than the other however, with that blood-curdling "let it be clear" he added, as he gave the table his fist bumps with both hands, "I want the chip to either be destroyed or returned to me."

Chapter Twenty-Seven

Earthquake to His Rescue

"Dear somebody,

The earth is coming apart at the seams. It is out of balance and those evil seeds are the cause of it.

Some say the world is currently differentiated into a-three. First are the ones who long for the blood, the second hide from the first, and the last are torn between either; but I don't believe the third existed in a flash of an eyelid.

I say there are only two kinds of people on this planet. Simply, the first is right for the world but the second is wrong, and the latter shall be eliminated from this earth the moment they were born. So it only makes sense for me that I use my brain to create a course of action to reveal them, and I will too call it the *brain*, I keep to myself and my only son. It will be able to detect the seed before it grows, kill the host before it spreads; and once the whole world is free from it, there will be no more foul to taint the peace - and this is my definition of a real heaven on earth.

No more blood, I was begged constantly, but it has to be done as it is the only way. If my son mentions benevolence, I'll know he'd be helpless, and I'll be dead. He will find out why, and he will weep at my ghost, should I not have the chance to live its glorious day. He will burn this filthy book he wrote, The Earth, and understand the real world will not settle for his fantasy - people controlling earth elements.

If this paper is out of the gap, that means he has gone past his furthest; my own, has turned into his own Code Black in a White, and I am glad, and I want the whole world to know, that I know, that it is all because of me and my *brain*.

Sign,
Homeron Beckett"

"You need to get this to Code White," Wyre screamed and jumped out beyond consciousness.

"No, WE need to get this to Code White. But, what are they going to do to us if they find out? Besides, it's not like this letter means anything, it just implies that the founder's dad was crazy and maybe evil, that's all," Elowen replied in a more calming way, but with a taste of her usual indecisiveness.

However, Wyre responded, "And thus the *brain* is evil," much to the woman's bewilderment.

Elowen was not sure that the *brain* was evil in her honesty because so far, everything in the Code White area seemed to be perfect. It was indeed a literal heaven on earth, and though she admitted that some of the ways were pretty cruel, they worked for the good. But she thought of something else too. So, the one who started The Earth belief was exactly the same one with the one who founded The World? Did it even make sense? How could it?

However, no matter which side was greener, or better, or finer, it only diverted her mind back to one thing. All she really wanted was to just go back home.

Wyre grew quiet for a while too and it was because he had been contemplating what was written on the letter. While doing so, his hands had been sleeping behind his two pockets for a warmer bed, when suddenly a few of his fingers felt they were adjoining something. Unconsciously, Wyre put out the brain chip he took that he had forgotten completely as he was trying to survive in the forest, and Elowen was caught by a surprise.

Wyre suddenly had an idea and suggested that maybe there was a hope if they looked at the programming. He felt that his father did not belong in the Code Black category, and that there were so many people in the Code Grey area (of course he was actually talking about himself) who tried their hardest to be good that there was probably more light in them already and they were more risk averse than probably any others in Code White. "No offense, Elowen," Wyre added.

"But I also don't think anyone here has the bravery to come up here like you did if given the citizenship in Code White,"

Wyre further commented, hoping that it was clear he meant well about her.

"Being born there, I guess I probably got used to it and didn't appreciate the privilege as much as I should have. Now I'm missing home again more than ever," Elowen responded with about the hundredth time she talked about missing home.

Early morning came, and birds chirping right around the torn-up ceiling was the only reason the two of them were brought back from dreaming. The atmosphere grew quiet again, just like the dusty air inside the abandoned warehouse. Their skin was cold not just from the chill ambience amassed from the night before, but the sudden awkwardness as if they turned to strangers the moment they woke up.

"I think I'm gonna get ourselves some food, you should stay here in the meantime," Wyre initiated while bending his right knee and smashing his palm right on it just so he could pull his body up. He was thinking that perhaps by getting some alone time with no pressure, he could summon his day-before self again. As Elowen was already back to her half-asleep state, she was grateful for the suggestion.

Fallen leaves on the forest ground were driven by the wind to move off quickly in all directions. Wyre's feet swished around them every distance just so he was sure there were no snakes and other crawling creeps offended while his hands brushed on every bushes he could find for non-poisonous berries he was half certain. He picked out some soft yellow flowers too just so Elowen could safely eat their petals, but when he realized that the gesture might look misleading, he took them off of their discs and scattered them into a giant leaf like a plate before he brought them to her.

As he was on his way back to where Elowen had already woken up hungry, he had just noticed that the wind breathed quite heavily on the shrubs. Or was it all of a sudden, which was almost never a good sign if it was. Having been hiding for days in the forest had taught him that it would not be smart to trace it back to its origin, thus he walked the quickest he knew how so as not to let his morning harvest fall.

He was not sure whether it was the gale he slapped against his body, his panting breath, or something else anonymous that was making that growling sound. As his pace was slowing down, the sound got closer and closer and closer towards his presence that he chose to close his eyes pro tem without turning back, until the earth decided to save him by shaking her ground. Alas, the horrid groan was no more.

When Wyre came back, he found Elowen chilling and reading the book written by Hayes instead with no sign of stress from the short earthquake, to his surprise.

"What earthquake?" Elowen responded and she did not sound like she was kidding, making Wyre want to scratch his head even more. He was confused but then he looked at the book she was reading, and his curiosity was diverted instead to what was inside that bound pile of papers.

"Why didn't you read that book in Code White before?" Wyre asked in full curiosity, wondering if she was just simply not fond of reading.

"Why haven't I read this before? Oh right, maybe because I

don't read that much, or I couldn't find it anywhere, or that I don't think I have ever seen the book before, or I don't know, perhaps the leader of The World doesn't want their people to know that they shared the same founder with their sibling they always mock?" Elowen responded sounding a bit upset and Wyre could not figure out why, but so did she. It might be all the stress building up in her and making her more sensitive to any question.

She was only still in the middle of the book, but she could already tell that Hayes used to be a full believer of The Earth belief. She brought this up with Wyre, how it just bedazzled her to have been living under the strong The World regime that never wasted a minute to mock how The Earth people live, and yet, their founder was just one of them, or maybe had been, she still had not figured out that part too.

"Actually, I've been meaning to ask. What's that? What's The Earth?" Wyre admitted in all honesty.

Elowen began to explain full-heartedly by saying that The Earth was quite well known in the Code White district, and that The Earth was established around the same time as the World. The Earth used to be a part of The World for a short moment when the brain scanner was first introduced, until they learned that the *brain* did not condemn the evil things done to Mother Nature. So it was not that The Earth believers did not belong in the Code White area, they refused to.

The Earth area was floating on the sea, and its members were living organically, while similarly against the wicked.

They lived without a single attachment to the land and who knew how they were able to survive living there for decades.

Their food was fully grown and harvested from what was called floating farms, and though already knew as much, Elowen had never seen a picture of how they looked somehow. She was told that they were serious about not eating meat because they did not believe in the spoiling of blood for the living, but some of The World members swore they had seen them do.

There was no ruler in The Earth district, everyone was for themselves. Even so, they never had the goal to be one. They simply wanted to live in peace away from the technology they believed was harming nature, and lived their own lives loving and treating all of Mother Earth elements and organs with full respect as the only way to bring complete peace and balance on the earth.

They even believed that once, a very long time ago, their ancestors were able to reign over the earth's elements, over some drawings on a cave. And such was what became the cornerstone of The World's joke towards what they perceived as The Earth's madness and over-idealist fantasy, with The World's foundation being their logical sense and paramount faith in modern technology they could not live without - matching Homeron's letter. That was why, The World government never considered them as a threat and decided to leave them be with whatever they wanted to do. They even ensured, if themselves, or their kids, or their grandkids wanted to join

The World once again or for the first time, they would always welcome them with open arms.

"Wait," Elowen suddenly had an epiphany, "I think I know how to get you in Code White, Wyre."

"Wait, what? How?" Wyre's hope skyrocketed to probable infinity.

Elowen then created a scenario, where Wyre was pretending to be one of The Earth members and going to Code White. However, he would still need to be tested, and if - "No offense, Wyre," she emphasized before she continued, just if he got another Code Grey result, then what was the point?

But, if he could somehow get into possession of the *bracelet* thrown away by some ex-The World's members turned The Earth's, he would have a higher chance not to get caught, and he could even probably skip the brain scanner. Of course, Elowen added, probably for a short while before he was called for a maintenance brain test.

All in all, Elowen's idea was to have Wyre pretending as one of The Earth members.

"But how?" Wyre seemed to be taking the idea as a definite possibility.

"Not sure to be honest. But to start, maybe you need to read this, very carefully."

XXVIII

Chapter Twenty-Eight

Brain Dwindling and Hungry

The morning was cut short by the great enthusiasm they harnessed to prepare for the long journey they had yet to have the idea where. It started out good as Wyre led the way to the deeper side of the forest he had not been, then when it was obvious that he was stuck, Elowen took advantage of her knowledge from having climbed only one particular mountain to use it to find the way in the unknown. Wyre accepted her standpoint until eventually he built his own school of thought from what he knew that unfortunately contradicted with the one who walked in front of him.

"Are you sure you know where we're going, Elowen? You don't think we should go that way instead?" Wyre then pointed out a big old tree where a flock of birds could be seen flying on top of it towards the other way the two were going.

"I'm sure, well, not quite. But I've been trying to remember the direction we've been taking so the Code White area should be at the end of that way, I think, sort of. This forest is so different from any other forests I've been to," Elowen responded.

"So, the answer is, no? I thought you'd know better than that, maybe you've given yourself too much credit," the constantly striking sunshine sent Wyre's frame of mind to a high heat of temper. His self-control remained to keep his voice down low but some of the words representing his bad mood still managed to slip out. Elowen afterward glared at Wyre in annoyance.

"No wonder they put you in Code Grey," she responded, prompting Wyre to glare at her in similar vexation.

They were quiet for a short moment afterward before Wyre made his attempt to neutralize the bellicose.

"You know, after reading the book, living in The Earth area doesn't sound so bad after all, but how can we really reach there?" Wyre started.

"Well, The Earth is well known to live on the water, so we just probably have to find the sea, somewhere, if you want to go there instead." Elowen responded.

It was not much of a time they had to mend the tension as an elevating guttural sound was abruptly overpowering their attention. The sound was getting louder as they stopped everything they were doing for trying to figure out what it was. But as they meditated the animals running away, they knew they needed to follow their steps in the expense of their fulfilled curiosity.

A short moment later after they started their race against their death, and as they span their head to the back for a few seconds, they witnessed the source of the sound. They were the ugliest frightening creatures anyone could have ever imagined, with great resemblance to mankind.

Collectively, they seemed to be in different stages, as in, some were more like humans, and some were less, kind of like they had probably mutated from their original form. Their bodies were rotten and mushy like bad pickles walking in uncertainty, and their faces were dried out of water like the dead.

As Wyre and Elowen were running for their life, they passed those who had lost theirs - all in bones and leftover fleshes. With a quick look, Wyre was positive that they were Code Grey runaways who did not make it. He hoped he was not going to be one of them, as long as he kept on running without looking back.

It was almost too impossible not to get caught, and the two were almost in the verge of giving up if the monsters were not slowing down. Fortunately, the wind was starting to get very strong from their fore, powerful enough to even knock some of those zombies down. Elowen, realizing the smell of the salty breeze and blowing sand, wondered if the sea was near, and the hope she screamed unconsciously gave them more strength to keep going.

"This way!" While they were running, Elowen saw more

hint of a water trail and followed it confidently. A couple of miles later, they finally reached the sea.

Without thinking straight, they forced their way through the shallow of the deep, hoping that those monsters were not able to swim. Most of them were drown as they were all cluelessly following them to the sea, however two were able to propel their body to stay afloat and chase them with their swinging arms, while the others chose to go back to the dark forest. Wyre and Elowen then noticed more Code Grey runaways' corpses were floating on the sea - barely unrecognizable, and they realized why no Code Greys were able to sneak into Code White area. In short, it came across as they had no way out, as two of those monsters were inches away from seemingly going to chew them to death with blood palette and then hurling their fleshes like the rest.

Bang. Bang.

Two bullets that breathed out fire when the trigger was pulled hit the two monsters perfectly at the chest. The flame was eating all of their faces and half of their bodies above the water, while half others descended to the sea ground slowly. Their painful screams sounded so confusing at the same time that it almost seemed they were quite enjoying the burn like they were looking forward to hell. Or maybe, they just preferred the eternal death over living like lingering corpses.

"Get in, quick!" Phoenix who had just saved them from the zombies, rescued them further from the cold water and brawny waves. Elowen and Wyre thanked him thrice afterward before Phoenix told them to stop or else, the two assumed he meant going back to the water.

"What are they? Dwindling-brain zombies?" Elowen started to wonder as she peacefully dried her hair with a towel without distraction and she sought confirmation as her eyes rolled left and right at the two men.

"I don't know, maybe?" Wyre seemed he agreed with the phrase, but he would prefer hungry zombies.

"So that's what they look like, humans," Phoenix on the other hand seemed to be talking to himself, "Weird how some of them know how to swim and some others don't," he added. Right, the two others' mind started to wonder. Phoenix's breakthrough of reasoning got all of them thinking, why?

"I've never seen that in Code White, where are they coming from?" Elowen pondered so deeply that she almost forgot Wyre's face who turned panic red as she mentioned Code White.

"You too from Code White? Because I cannot see your *bracelet*," Phoenix raised his question to Wyre in front of Elowen, and with an uncontrollable feeling of trepidation, she responded instead, "Yes, he's with me," much to Wyre's surprise.

"What's your story? How did you two get here? You know what, I don't want to know," Phoenix, who assumed that they were just some stranded lovers who were just in the wrong place at the wrong time, gave extreme relief to the other two.

Elowen then brought herself closer to Wyre's side, and her

mouth too to his right ear then whispered, "See the symbol on the edge? We call them House of Rules. They're leaders of Code Whites, government kind. We better be careful with our words." Wyre, who was surprised to hear this, nodded, and with more nervousness intact, stole moments to see the symbol with more attention, trying to remember perfectly what it looked like. The logo was of a planet earth hovering above the cloud.

Elowen and Wyre realized lady luck seemed to be on their side after the near tragedy, as Phoenix mentioned that he was on his way to The Earth before going back to Code White. Wyre jumped with his bottom bouncing as a result, struggling to contain his excitement while he was sitting down. Moments later however, Elowen and Wyre noticed that the wind and sea had been bringing them all back to where the dark forest was, just where they had just been. It was before they realized that it was Phoenix's skill instead and not his intention that was doing that. Apparently, he was forgetting he had never sailed before, while he was deciding on a free-android sailboat.

"Let me," Wyre initiated, as he steered the boat left and right accordingly, and fixed the twisted rope with the right rhythm like he was a natural.

"Who taught you?" Phoenix could not help but asked, totally impressed.

"My dad," Wyre responded, and Elowen's expression adjusted to showing concern, worrying that he would slip out.

"You've sailed before?" Phoenix was expecting an either 'yes, everyday' or 'yes, too often', but out of left field, he got a "Nope."

Curious, Phoenix enquired further where he got the knowledge from. Wyre briefly summarized his father's sentences, but some were obvious to all that he was going to keep for himself. The same way Phoenix knew more about those monsters, but he would not tell.

"So, what's our plan when we get to The Earth district?" Elowen rushed on her question, trying to swiftly change the topic so that she could remain calm, and less chance of Wyre letting out suspicious behavior. Phoenix then mentioned his plan to see Mistral.

"Who's Mistral? Do you know her well enough for us to trust her?" Elowen questioned.

"She's my ex, so it could be both ways," he responded.

"Was it, a bad breakup?" Elowen's body leaned forward unconsciously as she was getting anxious to risk her life on the boat longer. She was hoping for a 'no' answer for worry-free, or any answer at all just so she would not be in a teeter wondering if she should be worried at all. Instead, Phoenix did not respond.

Wyre and Elowen would bite their nails, but it would be so obvious. They could scream the frustration of not knowing the certainty, especially after escaping death like that, but that would probably get them thrown out to the water on purpose. Thus, they decided to go along with Phoenix's plan to go there anyway, as they discerned they had no other, better, choice.

Elowen put her chin close to the side of the boat, feeling

hopeless, but instead, what showed itself by the distance took her mind somewhere safe and wonderstruck. What was appearing before her eyes from afar was completely magical.

XXIX

Chapter Twenty-Nine

Mistral Clode

The vast ocean looked like a prodigious number of soldiers guarding a vulnerable modest kingdom. The Earth was floating, literally, and they resembled a group of beautiful water lilies in all kinds, refusing to go back to the pond where they were deemed to belong. The way they were scattered all over the surface, with big and small eco-friendly brown vessels powered by sunlight reaching in and out of each of the floating giant petals innately, was indescribably simple and magnificently beautiful.

The high-end parliament boat that was fully operated by Wyre was smelling soil more than water while it was bringing its passengers closer to their kinds. It shifted left and right, being forced to go along with the sailor's confusion as he was waiting for the owner's instruction on where to park. "This is not how I remember it," Phoenix mumbling in an awe speaking to himself had convinced Wyre that he would not be able to tell him where anyway.

The big boat stopped at the bottom edge of the wide district and the three were half surprised that they were greeted with warm smiles as well as direct ignorance. They strolled through what was called Floating Houses, one of many and separated from the others living on a different leaf each. The floating ground was built from a mysterious material that was light and incredibly strong at the same time. Some said that aliens felt sorry for how they saw the earth in pain that they donated their giant flying saucer to cheer her up, while others believed that their not-that-long-ago ancestors gained the trust briefly from The World just so they could lend their scientific brain in how to develop an eco-friendly floating land to help them build their runaway dominion. All in all, nobody could really explain how it really started, but maybe some just didn't.

The houses were very small compared to those in the Code White area and probably slightly the same size as the ones in the Code Grey district. They were all identical in size due to the obvious limited grounds with at least the sky being visible in the open and they were free to do whatever they wanted with them so long as the earth was not harmed.

All the houses were shaped like little pentagons, with each was uniquely colored in and out according to the inhabitants' preferences except the top. Their roofs bent down inward resembling the wing of a butterfly in black rectangles and white lines waiting for the sun to come in as their only source of electricity. As they were all surrounded by water, an extremely pungent camphorous scent of eucalyptus coming out of each was one of those things that reminded them of land, grown in by little distance of water from where they were.

Each of the Floating Houses' petals had a nearby floating ground filled with growing crops for together-consumption within the same house complex, they called it simply Floating Farm. Vessels in the shape of brown vases were the only way they traveled back and forth the house complex and the farm, the big ones fit for two humans and the smaller in size for their harvest. In addition, a two-way vessel rail served its second purpose to indicate which farm belonged to which complex.

The Floating Farm held many kinds of plants edible to the mouth when harvested and necessary for the consumption of the eye when cultivated. The view of it, of how humans paddled from one to another, how the greens were spreading across the floating land, and how submerged little lanterns fooled fishes to come then made their way out as soon as they were trapped, would draw a lot of interest for those who saw it for the first time. The three companions' attention however was undivided to a small ex-cave afloat about three miles far, seemingly standing on the surface by itself.

Their focus was distracted all of a sudden by the proof that the commitment The Earth members took about their life loving earth and living on the sea out of nowhere with limited resources was not for the faint hearted.

"You've taken more than you should!" A small guy with long hair and a loud scream lifted his fist toward below the chin of another male he could not reach. "You're not supposed to!" He continued when the other man just pretended that he could not see anyone below his shoulder.

Fed up with the accusation, the big buffy man put on the ground the basket of fresh vegetables he had just harvested from the Floating Farm, and screamed back, "Oh yeah? Where's your proof? Even if I was, who were you going to report this to anyway?"

The conversation freshened up the idea to the three strangers that The Earth did not have any House of Rules, or probably any rules at all except for their pity on the earth. Everyone was for themselves, loving the earth, whilst seemingly showing lack of interest in what The World was trying to achieve.

Wyre and Elowen were letting out their words of opinion until they realized that Phoenix was already gone. The tall guy with a red vegan leather jacket on his torso was already walking towards the scene, and by the time he stood in between the two males fighting with their mouth swords, the air around quickly changed from hot temper to confusion.

Phoenix then continued asking why the small accused the other. "He harvested and took back two portions of my plate size!" He answered, then the other defended himself, "This is one portion of my plate, look! See yourself if you don't believe me!"

Phoenix then truly realized what was really going on. As there were no rules enforced in how much a person could take, they just determined the portion themselves. As he gathered more people around to ask if that kind of issue happened all the time - which was more than ten times daily as it turned out, he walked to a big flat stone rounded on the edge, let the skin of his fingertips to scratch a little from making sure it was not wet, and managed to jump to its top without slipping.

"Let us start with this," he started by asking each of them a list of contributions. He then instructed his hovering phone to write them down in detail and flash a see-through projected screen in big font sizes so that everyone could see. The quick-witted was able to write them in headings and small descriptions for the details below, matching them accordingly as they went on and on.

Next, he grouped the activities and let all of them rank appropriately and collectively the list until they reached a consensus. He then let them decide how much of a portion one should have bigger than the other, and if one disagreed, he gave the others the chance to oppose until the minority was willing to give in to the majority vote and respect it. The discussion became a huge hit and even invited all of the others from nearby floating lands to come to watch. All in all, the democratic event ran for five hours long but to a great achievement, a fair portion system was established.

At the back of the crowd, a female with long braided black

hair to the back and a long sleeve white satin dress covering her whole body to her ankle had been watching quietly and pulling to the side her bow-shaped lips for the whole time. The Earth could use this kind of a leader, she believed, as she realized nobody else in there had yet to possess his kind of charisma.

Her cold bare feet came closer to the impromptu podium once the unplanned panel discussion was over with a big success, and she clapped her hands towards Phoenix along with the fully impressed Wyre and Elowen, as the others were leaving in peace.

"Mistral," Phoenix mumbled to himself as the shorter distance brought her face to look clearer under the bright sun.

"It's been a very, very long time, Phoenix, since the last time someone was able to step up like that in here," Mistral's words confirmed Wyre and Elowen's suspicion they gained from Phoenix's bewildered expression that she must have been Mistral.

"Well, it's been such exactly since something else too," he replied with a tense reveal just by looking at her, and Mistral responded with a smile without a single word.

Elowen and Wyre sensed the great awkwardness coming from their presence. They knew they should probably excuse themselves, but they could not help but stay within a distance where they could still hear what the two were saying.

"So you bring company this time," Mistral looked at the two who could not say anything to her except returning her smile, as Phoenix's glance at them were saying things that could mean just about anything in their minds, they still were not sure. But as soon as Mistral embraced them with a warm hug, they knew they should not be as afraid as they thought they should.

"I came here to see the people of The Earth," Phoenix responded to Mistral's question of why he came, as the four of them made their way to her little boat.

"Really? That's not an excuse for you to see how I'm doing here?" She replied with a joking sense, and the two others' quietness burst into laughter.

"You look so peaceful and happy here," Elowen always thought twice about what she would say to Mistral from the moment they first met, but the compliment was the only one she did not.

"The breakup made her that," Phoenix was calm saying it until he was aware, he said out loud what was on his mind.

Mistral took it as a joke and laughed, thus so did the others one by one. "Well, we can laugh about it now, but definitely not then. It's always like that, time always heals everything, fast or slow, we just have to be patient and try to move on with our life, until it steers by itself," Mistral responded as her hands drove the wheel the little boat ship them to, the Floating Houses next to the one they had just left.

"Where do you live?" Phoenix asked, and to that Mistral responded, "That one, the little red house over there next to the blue one, is where me and my husband live."

Mistral's words however almost caught Elowen and Wyre off guard to open a big hole in their mouths conveying disappointment. They were rooting for Phoenix and Mistral to get back together for a short while when they saw them reuniting like there was no breakup, and then the word 'husband' came out and ruined their hypothesis. Phoenix however, showed off afterward the most genuine smile the two had ever seen of him, and if it was just an act, he had played it really well, they thought. In fact, he looked veritably happy for her.

"How's that Dagger beauty you had a crush on before me? The one with the charming older brother, and whose mom's as scary as your dad." Mistral then continued giving more confusing information for the clueless other two. So there was another lady, they nodded agreeing to what they asked silently to themselves, and they then tried to make up another story in their own mind while appearing ignorant for the rest of the conversation.

Realizing how Elowen and Wyre kept unconsciously looking at him with a swinging smile and teeter-totter eyebrows while they were writing romantic novels in their own brain, Phoenix quickly changed the topic.

"Does The Earth move constantly? It isn't in the same coordinates as before, and it took a while for me to find it," Phoenix spoke while he spun his flying mobile phone left and right with his pointy finger.

"We're moving wherever the water brings us to. We believe they get us away from disasters," Mistral replied, much to everyone's shock.

Elowen and Wyre were more surprised Phoenix never said a word about them getting lost. For all they knew, the trip seemed to be going smoothly and not as long as they thought. The way they had seen him on the way, other than looking like he did not belong at sea for his constant failures at driving the boat the right way, he did not at all give a vibe that something was even slightly wrong. In fact, he looked like he had known the way all along where actually he turned on his poker face just so the two who had just escaped death, did not think that they were on their way to another one. Guess he just did not like his panicked look to be seen by anyone else except a lonely mirror in the room.

Phoenix however was more interested to know about the disaster. "Not at all, we haven't even had any disaster in a decade," Mistral answered.

"Really? No tsunami, big waves, anything that can tore this place apart, nothing?" Phoenix asked for confirmation again because he was surprised to the bone. He was almost positive that there would have been at least one, for even the Code White and Grey area were still hit at least a few times a year.

"Some others think it's complex coincidental science, but we think it's because our belief works," Mistral then explained further by pointing out a round hardstone chamber crafted by nature. It was located right at the heart of The Earth district as clear as daylight even though it was obvious it should have been underground. Indeed, it was that one ex-cave the three actually had been wondering about.

Mistral then brought them to the peculiar floating cave. As they were walking, she mentioned that what kept everything afloat was the exact same material to the floor where their feet were attached to. "How so?" Elowen shouted in curiosity, but to that, Mistral and everyone else there had been asking the same question their whole life. And it was not that they had not been trying to solve it. When they swam under all the floating material, nothing was under but water, and the only explanation they could think of was that the cave was the head and it was bringing along the other parts of its body with it as it ran away from the only land on the planet.

The cave was only a few meters long and wide, and inside there was nothing but a cold bed of rocks, a pillar of boulders, and a rough ceiling that shed tears of sand.

"What are these drawings?" Phoenix wondered as his fingers glazed on the wall with wonder and discombobulation.

Wyre and Elowen then went to the other side to see what Phoenix was talking about, because their side had none of such. While their eyes were scrutinizing each line carved on the surface trying to make up the idea behind the illustration themselves, Mistral was speaking as a background, "'Four men were lifting their hands to the earth the same way; then the first was flickering five fingers to his front and five others to his back, the second pushing his left arm to the left and right one to his right, the third kneeling and placing both of his hands on the ground, while the fourth lifting both arms up high. Afterward, the four of them stood side by side in various positions, and from the first to the fourth, their linked arms formed a peaceful resting heart pulse of a body and soul' - 'twas in the book," she communicated, but with a much lower voice only her could hear during the last four words. Elowen's expression was mirroring a trip to a memory lane, not long ago. Wyre would have been too if he had done thoroughly what he was strongly suggested as well as Phoenix if he had been stranded in the forest with them.

"What happened afterward?" Phoenix struck a question out of curiosity.

"No one really knows," Mistral responded, "but the book says they purportedly put a strike on the enemy, cleaned the battlefield," she added, but halfway Elowen jumped in to finish the sentence together with her as their heads met face to face mildly startled, "sang their child to sleep, and kiss the earth long good night."

"That book," Wyre said as he then noticed the answer from Elowen's rolling her eyes to her right waist, where she kept it as known by him.

"What is going on? What book? What else does it say?" Phoenix, who was the only one who did not know what was really going on, could not contain his train of unanswered questions.

"Something about a seed, where the fire has to come first. The book ends there," Elowen responded, "Who knows what kind of seed that does that?" She continued.

Mistral's face twinkled with her front teeth exposed as she heard Elowen. She lifted her hands up to her chest and responded with excitement, "I do!"

XXX

Chapter Thirty

The Fire Has to Come First

"What blasted gun?" Phoenix screamed at Wyre, and his high pitch turning in a trice just proved how nervous he was to pretend. The truth was, he did not feel safe to shoot it on any land but water for he knew how fast the fire could easily be out of control, and so he finally admitted when he gave up the sham.

Wyre then swam to the ocean and brought the seeds that looked like brown flowerpots sharing a room in a small canister. He drowned his face downward below so that only his palms holding the container upward could be seen above the water surface. "I will not panic, promise," he assured before.

Phoenix then set the gun power to extremely low and fired it out as trial on a floating little vase on the other side, to ensure the bullet would only breathe its flame on the seeds without burning them. The vase was still intact but slightly moved to the right, dropping fish pellets out of the vessel ready for swimming creatures' early dinner. "Ready, Phoenix?" He talked to himself and then fired the bullet to where the seeds were on the sea.

Wyre's palms below protected the canister from moving to its sides so that the seeds remained inside. Feeling the small impact, he got out of the water slowly and brought himself back to the very narrow side of the floating cave on its front, the only spot where the sunlight could still sneak into, along with the others.

The four of them watched together the serotinous cones of those cracked while Mistral at the same time tried to contain the hot air inside the container with her hands acting like a fan. Their resins were melted by the heat and they released their seeds from inside.

Elowen put fertilizer on the rocky ground and massaged it gently until it formed a ring of soil where those stardust-shaped seeds could sleep comfortably, then covered them like she was pulling a thin blanket all over them.

"Look at that, you're a natural. You must have a really good understanding about the ground," Mistral was applauding at Elowen, meanwhile, she was looking at Wyre proudly, considering he looked down on her before when they got lost in the forest. The way Wyre splashed some good water on the soil in the end afterward was clear that he was slightly annoyed by Elowen's fulfilling look at the compliment.

"I still think the Eucalyptus won't grow in here, it'll take a miracle to be otherwise," Phoenix implied how he still thought what they had done was just a waste of time, pointless, and completely out of track - no wonder they were the first to do it there.

As they were going back to where Elowen lived, they talked about how all the Earth members removed themselves from The World's Code White area, and grew their population ever since, living far from the mainland. Three of them then continued to talk about their time in the Code White area, while Wyre became quiet as a result.

Talking about the Code White territory made Elowen miss her hometown even more, even though she had only left for a few days. She just wanted to go back home, as she realized she had got used to living too comfortably for too long that she needed to leave it and see a possibility of never going back, to know she should have never taken it for granted. Wondering if Mistral could relate, she asked her if she ever missed it, living there. Expecting her to say 'yes', she said "no" instead. "And none of most of The Earth are," she added.

She then continued explaining how they had made a commitment when they separated themselves, that they would never go back there. Maybe they were still a part of The World in some ways, but they became fully committed to The Earth and remained separate, nevertheless. In fact, they really held the promise seriously that they even threw away their Code White *bracelet*.

Hearing that, Wyre's body went numb, finding out that

the idea was hopeless after all. There went his chance to pretend to be The Earth member, he thought, and he was glad he had not wasted his time reading that The Earth book word by word as suggested by Elowen. Hidden from Phoenix and Mistral, Elowen softly put his palm on top of Wyre's and her fingers hugged his; and though without her making eye contact on purpose to avoid suspicion, he still smiled just a little as he felt his heart grew warmer from her gentle touch.

"And you, you do too, like Elowen?" Mistral asked Wyre, realizing he had grown suspiciously quiet all of a sudden.

"Yes, I want to go to the Code White area. I mean, go back to, I mean, go back home," Wyre stuttered a little while responding, sending a red flag to Phoenix's instinct.

When Elowen and Wyre left momentarily to get them all some water to drink, as their throat was drying up from the cold ocean breeze and long night conversation, Phoenix felt that the timing could not be more perfect to let Mistral know of his concern that prompted him to run away from the Code White area for a short while.

Phoenix wanted to know more about The Earth so he could try to fix whatever was going wrong with The World's system. He was almost sure that Zirilo was up to something mad and aggressive as the new leader slowly introduced the inner circle to a seemingly more no-mercy policy to establish a definite world with no evil tangled to his grief-stricken past, and he believed the only ones who could support him were The Earth members as they loudly proclaimed The World's problem according to their mind. But still, The World underestimated them for never taking the action to try to change their minds. "Or maybe," Phoenix added, "two is indeed better than one, if you know what I mean." Unity between The World and The Earth idea popped up in his mind in the fullness of time.

"Then coming here is a waste because everyone here just wants to live in peace with nature. We may have different beliefs with The World, and sure we want them to change theirs, but we really take this 'living in quietude' seriously. We never want to fight them but rather avoid as much as we can," Mistral responded with fierce-looking eyes, inviting Phoenix vividly in a mouth war.

"Right, peace, like people still arguing, that kind of peace," he responded. The way he spoke was like attracting fire to ignite.

Mistral and Phoenix continued their almost-endless argument about The Earth and The World. Phoenix was still firm with his conclusion that there should be a reaction from The Earth to clean the world from its appearing invisible stains but they were just too scared to fight for what they believed in, whereas Mistral said avoiding war was what brought peace to the earth, not the other way around. The opposite views were brought up in cycle on and on, where none was willing to give up.

When Elowen and Wyre came back, the water inside the glasses they were holding almost broke free out of purpose as they were surprised and confused to see them suddenly get into a mouth fight. Scared to straight peacefully the twisted tangle, they stood quietly to summarize the long argument.

"So, what do you think?" Wyre attempted to confirm if his bullet points were the same as Elowen.

"The World - no evil in humans. The Earth - no harm to nature. Phoenix wants to take action, Mistral doesn't, then blablabla, but I think that's about it," she responded, tired at hearing them. "This will go all night long, I can see it," she added as she began to snooze.

Out of the blue, a man the three companions had never seen before came in the middle of the heated argument between Phoenix and Mistral. He had a low man bun and a small lotus tattoo on the back of his neck. His expression was somewhat a crystal of peace, one that even when strangers were looking at him for the first time, they could visualize giving him a piece of rock for his birthday, but he would still place it to keep and thank them twice. The name of the man with the light black coffee colored skin was Udoka, and he was revealed to be Mistral's husband.

"I know this may sound weird, but I think you two should talk privately somewhere. It's been a while, there must be a lot to be filled in," he spoke like water pouring to the two minds on fire, smiling kindly at them the whole time. He could read wisely that they had never had a proper closure and it would be a good time for giving them the chance to have one that night.

And off the two went to the edge of the floating ground near the vessel port, with a view of the tranquil Floating Farm in the hours of darkness.

XXXI

Chapter Thirty-One

Closure

It was either the long quiet walk to the port or the wintry breeze that slowly put off the heat tension between Phoenix and Mistral. As they were sitting down, they realized their mouth slowly turned numb from the cold and they had to start talking to keep them warm. Thus, the two started the conversation, beginning with how they separated because of their different beliefs.

Phoenix used to think that The Earth movement was simply too boring, whereas Mistral thought the way The World determined the definition of evil was incomplete - they excluded the foul done to Mother Nature.

However, as he evolved, he did not think some of the ways The Earth believers lived were all bad after all; in fact, they lived in a complete peace with the earth and were free from her temper, though apparently not so much within themselves human beings. She thought it was common, as one grew more mature, it was natural to want peace more instead of unlimited wasteless fun. They realized that their preference had merged since many years before, and he could not help but wonder, if they had grown back then into who they had become, would they have still been together?

Mistral raised her body up and stood tall on the ground. Phoenix, who did not know why, imitated her move. Surprisingly, she embraced his neck and laid her chin on his left shoulder. Both of her cheeks felt the smoothness of his covering leather as she shook her head, then said, "There'll be other things that separate us, I'm sure. We're better off as friends."

Phoenix's eyes widened from the two sentences but shivered slightly as he embraced her back. Mistral then admitted that after the breakup, she too unintentionally absorbed some of his behaviors like he did too of hers. She thought she would not want him to know, but she did eventually. When they had believed that they had broken up because they were too different, they realized they were just too the same that it would never work. However, even when it had taken a longer time for both to heal, they ended up being happy for each other sincerely.

As Phoenix finally nodded back, he told her what a great guy the man she called her husband was. From afar, Udoka had been holding the curtain to the side, watching. He looked at them and pulled his lips to the side both ways inattentively, happy that he witnessed the two finally getting their closure.

While they were walking back, the small space of ambience between the two was releasing a fresh scent of blossoming friendship that triggered many different topics showing how similar their way of thinking had been, if let out.

"By the way, about Wyre, do you think he's really from the Code White area? Why do I have this feeling that he isn't, but at the same time he is?" Phoenix tucked his hands hidden inside his jacket pockets as opposed to his wandering mind that he set free.

"And how do they know each other in the first place? That part is the biggest mystery to me," Mistral responded, but she came to feel strongly positive that Wyre was Code White too afterward, solely from what Phoenix had said to her.

They looked at each other and knew exactly what the other thought they should do, to beware and quietly observe. They realized afterward, there were too many occasions they were the same, in fact, a full resemblance in some cases due to one simply brought it up first. After the sight's conclusion, the conversation about Wyre thus repelled back to them instead.

Phoenix mentioned he felt peace in there. He did not know if it was the pungent smell of eucalyptus essence all over The Earth, but he felt like he wanted to bring, maybe, his future wife there someday and start a new life together. Mistral grinned widely thinking how it was a good idea, and that she and her husband would always welcome him and whoever his wife was going to be.

"But, if things were left out in the Code White area as it is, I'm afraid more problems will grow further and never eventually be solved. Running away is never the option, if you never want to be chased again," Phoenix said, hoping Mistral knew it was not only his fight, but it could also be hers someday.

If birds were watching, they would stop right on top to see if the two would fight again. And if it were, they would just fly away again afterward knowing they would not, as Mistral took in air deeply, let it out slowly, and smiled instead.

Mistral agreed and explained how the people there, including her, were so in peace that they seemed to always forget that there was still a concealed war they were a part of. She also talked about the need for balance between nature (earth) and the people (world) living on the very same body parts and how every single person on the planet had the responsibility to manage those resources - unlike letting people live like they did in the Code White area with no responsibility, because the earth did not really need them to live on her skin in the first place.

Phoenix responded with his own world of thoughts. Even though the earth could live without humans where the other way could not, humans had done so much that it was almost impossible to clean their trace out of her without still hurting her in the process. Imagine glitches in nuclear plants that went unnoticed without human supervision, it would not be long before they broke out of their containment and ran freely in violent shattering and flames. With deep underground pumps left unmaintained, rain would no longer be able to be diverted back to the sea where it came, thus claiming flowing rights on the whole land. Those polluted chemical waste that were absorbed by the soil as factories melted in rumbles, it would take her long or never to remove the after taste. And as she lost hope from the inexistence, the wind would flurry directionless following her sight and mind that lost sanity. Before she knew it, it would be the other way around, as she had to fight the temper of ghosted recalcitrant mechanical disasters randomly tempered on the peaceful earth for pleasure. And yes, Phoenix slowly learned how the earth thought somehow even without The Earth book, and it was not that hard to relate when he thought about it that way, like she had feelings too, and senses, just like humans.

"But nature will always find a way, don't you think?" Mistral responded as she looked up to the sky, trusting the elements around. Phoenix smiled in return.

As their walk nearly brought them to where the others were waiting, or probably already sleeping, Mistral wondered, expecting that Phoenix had come up with a draft plan in his head by then.

"Just some bullet points, I still feel I'm missing something," he revealed unconfidently.

"By the way, about Wyre," she then continued, "I see good in his eyes, but still, you should keep an eye on him there."

"Don't worry, I think the system will take care of that. It's changing, but I trust it's still working, for now," he responded, this time, with full confidence.

Elowen was already sleeping in the living room and Udoka

too in the bedroom, but out of their expectation, Wyre had been waiting for their return alone in the dark, not far from the window next to the door. As soon as four feet stepped a few centimeters away from the entrance inward, the other two were pulling them out for a talk under the half moon.

Wyre admitted he was from Code Grey and told them everything they went through without leaving out a single hour of memory, except about the chip. With his left palm thumped into the other, then swung like a mad tree, he begged them not to blame Elowen for lying about where he really came from.

"Why the hell would she do that, like what's the benefit for her?" Phoenix said but rather in a calming way and his fingers touched his chin on purpose just so the others would know he was trying to find his own reason, sending Wyre to confusion that he was more surprised about that.

Mistral responded that no one would understand why better than her. She then looked at Wyre's eyes with a smile and raised her eyebrows, suggesting she believed he too knew the answer, and so Wyre understood and said, "I think I do know why." Wyre's heart was beating faster than a bullet fired from Phoenix's gun, and so he had no other option but to smile, just so he would not scream out of excitement.

Phoenix, still clueless, responded, "Why? Can someone tell me?"

"Now I remember why we really broke up. Well, I'd better get back to my husband now, night," Mistral responded with a twinkling attitude and a tap on his shoulder, leaving Phoenix utterly more and more confused as he tried to recall the blurry past for a reason.

"So, what are you planning to do when you reach Code White?" Phoenix asked Wyre, diverting the previous unanswered question intentionally to a harder yet with highly more chance for him to know the answer.

"I'm so tired now, I think I'll just follow what my father wanted of me, to start over in Code White, if possible. The World with no evil, seems like a good place to grow old in," Wyre's eyes were tingling as he was reminded of him.

Phoenix's eyes instead rolled extensively, suggesting that, knowing the system, he did not think that Wyre going to the Code White area was a good idea. But as the both of them entered the dark room, the simmering light of the moon from the temporary gap of the open door, managed to make Elowen's sleeping face visible by a glance. Seeing that, Phoenix came to realize that it might not be a good idea to separate them too.

The next morning, Phoenix woke up the earliest. "I need to talk to you both, seriously," he said to both Elowen and Wyre, and when Mistral and Udoka saw the seriousness he was embodying, they made an excuse to let themselves out the door - of their own house.

"Wyre has told the entire truth," he started, and Elowen tapped on her chest for she felt she was surely at the brink of having a heart attack.

"I need to be sure that both of you have told me absolutely everything I need to know before we start our journey back, or the first time for you, to Code White," he continued, "And when I said everything, I meant EVERYTHING." The little seed of trust towards Wyre seemed to grow in his heart to decide to let him in the area specially restricted to him alike.

Phoenix concurred with the plan to let them think that Wyre was born in The Earth and let him go there. Elowen and Wyre were glad that he got to trust them so quickly, but little did they know it was substantially because he wanted something out of Wyre - something he accidently took a look at, when Wyre took it out of his pocket for a brief spin of wonder, forgetting about the window that could still shed some light in the pitch dark. Still, if he had not believed there was just a bit more light than the dark in his heart, I repeat, he would have not let him in at all.

"What do you think?" Phoenix hugged his own arms on the table after laying down his simple plan, waiting for a positive answer.

"Let's just do it," Wyre responded, "What's gonna happen next, I don't want to know now."

XXXII

Chapter Thirty-Two

Reaching the Shore

"Okay, so here's what we're gonna do," Phoenix rattled his right hand on the side of the ship, reminding them that it was that time again for the third time to recap their goals and missions, for he had actually nothing to do as Wyre was driving his boat. The excitement on the execution of the plan slowly forced himself to take off the mask he never knew he had. If Elowen had not been helping Mistral in preparing breakfast, she would have been sure that his ex-girlfriend had put some long-active stimulants on his meal that made him super hyperactive.

"Three issues to solve. You," he then blasted his pointy finger at Wyre from a short distance, "you want to keep your promise to your dad and start over in the Code White district."

"And you," he continued while sliding his pointy finger to the left to where Elowen was sitting on the floor, "you just want to go home."

"Hey, why do you have to say it like that?" She responded, noticing how he looked down on her deemed-simple wish, whereas for someone who had realized she had taken her simple beautiful life for granted, the wait was not easy to bear at all. But inside her mind she still sometimes contemplated, about the nature and nurture of evil concepts she never shared, would she be as excited to continue it once she returned?

Getting dizzy from either the motion of the boat getting through the small waves or her own mind turnover, she walked towards Wyre while Phoenix was nowhere to be seen from their sight.

"Don't you think he sounds a bit bossy?" She mumbled only loud enough for Wyre to hear.

"I think he's just a natural born leader, though I don't think he has fully realized that yet," he responded while his eyes still looked straight into the ocean.

"Well, he did ask us what we think about his plan," she replied, feeling uneasy all of a sudden for talking negatively about Phoenix behind his back.

The boat with the House of Rules symbol on both of its outer sides too finally reached the shore of the Code White area without an issue, except for what was coming after. As the snow-colored pole on their way out of the port blocked any visitors to come through without scanning their *bracelet* first, Wyre was stopped by one of the human-size robots when he could not.

"He's from The Earth," Phoenix stepped in the conversation.

"You... will need to... be tested... Sir... next morning... in Grey Chamber... South-East," the robot commanded, and from the gap between his words, it was obvious that it was thinking while talking at the same time.

"We... will put you... in quarantine... safe," the robot continued, and soon after, two more robots rolled in to take him away.

"Wait! What's happening? What's gonna happen?" Elowen blocked the robots' way all of a sudden, then the first robot looked at her *bracelet* and conveyed another piece of order, "You... will need to... step away... Madam... now."

"Let them," Phoenix gently pulled Elowen's arms.

Phoenix first said to her to ask the guard to find a place to stay near the chamber if she wanted to stay, while he took care of things with Wyre, as he mentioned she should not worry. But considering Elowen was one of those Code Whites who got used to getting what they wanted, sort of, she screamed and insisted on coming along. Phoenix sighed, then used his *bracelet* to let the robot know he was part of the prestigious parliament and thus, the two were able to come along with the trip on the bus.

Wyre's right cheek was pressed against the window as he was so amazed with what his eyes were seeing.

"It's beautiful, isn't it? Though probably not as beautiful as where we were," Phoenix spoke two chairs away to the left.

"There are other chambers?" Wyre shouted as he saw colorful chambers explained by Elowen who was sitting by his side. From that, Wyre almost forgot of his nervousness to do the test the next day.

"I'm surprised there's no other chamber but Grey in the Code Grey area, I wonder why," Elowen pondered and Wyre lifted his shoulders up, while Phoenix stayed quiet for he thought he started to probably know why.

Elowen then continued explaining to Wyre more details about some of the other six chambers. "See those two people there? They look like they have just been in a fight, they must be going to the Orange Chamber - that is where people find forgiveness," then she continued, "And that girl over there, the one bringing two same dresses with two different colors, she must be going to the Yellow Chamber, for indecisiveness."

"So unimportant, that chamber can do better than that," Phoenix mumbled loudly, "and do you know how much budget needs to be increased for building more Yellow Chamber? Soon there'll be thousands in each direction."

"So, what rehabilitation efforts do they even make for Code Grey people then to be Code White, if they don't even have more chambers other than just Grey? This doesn't really make sense," Elowen raised her question.

"Unless, there isn't any," Phoenix responded unconsciously, then suddenly a small gap in his mouth was formed accidentally as he panicked when he realized he said it out loud. Fortunately the driverless bus put on the brake just in time for him to smoothly shift the topic to "Let's go!"

"But you, Elowen, you need to stay here. The bus will take you to another hotel," Phoenix's right palm suddenly tapped on Elowen's shoulder, politely forcing her not to get up.

"Why can't I just stay in the same hotel with you guys?"

"Trust me, it's for the best," he continued.

The two guard robots were already waiting by the door. They talked to themselves counting down from a hundred, and Wyre assumed that if he had not got out before that, they would have probably re-entered the bus and forced his way out.

As they stopped by in the lobby waiting, Wyre saw how Phoenix used the *bracelet* to pay for everything he needed - unlike in the Code Grey area where he had to work hard for even a single Durum, like everyone in there too. While Phoenix was on his way back to where he sat, Wyre could not help but keep looking at the *bracelet*. He wanted it too. Then he thought to himself, if he did not pass the Code White test however, his new dream of owning his own *bracelet* would shatter and he would probably be punished to death, or worst, going back to live in the Code Grey area; unless – a dark idea suddenly came across his mind, unless he could somehow get that *bracelet* to be his...

"Wyre, Wyre?" Phoenix snapped his fingers right in front of Wyre's nose, and his eyes could see more closely how the *bracelet* really looked, prompting him to come back immediately from his blurry imaginary lane.

"I'm gonna go now, you're good?" Then Wyre nodded, "Alright," Phoenix added.

The two robots walked right beside him one on each side on his way to the room he was allocated too, very quietly. Wyre asked them some friendly questions, but they just spun their heads towards him and spun them back right away. Even when he entered the hotel room, they did not say a word and left.

The hotel room was so much better than what he had imagined. The size of the room was thrice the size of his house back in the Code Grey area. The window looked like a painting of real blue sky seen from inside a golden jail, but as it was opened, the air coming in oddly smelled of lemon, very refreshing.

The bathroom look made his painful run in the forest feel more than worth it, and the velvet silky robe hanging on the mirror wall made him feel like a king when he saw himself wearing it. While he pampered himself with the most relaxing hot-water shower he had ever had, he lost awareness of his thick skin forming wrinkles from the very, very long bath.

Not long after his damp bare feet touched the living room floor, he heard a bell ringing. Must be someone at the front door, he thought, and he began to wonder who it might be. When he took a peek on the peephole, his nervousness was gone immediately - it was just Phoenix alone.

Wyre opened the door and he realized one thing he did not really shortly before. The man in front of him was standing with both of his hands on his back, looking like he was holding something big but did not want to let him see it just yet.

"Can I come in?"

XXXIII

Chapter Thirty-Three

Inside the Chip

"A laptop?" Wyre's mind was spinning of the reason, but Phoenix stayed quiet knowing his sleepy brain would eventually find the answer.

"Unless, you know?" Wyre was getting there.

"Yes, that little thing you always kept in your pocket, without knowing what to do with it; well, I do," Phoenix was tired of waiting.

Soon enough, they found themselves plugging the chip in with their upper and lower teeth punching each other repetitively, completely nervous of what they might find. What they discovered sent them to an almost disbelief.

"Don't tell anyone about this just yet," Phoenix spoke with

his voice kept down to the low still looking at the screen, and to that Wyre nodded heavily.

The next morning, Wyre was encountered by probably the same two robots from the day before, to bring him to enter the brain scanner in the Grey Chamber. He took off his shoes as if he was going to go to bed, and lay his body slowly trying to find the most comfortable position he could. Afterward, he simply went to sleep.

Phoenix and Elowen were waiting anxiously at the front of the chamber, but when they saw Wyre coming out with a *bracelet* of his own, they knew - Code White result! But for Wyre, he was not just happy because of the result he had been waiting for his whole life he finally got. He had just realized that it was his first time getting his own form of identity, something Code Greys never had; something he had never thought he needed, until it was coming to him.

"What name do you use?" Asked Phoenix curiously.

"River," then he put his biggest smile under the sun.

"Did you already know that you're gonna get Code White?" Elowen wondered, as Wyre was looking extremely calm before he entered the machine, even more than her.

"I didn't," he replied, but then he looked at Phoenix momentarily with the same kind of beaming expression the other was giving too, slightly reminiscing about the thing Zirilo did not want anyone to know - the one reason the leader was so desperately wanting to get the chip back.

After having a long brunch, paid by the mere touch of a *bracelet* on Wyre's wrist (he never looked happier), they made their next move to accompany the new Code White to one of the housing agents fully operating without human assistance.

"They don't have a lot remaining in the East, but, oh! This one's actually pretty close to my neighborhood," Elowen swung Wyre's left arm back and forth so hard that her fingers drew a temporary tattoo on his skin.

"So you're saying that I can choose any house I want at only the cost of a single touch of my *bracelet*?" Wyre did not seem to care about where he was going to live apart from the fact that he was already enjoying living free of responsibility.

"You know, her neighborhood is the closest to where the forest is. I'll think twice if I were you," Phoenix spoke without making eye contact with the two. He also looked like he was really enjoying rolling his eyes up and down his flying mobile phone across his face.

"I'm sorry that not everyone gets to live in the glamorous House of Rules like you do," Elowen replied in annoyance.

"Where is that actually?" Wyre was clueless, and Elowen answered straight away, "Right at the center, lucky guy," she was rolling his eyes on Phoenix while saying the last two words.

The three went to where Phoenix stayed afterward, the most luxurious hotel branch only allowed for the House of Rules residents to stay. The size of the hotel room was even twice the size of the one they stayed at the night before. The smell in the room was of a floral bouquet of lavender with a touch of a vanilla essence, and a giant chandelier on top of the ceiling almost blinded Wyre and Elowen's eyes for it was shining so brightly that Phoenix had to turn it off; it was that majestic.

The information Elowen heard from Phoenix and Wyre was not at all relaxing like the scent in the room, as they told her that the chip in the Code Grey area was rigged, but apparently not for the ones in the Code White area.

The *brain* that changed ownership to be on Phoenix's pocket concluded that Code Grey people never went back to Code White for a reason, as programmed in the chip, once they had the Code Grey result they would only either have Code Grey or Code Black but never Code White, and once a Code Black they would never have the chance to be other than that. That was simply why Code Greys never went back to the Code White district. Elowen's hidden question was finally answered.

"I don't think I can trust the system more than I ever was," Phoenix covered his forehead while closing his eyes, disappointed.

"Maybe that's just what always happens when humans make the system, humans are always prone to error," Wyre bowed his back frontward while his long arms stayed on top of his thighs.

"Well, now that you can live in the Code White area without fear anymore, what are you going to do now, Wyre?" Elowen landed her palm on top of Wyre's left arm and it was able to ease his dizziness just a little bit.

"Maybe start a new life with Elowen?" Phoenix grinned while saying it.

"That sounds nice," Wyre then smiled sincerely at Elowen and so did she, but slowly, his smile turned into a forced one.

"But there's always a but," Phoenix knew as he looked at Wyre's expression of regret and sorrow.

Indeed there was, as Wyre reminded them that his mom was still in the Code Grey area. Imagining how lonely she must be without her son and her husband too, he asked Phoenix what he knew about the people who got Code Black and taken away. He simply wondered, would there still be a hope? But to his disappointment, the man who decided not to give him false hope answered that he did not think so, as the only "prison" he knew was the Code Grey area. Widening the tear in his aching heart, Elowen nodded.

"Maybe there's still hope," Wyre shrieked. Phoenix and Elowen really highly doubted it and they suggested instead that it was best that he moved on with his life, just as his father wished.

As they succeeded in getting their life back in the Code White territory safely, in where just a few hours before they were still not even certain if one of them belonged in where they were, it seemed that things were getting normal or better for sure if they just followed the system's rules of good and happiness blindly. Nevertheless, as it turned out, the rise and fall of their chests would never be the same. In their mind, they each still thought about, "What's really next?"

XXXIV

Chapter Thirty-Four

Under Pressure

One day, two days, then three days passed but the feeling was like years for them. That was probably why some said that the worst advice someone could ever give to anyone was to wait. Patience was the highly arduous virtue of all and there should have probably been a special chamber just for being forbearance.

Regardless, Wyre still could hardly believe that such a world was possible, a world free from evil mankind and crimes, a feeling full of content in assisting anyone in the middle of the night without the fear of being a target of a serial killer, and a sanctuary free from the judgment of sins and disdain unless for the people that were not there. Elowen too had been helping him to recognize how good life would be if he just gave in to ignorance and moved forward.

The bond between Wyre and Elowen became a little stronger, if not far driven by the dangerous adventure that almost killed them into no one really knew; however, the magnetic pull from a vague existence of his dad and vivid loneliness of his mother from time to time, coming from way behind beyond the unknown of the Code Black and Grey expanse, pushed Wyre more and more away from the promise of moving forward, and his one true love.

Once upon a warm sunny day, the two of them gathered to discuss what they could do in oppose to the reigning government power who provided the free-of-charge opulent prerogative system that they enjoyed so much, only to realize that this was not some kind of a movie they just watched a day ago, about one rebellious hero who single-handedly came second to none beyond millions of armies.

No, this was a real world, where they probably only had one chance to do it right, or maybe did not have the chance at all, unless they were one of the ones with power. The only person they knew who held such a concession that could open the door for them, was Phoenix, the precious inside man, which they made clear for him to know. On the other hand, he was just on the other side of the better land, dealing with his own setbacks.

The pressure the two had been constantly giving him had put his mind on fire. He could no longer concentrate on the inner circle meeting for he realized that the 'inner' group he was a part of was barely the shell of where the truth was stored, and he almost ran out of excuses to reject Zirilo's invitation to hang out casually in the bar like they used to.

The stress from the thought of the two who deeply believed he had the power he could barely hold managed to drive him to do one of two ways he could do, out of desperation. He started by going into one of the training rooms, going on a rampage. He swung his arms and legs against the air and even his body could not handle the anger he had for himself. All he realized that day, he was not happy being powerless.

The next day, he was standing at the front of the Blue Chamber door, his second option. He was just standing there, breathing, thinking, and he did not care if the people passing by might think he was turning mad. However, he finally managed to bring himself in, and into the machine.

"You're in the right place," the *brain* verbalized the chip's intelligence in a soothing woman's voice. "I can see that you're under a lot of pressure. Indeed, they're expecting a lot from you," it continued.

"You really know exactly who they are?" He tried to understand its way of thinking.

"Well, not exactly, but I can sense it. You are also hurt, bored, angry, confused - the other twenty-five levels of emotions would be detailed if you say 'detail', but say 'continue' to move on."

"Continue."

"Your ambition and pride set you apart today. Tell them the truth. You will not be able to rest until you reveal to them that whatever it is they expect you to do, you simply cannot deliver. When those who walk with nothing but darkness are granted to see the light, they can better decide between staying and leaving the path they are on. If you try it, it will make you feel better. Something to think…"

"I'm done."

"Are you sure? I have not finished with…"

"Yes."

"Thank you for coming in. Please come again whenever you feel you need to."

Phoenix got out of the machine looking bright and sharp, standing like a new man with that gleaming expression of his. He was positive he was going to take what the *brain* suggested him to do, but not at all what it meant. In fact, his arriving idea was something else, something his inner circle peers would perceive as dark, and there would be no way back from there.

"Phoenix? What are you doing here, coming from a long way?" Wyre was surprised to see him right in front of his door in the East.

"I've got a plan, but I need your help."

XXXV

Chapter Thirty-Five

The Revelation

The palatial golden seat where Phoenix was sitting did not look as comfortable as the others, seeing how his globular organs of sight narrowed whilst his lips were up on one side and low on the other. His mood suddenly changed however as the leader, whose age was only about a decade older than him, brought his steps closer to his usual seat, probably best to call it the grand chair as it was surely the best one in the room and different from the others.

"Please be seated," Zirilo commanded while scanning the rest of the hall, but as his eyes got to where Phoenix was sitting, his face turned pink from happiness. He was extremely glad he was looking like he was really back.

The ambience in the room changed immediately as they

discussed further the limited resources issue that had been going on for a while with yet a resolution. The heated discussions were flying here and there as usual, but much to everyone's surprise that there was one more active person in the room joining the peaceful war. It was Phoenix.

His hands were no longer attached to his chin as they had always been before, his blue eyeballs were not constantly covered anymore by their lids, and his mouth was firing bullets of opinion that hit right at the center of the bullseye. His energy was out of control. He was on fire.

"Good job, kid. Didn't know you've had it in you," one of his father's friends spoke, impressed, and his old man showed nothing but pride.

"You're different, but in a good way," Zirilo brushed his left shoulder from behind and Phoenix's eyes were enlarged from both surprise and relief. He thought it would have taken more to have him back on the leader's good side, and his later invitation to their usual bar-hangout day proved otherwise.

Phoenix had never realized that it was not that hard for him to behave naturally so obsequiously towards the crucial men and women in the House of Rules, including his father, only if there was something behind it all he needed. He came to an understanding of those mass-proclaimed phonies who faked every loath they could just to get on someone's good side for a great purpose, as the only or quickest way to get the mission done. He just never really tried that hard, or even at all, before. But he eventually realized, with all the things provided for him, they had him stuck in a comfort zone while at the same time excruciatingly bored and painfully directionless, that he had not felt as such was necessary.

One year had quickly passed; with Phoenix adjusting to his new self, Elowen and Wyre moving to live with The Earth members, everything had changed drastically.

"You're nervous, Phoenix? After all, this is going to be your first speech to tell the whole world the things I don't even want to say," Zirilo tried to calm Phoenix who was looking very nervous with his sweats clustered around his forehead in the very cold backstage room, a few minutes before rundown.

"Is that supposed to make me feel better?" Phoenix responded with a smirk.

"Don't worry, we'll soon be off partying on that big cruise ship you've requested, celebrating today." Zirilo then bumped his arm with Phoenix's, saying afterward there was nothing for him to worry about for he was sure he was going to do a great job with his first assignment as the leader's official right hand man. Little did the leader know, that was not at all the agenda his most-trusted assistant was worried about.

The lights were set very brightly right on top and Phoenix was standing in where Zirilo usually was in the big meeting hall. Not all the seats were taken for they were only filled with the inner circle, Zirilo's most trusted men and women.

Phoenix was grasping strongly at his speech paper like he was holding a rock to throw. The camera was pointing solely at him and he imagined if he was allowed to throw it, the familiar camera would be the first thing it would go to.

His throat was sore from the dryness built up from his

many emotions, and so he started the speech he should have started a minute ago with a cough instead. An alibi would do, he convinced himself. Then, he started reading.

It was going really well, surprisingly, and everyone thought so too. How could it not, for Phoenix was loyal to every word written on the paper, and he never once tried to look at the livings in the room; no, he was better off glancing at the empty seats, and he knew it too.

Once the meeting hall was opened, it was surprisingly crowded for Zirilo, filled with Code Whites demanding an explanation.

"I know, I know, about the decrease in the resources, but we're doing the best we can and we're gonna be fine, everything's gonna be fine," the leader lifted his palms and pushed it to the air, attempting to back in the crowd. Good thing the robots were doing their job perfectly that he was perfectly untouched by the mass.

"What are you talking about?" Many of them were furiously confused.

"You were not talking about the recent speech? The limited resources? The new restriction in quantity?" Zirilo became the most discombobulated of all. He turned his head to where the stage was and Phoenix was nowhere to be found. He went backstage and even as far as where he lived and he was not there either. What was going on, he wondered, and he and his other trusted people, including Phoenix's father, who had all been near him on the short trip too had a bad feeling about this.

"This can't be happening," Maredine shouted in disbelief in the midst of quiet confusion with her phone screen hovering against her face. She was the first one to find out the reason. The others including Phoenix's father, but excluding the leader himself, ran towards her and they almost forced her to fall on the floor as they were fighting for the front audience standing until they realized they too could see the recorded broadcast themselves from their own devices, out of panic.

"Just tell me," Zirilo sounded like his loud angry voice was just a mumble as his right fingers were still locking up his mouth like a prison, and he stayed still to his stand far away from the minor crowd.

His heart moved to and fro like a tree in the summer blown away by an unforeseen winter hurricane. As it turned out, what was played for the whole world was not the speech he thought was going live. On the contrary, it was a recorded testimony authored by the very same person who performed the fake speech, revealing what he believed as everything no one was supposed to know.

The revelation.

The nature of the chip that possessed the immediate killing ability for all Code Black results, the mysterious death schemes orchestrated by the hidden warriors who had no other choice with the order given to them - some too had volunteered their faces and facts for the testimony bravely, recycled corpses turned zombies hidden in the dark forest and Zirilo's plan to release them to the Code Grey area to *clean* all the people there as he said it himself in the recording unknowingly to him, and last but not least, the rigged chip also in the Code Grey district as Phoenix emphasized the program altered to, "Once a Code Grey could only be either a Code Grey or Code Black, once a Code Black will always be a Code Black. Code Greys and Code Blacks are never given the chance to be good." Meanwhile, The Earth members were living in peace without natural disasters, unlike Code Whites, though not with a complete harmony he could not lie. Thus, in the end, Phoenix asked them to come to The Earth, and if they wanted to, they would know how.

All in all, it was the recording of all the leader's plans to conclude a valid heaven on earth, at the expense of most human rights that were intentionally secluded, and all this time, Phoenix had been patiently collecting concrete evidence to back up the reveal of truth he had planned. But he was not doing it alone; clearly, as Elowen, Wyre, and Mistral were arriving at the Code White shore with an army of their own. They, along with all of The Earth members, were there to back him up, as a big white cruise ship with an emblemed House of Rules logo all over the blank set safely on the dock, waiting.

Soon enough, everything was coming to light. Phoenix's sudden change of wanting-to-be-liked behavior for nepotisms though he did not want to, he realized it was the only way to speed up the plan. His sudden ambition to be the only right hand the leader could trust. Not to mention his two companions he could barely trust before who sailed back to The Earth to tell Mistral about the plan and made sure the plan was heard. Also, Mistral's effort to convince the others to finally make a move, inspired by Phoenix's braveness and endeavor to no longer stay silent or give in to the other side's definition of a world with no evil.

By the time everything was let out of the dirty bag, Zirilo ordered all of the armies, warriors, and robot guards, everyone, to search for Phoenix. However, Phoenix was already long gone with his plane, on his way to the shore.

The next day, the wind blew so strongly out of anticipation of what yet to come. Even the trees guarding the port on both sides had their heads elbowed by the air as it was trying to get a better look at what was going on.

As expected by Phoenix, Zirilo had agreed to have a peaceful meeting with just him. Zirilo had no other choice, Phoenix knew, for the leader never led a war and less than a day was not definitely enough for him to learn how. No, he always preferred the underground way, like killing the citizens silently and blaming it on the unknown or creating monsters that were eating people alive and having them throw out their flesh on the ground - all just to ensure the solemnity of his unrealistic goal.

The discussion between Phoenix and Zirilo gave everyone in the room who were watching from a close distance chills to their bones.

"The point is, we're just trying to bring awareness to all the people about the transparency of the system, everything, and let them decide," the sentence was then elaborated in a slightly different structure and similar wordings, "We don't want to keep them in blindness, to let them decide of their own definition of the world with no evil," Phoenix started out strong, the way the others saw it, that Zirilo didn't have anything to respond for a short while.

"How could you? After I put my trust in you?" Zirilo's eyes could be seen trembling. He then quickly got up from his seat and seemingly rushed to get out of the door.

"I'm sorry," Phoenix responded while he was still sitting down, looking in another direction - any other without Zirilo on his sight would do, he thought. Hearing that, Zirilo froze in tears with his hand landed above the knob. But then Phoenix continued, "Maybe, we should not put our trust in humans, not even how we judge good and evil."

"Then who should we trust?"

"I don't know."

Just like that, Zirilo vanished from Phoenix's sight, with only the sound of the door closed and for sure it almost crumbled into pieces from the impact. A very short meeting indeed.

Phoenix brought himself out a few short minutes later and could still see Zirilo's plane rising up to the cloud. Mistral then approached him. While pointing out to the same kind of camera he remembered seeing that day in the House of Rules' meeting hall, she forwarded the message that the whole world was ready to hear him speak and that they were coming close to his last step of the plan.

Phoenix's hands placed on the side of his body were trembling, though his throat was not as dry as the last time he stood up to give a speech. He was still in between regretting and applauding the progress he had made, or whether he was making the right choice or not. He could probably use some Yellow, Green, or Blue Chamber; with that being said, he did not think he could trust them as much anymore. But then he realized, he just had to let the people know what made him change his mind about the system. Trust.

"I'd say the brain scanner is not as accurate as it is claimed to be. It judges that some people were born evil when the real truth is, everyone's got a bit of a devil inside. It just depends on which side you let to rule your life, but the temptation will always be there. Everyone, without a doubt, has an equal right to determine themselves which they get to be and let the consequence decide." He took a short pause then he continued.

"No one gets to tell you that you can't turn your way. It has taken The World to rig the *brain* to prove you Code Greys wrong, but their action has admitted otherwise..."

Suddenly, his speech was cut off by a scream of questions coming from a few of the audience. Standing with their puffy jackets defending their body from the strong blow of the wind, they claimed.

"So, what's in it for us?"

"I don't see why we have to live with clean rules miserably, when the rigged system does us just fine."

"It's Code Greys' problem! Not us!"

"So what if Code Blacks are killed? They should!"

"This is heaven on earth!"

"Hail The World with no evil!"

"You ungrateful moron!"

"Yeah!"

It all became apparent, not everything was about the merit of morality, or what the virtue stood for.

The loud piercing caterwaul of words were fired out collectively from their cannonball of a mouth. Phoenix and the others were starting to walk a few steps behind, ready to run back to the ship, until a small woman with a ponytail and white lab coat they all had never seen before came forward to the podium uninvitedly.

"It is true that if the plan is to be initiated, those monsters will be released to invade and kill all residents of the Code Grey area, so unwillingly be claimed as an accident," she screamed at the microphone - clear as a crystal that she was extremely terrified and had never spoken in public before as she accidentally got her front teeth hit by the microphone that didn't move, but she still had the courage to continue regardless. She also made it clear that she was not finished. "But in the long term, those monsters will be released to the Code White area when the population here is getting too high."

She then further disclosed that Zirilo instructed scientists to recycle all Code Black corpses and *alter* them to become deadly creatures in the forest, so no one could go between the Code White and Code Grey area. He no longer considered the Code Grey result to be a rehabilitation code, and he wanted it to be treated as Code Black. His idea was to have no mercy at all. Finally, he wanted a clean peaceful world free from evil based solely on the *brain*'s judgment, only to be filled with a limited number of those chosen ones as he saw overpopulation as a potential problem that started to destroy the existing heaven on earth the leader ascertained. After all that, the strange woman sighed a very long breath, and came to the side to meet the four others, who were still wondering who in the abyss was she?

"Mide Holmes," she introduced herself, and soon it rang a bell for Phoenix and Elowen that she must be the daughter of Meng Holmes, and to that fact the female scientist nodded with a giant smile on her face.

After talking to her for a while, they could hardly believe how many important figures in the Code White area had been thinking of the exact same thing but never dared to make a move.

"I guess, now we wait. Let's see who of those who agree with us will finally dare to make a move like you do, Mide," Phoenix then turned his head towards the sea of people who were increasing in number, curious and puzzled between staying and leaving.

XXXVI

Chapter Thirty-Six

"A Couple of Winds Told Me"

A shockwave of continuous rumbles confiscated the bright blue sky's quietness, and it was not at all coming from the thunder. A brand-new ultimatum dominating all the media channels was the cause of it, and it was broadcasted straight from The World's leader's moving mouth.

"Those of you who decide you are to follow the foolish who do not respect our heavenly way of living system that has been proven to work for decades long may follow the white cruise ship that will lead its followers to hunger, responsibility, and no freedom. You will have to work hard for a spoon to eat, work harder for a place to live, and say goodbye to the leisure you gain so easily in this country. Soon, you will find that your surroundings, or even yourself, will carry the weight of crime and its consequences just for a single taste of your old ways of living, and eventually realize that you are no longer welcome here." Then he continued, with a much louder voice than before.

"Yes. All The Earth members will be banished and no longer be a part of The World. You were considered our long-lost twin who were just trying to find your way back home to us, but from here onwards, you are our enemy. The World residents must not travel to The Earth district, and the other way around, or else, you will be punished." He did not stop there, nonetheless.

"And for you all The Earth members, you will be given seven days to change your mind, and after that, consider the punishment that will be given for your overstay should you choose to remain here. My men will ensure that."

The four were watching nervously inside the big ship. They were a little glad that at least Zirilo did not declare the word 'war' in his speech but the cold version of it was obvious. Their anxiety did not stop there, as they and all The Earth members were anxious about which Code White residents would step into their ship, if any. Not stopping there too, the 'my men' he mentioned, five-hundred soldiers in total, were coming shortly after and standing close by the port, suggesting the leader was not bluffing at all.

Meanwhile, the front of all Yellow Chambers in the land was packed up with crowds that were waiting their turn to step in the brain machine. They were targeting to have their brain scanned before the seven-day limit so that they would know what they should do.

The fact was, they did not really need to wait any longer for their decision to queue. Unknowingly to them, the moment they chose to go to the Yellow Chamber instead of their heart, that was when they had already made their choice pretty clear. They still trusted the system unlike Phoenix, Mistral, Elowen, Wyre, and the other The Earth members. Just like the *brain* of course suggestively confirmed, they still chose The World, and there would be no other hope to turn them otherwise. Human rights to live and change were tainted but it was only made an issue for the minority whose lives were directly impacted by it, such as a certain Code White female who was the first to enter the ship the next day.

Her eyes had not healed from many years after she first lost her baby. Those lenses had ever since stayed red like they were always created that way and the puffs below were just waiting for the bursting water that tasted like the sea coming daily.

"I've always known and they thought I was delusional. Mother always knows," she shrieked her shattered good opinion about The World, and her husband caught her elbow just in time again to lift her so she was not to fall. They did not even think about going to any of the chambers ever since, as they thought of them just as the one that made the country kill their only child in silence.

After the long-grieving pair, came about one couple at a time approximately a hundred more with the similar mysterious death cases. Whether it was another person's innocent infant, their grown-up sons and daughters, husbands and wives, parents, grandparents, or their close friends and family members, the hole created by the emptiness of those dead presence could never be filled with any of the luxurious perquisites offered in exchange for their mere loyalty. They had too lost their full trust in the system ever since the revelation.

The next person who came was very familiar to Phoenix even from afar, for he was no other than his father. He had these three scenarios in his mind, first was him to come along, second was to yell at him, and third was both.

The middle-aged man came with seemingly the most luxurious clothes he ever had and with no baggage at all, so of course Phoenix was expecting him not to come along at all. But then two android robots came and brought two big luggage each, and Phoenix could not contain his excitement. He did not know if the robots were allowed, or even earth-friendly, but all that mattered for him was that his father was coming along.

"I'm still not happy," he put out his worst frown in front of his son, and a few times looking back of what was left within his vision of the glorious land, "but I know I won't regret this for the rest of my long happy life, that is," and he held both Phoenix's cheeks with his cold hands from the chill breeze, suggesting proudness with his eyes but at the same time enough anger for him to leave his fingerprints in red on.

"If your mother had not been sick, I know she would have urged us to come sooner. I would understand if she had been one of those mysterious deaths, but this, I still don't get where your courage's coming from. You know, to realize something's wrong when everything has been going well in your life, still choose to fight for those who have been unjustly imprisoned at the expense of your own freedom - those are enough signs of true integrity, sincerity, and bravery; all are good qualities of a fine leader, my son," he added while his hand resting on Phoenix's shoulder.

When the father was a meter away from his son, Phoenix joked that he might not be able to have his hair extension in there, however, he would love the beauty of where he was going. The old man chuckled in response, "Well Son, that sounds like a place I want to grow bold in," and his overcoming love was able to make his next steps lighter than it would have been. "Already bold but anyway," Phoenix mumbled quietly, making sure the sentence was not heard by anyone else.

A few hours after that, a very big group of seemingly almost all of the scientists working closely with Zirilo, about two hundred of them in fact, were queuing in front of the white ship. Mide could name every single person just by a glance as she was one of them. She thus ran downstairs to greet them personally and welcome them in. Just before she had taken the last step of the stairs, the scientists made way for an old bald man with his very same glasses from his bunker days to come towards her right in the center. It was Meng Holmes.

"You've inspired us to get out of fear out of command," he spoke slowly in trembling eyes. Mide thus jumped one tread down to hug him out of relief, almost forgetting of his backbone problem that he could not keep his moan to himself.

Following them right behind were about a hundred shadow warriors who were tired of committing what Zirilo said as noble murders for the good, including innocent newborns. They were coming with nothing else but their armor and dignity, and they walked naturally so organized that those who watched would suspect they had the way rehearsed for sure. Those who used to live in the bunkers, would see that their suits looked exactly like those in the past. Well, slightly almost with the brighter colors and stronger materials as well as few adjustments on the shoulder pads and the weapons. After coming in, they all came out straight after and decided to guard the ship by the front, almost at every edge of the port near the cruise, standing proud and tall. All of the on-post soldiers who witnessed that could not take their eyes off of them. One by one of those, totaled to only a few, began to stand closer to the port, did not come in, but instead still suggested they were on The Earth side, and they smiled with the warriors quietly.

Some other commoners also chose to neglect the Yellow Chamber and moved to The Earth, about a hundred of them and that included very grown-up Bolin, his wife and children as well as his parents. Maccush, the captain of all soldiers, could still recognize Bolin somehow and was more than surprised to see him alive that he accidentally dropped his gun he had been holding so dearly close to his chest. There the Code White authority had been building him the fear of obeying order, he thought, and consciously he felt manipulated. He then left the spot where he was standing and grabbed Bolin by the arm, and to his surprise, Bolin recognized him too as he mentioned his name, "Maccush."

"Why?" Maccush asked, "They didn't kill you, and you seem to have been living just fine, so why do you want to leave?"

"It's true, I've lived a good life here, really good in fact, but that almost made me forget about those who don't. That could one day be one of my family, or one of us because I am pretty sure I was almost one of them, well, we to be precise," and Bolin's words quickly took Maccush back to that day in the bunker.

Without further hesitation, Maccush came with him instead to the ship, and that urged Bolin to ask him instead with the familiar "Why?"

"Well, I want to know what has been happening with you," and the captain's decision to move to the other side of the cold war prompted half of his soldiers to stand among all the warriors.

At the end of the seventh day given by Zirilo, a young female of twenty-seven years old, wearing the most trending and fashionable style the year ever had, along with a black leather bag and golden chains strapping around her shoulder, dragging a medium-size light-brown luggage with her right hand was seen coming towards the cruise. Her long black hair resembled a dark-brown silky scarf hand painted by the sun's long arm and her face was one of a goddess.

"Phoenix, that's... that's that girl, Kindra, isn't it?" Mistral's scream pushed Phoenix voluntarily to run to the nearest window looking the same way as her.

Behind the young beauty was her mother, Maredine Dagger, along with her son and her husband. Altogether, they looked like a family no one would dare to approach unless being asked to but turned out to be more friendly than what they appeared to be. Kindra Dagger's eyes were like two magnets for Phoenix impossible to let go. Seeing her from up on the cruise head made him feel safe somehow as not to get caught, but he eventually knew he was wrong when she looked straight right at him from down below with that 'I know' look.

As they finally met face to face, Phoenix asked nervously why she was willing to come, and to that she responded with a smile, "I have more to learn about how to live peacefully with the earth, so not to get her mad." For one second there he was hoping that he would be one of the reasons, foolishly, but that second smile she gave before she was out of his sight made him wish for another that he might be.

The Daggers were apparently the last Code White area residents to enter the ship. Mostly who came were those involved directly or had been heavily negatively impacted with Zirilo's decision where their conscience had been screaming the wrong of it for quite some time. However, the total was only close to ten percent of the whole Code White population and thus the big ship did not even have to leave and make a return back to where it was to have more space for more passengers. Eventually, by the time the limit hour was met, the four had realized no one else was coming.

The World had won.

It was no surprise that Zirilo decided to come to see their losing face and he was looking forward the most to Phoenix's defeated expression.

"I'm willing to let this all go and give you a second chance. But let me make it clear that if you miss this opportunity, there surely will not be another. The ties between The World and The Earth will officially be cut, forever."

The discussion was watched by many The Earth members. Some of them glanced at each other to know what they all were thinking, but in the end, they passed on the second chance. Phoenix considered this as their win instead, not his solely, but The Earth's.

"And those Code Greys, they're coming with us," Phoenix said firmly with his voice and Zirilo laughed his hardest as he responded, "I don't care, that's one problem solved for me, and a new one for you instead."

"Oh, I almost forgot, I got this gift for you," and Zirilo ordered his remaining soldiers to bring inside a tired-looking man that made Wyre run through the crowd in tears. It was his father, and he was alive.

Zirilo then walked towards Phoenix and put his face very close to him, "Where's the chip?" He asked, and his eyes were expecting no less than a desirable answer. Phoenix saw Wyre's mouth moving with no voice and his lips still tight closed, then he looked at Wyre's dad and his. To that however Phoenix put both of his hands in his pants' pockets and answered calmly, "What chip?"

Regardless, Zirilo let the dad go unexpectedly, in where he was actually hoping that he would be the Code Black that would someday ruin The Earth.

Zirilo then looked at all The Earth members in the room, old and new, "I bet even the earth will see the evil in every one of you and everyone else here for breaking *its* heaven apart, our nation."

"Why don't you put if harming the earth is evil or not on that smart chip of yours, then maybe, every one of you instead might get that Code Black result for once."

"Who are you to judge?"

"Who are we to judge?" Phoenix responded with a tone that made Zirilo speechless and his charisma managed to blind Zirilo for a moment, for his voice was firm but his eyes were soft, and they all realized he was genuine.

Surprisingly for Zirilo, a man with complete wrinkles all over came inside the ship.

"Father?"

"Son?" The old man replied who in turn was also surprised to see the nephew he brought up as his own son, until he realized that he was not there to stay at all.

When the founder of The World claimed he wanted to join The Earth, he sent Zirilo into an outrage that he threw the chair he was sitting on to one of his soldiers, who was able to avoid it just in time, but barely. The leader mumbled angrily in curses nobody could clearly hear and he repeated three times the banishment rule to the old man, but he did not at all nudge to the decision still. Instead, the old man suggested Zirilo work with Phoenix and change the system as he added, "You know, one thing I wish I had known long ago, that people who will fight for the good no matter what, can do bad things too. But does that make him good, or bad?"

To his response however, Zirilo stood so closely to Hayes and bowed just slightly so his eyes could see right through his, "I did all of this for you. You said, if someone knew the solution to those corpses, you'd be impressed, so I did; and that heaven on earth bed story you once never stopped talking about - this is here, finally, the world with no evil, and you're leaving?"

"Son, this is no world without evil. What you did, what we did, those were as good as evil."

"I bet that everyday you wish too that it were Siva you took outside the bunker with you, not me. Admit that at least before you go," he said with little tears below his eyes, trying to be pulled back up with his pride to where they had been.

"On the contrary, I think it is you who wish so," Hayes responded, and with that last sentence Zirilo heard before he left, he could no longer hold the stockpile of tears that exploded by the anger and disappointment, just as much as the old man could not too.

From that minute on, Zirilo stayed as the sole leader of The World as he had always been while Phoenix, Wyre, Elowen, Mistral, and the other The Earth members were officially banished from the land they once called a home. They then had the ship moving to what was still and what was to be, their abode.

Arriving at the ship, one of The Earth members could no longer restrain his question as to how Hayes wrote all of those things in his book. Yes, the initial 'HB' was no longer a mystery that his father's letter needed confirmation from, once the founder was on board. How Hayes knew, everyone else too was wondering. Those who had read the book put their fingers close to their chin waiting for the answer, while the others solely focused on getting the front seats to the windows, looking at the miraculous beauty the floating grounds possessed.

The man, followed by many others, went out in the open area and approached the founder who seemed to have just thrown a little something out into the vast ocean from the edge of the ship, intended for the peculiar rustic fragment to never be found. Indeed, it was a chip that he let go forever from his possession.

"A couple of winds told me," he answered, "I just wrote blindly what they told me," much to a confusion and sighed from most of them, thinking that he had turned into a crazy old man, and if they had made the wrong decision of choosing the loving-earth lifestyle. Mistral however in particular was the only one that took the answer very seriously, way more than considering it being just a figurative speech.

When Hayes saw the floating cave, he added what he considered as his words of wisdom, "There is nothing the rock doesn't share with the wind and vice versa. I thought for a long time that I was dreaming. The blood on my hands covered my ears just like that telling me I was not worthy to even speak to the wind. But I know now that it was not a dream," and when they were seeing what he was seeing too, they knew they had made the right decision. Hayes afterward looked at Mistral, which confused her the most as in the reason why. He gave her the look that she could somehow understand, that the floating cave was all where it all started for him.

After the ship parked safely in one of the nearest Floating Houses, letting out passengers, Phoenix and Wyre were quickly running back to the cruise, accompanied by all warriors and half of the soldiers including Maccush.

"Where are you going, Wyre?" Elowen grabbed Wyre's right arm just in time, demanding an answer.

"Where the others are waiting."

"Who?"

"Code Greys, of course. Phoenix said we might not have much time."

XXXVII

Chapter Thirty-Seven

A Close Call

A mechanical breath of fire was dispersing with the help of air but out of control throughout the body of one then two mindless creatures that were once dead reasoning beings. Acting like scorching cannibals, they still threw up meanwhile, expressing their dislike over the taste of raw flesh bits, but then doing it all over again regardless. It was easily perceived that the chemical fluid injected to their defunct encephalon was invented for them to kill and only kill with no preference to flesh and blood.

The monsters refused to die a second time. Even when they were burning in flame, they did not stop to run in twisted agony for their brain had no memory of pain, crawl whereby doing so spread the flame across the forest ground and try to bite more of another living creature until they no longer could. They still turned into ashes eventually, but the time was not short enough to stop the extension of the fire rage.

"Hold! Hold! Remember, don't let the forest burn!" Phoenix shouted as his fire-bullet gun he put away forthwith was followed by some warriors and half of the soldiers to stop their form of attack - throwing their flaming fire matches. The plan was continued by some man-made heavy rain with the height of a tree, operated by Wyre and some of The Earth members tight-roping on the branches who had helped with the odd fat-fishing-rod-looking invention, while the rest of the warriors and soldiers were cleaning the ground with their regular weapons.

They made it out alive, every single one of them, and into the Code Grey area. As Phoenix had prepared with the prediction from all of the scientists combined, the seven-day limit was just more than enough time for Zirilo to set out the monsters into the middle town on loose by mere trace of fresh meat aroma he set as bait on drones to give the mindless creations the direction he wanted them to follow. Grounds were shaking and covered in blood, and most who had not thought of keeping a five-day supply of food and water had almost already died out of hunger, if not outside by the monsters. Once again, a little part of the world was fighting for supplies with their life at the stake.

The number of monsters flooding the little secluded town were more than anyone could ever conjecture. Imagine, the amount of people who had passed their life long or short with all the reasons, for the past five years they were gone and ten years more that were embalmed, times twice the danger then thrice the madness. So when they made up their cloudy mind raining in circle barricades against little shabby houses to form reckless battering ram with their own fragile bodies, they were prone to have the happenstance victory.

Not all the luck was sided with the one who planned the heaven on earth minus the pathway for mercy, however. Amidst all the affairs that had put the young leader to his utter disturbed, the incredible brain of his was skipping one particular pop-up prison where a few heavy-metal machines were ordered to guard one shabby little house by a lake that purposely gave rise to its lonely resident isolation with her basic needs taken care of to the minimum. During the lamentable invasion, the place soon became the safest haven without being intended so, detention for the noble, as the smell of the flesh and blood was tainted by the whiff coming from ten of those big androids circling the property.

Getting the female out next was not easy. Her kismet put her eyes on the bottom edge of the window, peeping, enough time to drive her to abort breaking through the glass with her frying pan when the raging zombies were visible for her from afar. Since then, she dragged her body to the edge of the room as far as possible from where she was. Her feet and back were glued onto the floor and the wall respectively, and she did not plan to move an inch closer to any other direction. She started to bite her nails and write her own eulogy in her mind in the meantime, while thinking about her husband and son who she believed were as good as dead.

The sound of what was like two giants' steps was heard to be just coming close towards the door. Hearing that, she folded both of her ears and closed her eyes so very tightly that her lips were coming-with all the way up. She was sure her time was coming to an end and she did not want to anticipate what her death would be or feel like.

"Mom."

"Is that it? Am I already in heaven?" The female was able to hear her son's voice. As both her eyelids were unfolded, she realized her hands were trembling so much that her earholes were not effectively covered. That, and the fact that it was really her son who was standing then kneeling right before her.

"Am I dead, son?" She suddenly lost sight of the messy table, three unstable chairs, and all other things that made up the little living room. Still, she thought she was hovering in a spirit form, until his gentle touch to her arms brought her mind back to earth.

Wyre's hands were cold and his eyes were a little bit soft from bottling up the yearn for too long. He knew he should not waste even a second to get out of there, but when he lifted his mother up to rest on his shoulder, he embraced her for ten seconds regardless. Feeling her bones, he decided to swing her body across his back and told her to hold on. Her mother then moved her face towards his neck and she promised herself to look the other way only when the sound was tranquil.

Wyre's mother was not the only one the team was able to

save. They also managed to bring hundreds of others, whoever were left of them; some were still able to walk, few others were even lucky to still be able to breathe comfortably. As they all had already had their feet nervously standing in the middle of the forest, both the sky leaving for a brand-new day and the long distance left to the shore unintentionally forced them to find a place to stay in the forest. Fortunately, a familiar abandoned structure was seen by Wyre, and he then urged Phoenix to call out the team to bring the others to stay there.

"What if that place is full of them?" Phoenix stated his worry, but as he looked back to the end of the crowd, seeing those weeping eyes and dying expression, he realized he had no other choice. "Move, move!" He screamed then made sure he was the last to enter the brittle premises to make sure he did not miss a single one. While he was about ten meters away to enter, two zombies suddenly grabbed his ankle each and dragged him far away from the door until he was left unseen.

"Nooooooo!" Wyre screamed as he ran towards the entrance from inside.

"Close the door!" Phoenix's yell was heard barely clearly as the sound of his voice was toning down by the distance, and all the warriors closed and barricaded it as instructed, sobbing in tears.

While Phoenix's body was moving without his own command, he looked up to the sky and was a bit glad that he at least was not facing the ground. His free hand slid through his gun pocket; he wanted to fire the bullets to save himself, but as he saw the trees hugging shoulders to each other's branches, he realized that even a single one of those could potentially burn the whole forest. So, he was going to give up, until he felt a drop of water on his nose.

It was a close call. He was not sure if the sky was crying on purpose to save him or he was just being lucky, but he perceived he would not have a chance at all once the rain got heavy.

Two bullets were fired out in total. They landed into the lobe of those who were dragging him and knocked them down to whirl around on the ground in burning pain. Their friends, probably coming close to a hundred in an amount the way he saw them, were running towards, but jumping to the other side afterward far away from them; unfortunately, that was the same direction Phoenix was moving. He was going to run as fast as he could back to where the others were, but realizing that might give those monsters enough to break through the entrance and harm the others, he decided to fight as many of them with his bare hands in the pouring rain and fired all of his bullets to the last for the rain to sort later.

He was sure the amount was more than a hundred when he almost finished the first group in a speed of light by probably the exact same miracle his father once had too, but as he felt the shivering ground giving him a quick update that the second was coming, he let loose the other five left from the first just so he could have enough time to spare his life.

Phoenix was screaming for the warriors to open the door, in which they immediately did. The view of him running for his life was enough instruction for them to kill the other five once they got close. Just five meters away from the entrance however, the zombies put a sudden brake on their chase. Their spongy skin looked more dehydrated, horrified by something they saw outside the building, and they lost their guts to come even an inch closer. Phoenix started to notice the oddness of this while seeing the warriors' faces confused. When he was back safely with them, he had more time to analyze what was happening. He went out again, keeping about three-meter distance from the walls, and followed where those monsters' eyes were looking into. The burning marks outside the building were what horrified them to their second death. An answer to a question Wyre had yet to have in his mind until then.

Going back to the shore from the Code Grey area for Phoenix, Wyre, and all the warriors and soldiers was like bringing a bucket of humans in water form. The amount of them was dripping out slowly little by little where once they reached the ship, they realized they were only able to bring about half of them, the very best they could.

Phoenix watched the forest from the edge of the quarter deck on the ship as it sailed, seeing all of those monsters were left alone to kill another day. They were just lucky that they were living so closely with what The Earth wanted to protect from burning into nothing, otherwise, they would all be wiped out. Wyre then came next to see them too from afar, standing beside Phoenix, thinking of exactly the same thing.

"Do you think we'll ever come back here?" Wyre asked, and hearing that, Phoenix's forehead formed lines of wrinkles and answered, "I think there'll always be a reason to, I just can't think of one at this moment." Wyre then rested his right palm on Phoenix's left shoulder and they continued watching the land as it slowly disappeared from their sight.

Chapter Thirty-Eight

The Creator

The Earth members were living peacefully with the planet, but not with each other. Once one social problem was solved, another always came down, and it was obvious that it was so only because the little born kingdom was without a king to guide them. The floating ground was getting more and more chaotic, and Mistral's patience to wait for Phoenix to step out as one, like he unconsciously did before, was due.

Maybe no leader was a good thing, Phoenix thought to himself a few times, and he was not sure why, but he could sometimes see him turning into his own version of Zirilo, for better or for worse; that was the part he felt he still needed to figure out, and so he preferred to wait, while lingering in his life with no duty comfortably. Heck, he did not even mind if someone else was going to step up as the leader. Funny that while he was standing by to see who was willing to take the first action to lead, the others were waiting for him to do so instead, and that very much explained their lack of enthusiasm to lead. They already saw him as a leader; everything he told them, they would already trust.

Shouts were getting louder day by day and they disturbed the wind who was blowing harder from such a consequence. When the new members had chosen to leave The World for good, the fact that they refused to put in longer their trust into its system did not necessarily mean they had faith in The Earth. They just had no other option but, and it was evidently seen in how hard it was for them to live in harmony. As it was apparent too how they were trained to avoid confrontation, the new members of The Earth decided to just live in the big cruise ship, separating themselves.

"Why did you do it?" Mistral one day approached Phoenix who was just reading The Earth book peacefully by the dock, looking like he was either enjoying the similar no-responsibility life in tranquility, or doing it out of boredom.

"What do you mean?" Phoenix closed his book, turning all of his focus towards the lady who was sitting next to him.

"Why did you decide to separate yourself from The World?"

"I thought it was pretty obvious, I didn't trust the system anymore, and I still don't, so do the others who came with us."

"And somehow, you suddenly don't trust yourself anymore, after what you've done? Or you just feel fulfilled that you could somehow pull it off, doing something really big out of curios-ity?"

Phoenix, who kind of knew where her question was lead-ing, decided to change the subject of the topic.

"I should ask you the same thing, why do you think the ex-isting members of The Earth such as yourself wanted to help us eventually? I have to admit, Wyre and Elowen must have done a very good job in convincing all of you, otherwise, I would have not even had the courage to broadcast the truth."

Mistral was quiet for a while. She looked up to the bright sky and finally responded, "Actually, it was all you."

Mistral then further told him a brief story of The Earth before and after he came that day with Wyre and Elowen. The Earth members were always just wanting to live peacefully with the earth, but they had been too busy in getting the planet to like them so much that they forgot about the people. Soon enough, they had lost sight of what it felt to trust one an-other, until they first saw a stranger from the Code White area coming up with his own solution and stepping up by turn-ing those ideas into his charismatic words spoken out - that worked. So, when Wyre and Elowen told them about his idea, they were reminded of him to agree, actually, they were more reminded of a new hope, coming from him.

"So you're probably bored and don't know what to do after-ward and think that that was just a one-time heroic thing you wanted to do because you can finally know how it feels. But this is not like in the Code White area there, where you can try to work as a soldier or a hairdresser for a day just out of curiosity, and the next day you can just get out of it and give the job back to the robots, starting again with a clean slate. No, there is always a consequence for things like this, Phoenix. Don't you understand?"

"So you're blaming me for all of these changes? Because I too know it's all my fault if you do."

"No, I'm blaming you only because you don't even want to try to become the good leader I know you will be," and Mistral left afterward, furious.

Her words had definitely made a difference. A few months after, where it was more than obvious the importance of the existence of a leader, The Earth residents found themselves in a significant change from no leader at all to two leaders at once. Wyre was leading those who were once Code Greys, while Phoenix the rest. "Let's keep each other at our best behavior," they said constantly to one another.

The difference in leadership style between the two of them raised questions however, not just how they were each doing it, but why there had to be two of them instead of just one in the first place.

"I thought there would be no more separation like this," one resident was complaining in front of Wyre during the meeting.

"There isn't anymore. I'm telling you; it is because I was once a Code Grey too," Wyre responded with his right fingers on his forehead, he sighed very deeply after that too. He was so stressed out that they were seen as the most out of control compared to the others led by Phoenix where he seemed to be doing just fine.

"I think it's because I just don't have that charisma Phoenix has, you know," Wyre talked to Elowen in private.

"It's not you, I'm sure you're a better leader than him, if not the same. Maybe, Code Greys, well, they're just harder to lead because... they're Code Greys."

"What's that supposed to mean?"

Wyre soon became more sensitive with Elowen's defense that she did not mean it like that at all. He put it all out of the stress, she believed, and she tried to be as patient as she could in the midst of her annoyance that grew towards him, and afterward, their conversation went downhill all the way.

"You need some alone time, and I think I need it too," Elowen said to Wyre then kissed him on the cheek, of what she hoped was not a kiss of forever goodbye.

Wyre dealt with the heat by doing what he always did in the Code Grey district, threw himself into the water and breathed through the hazard of drowning. He maneuvered his body to move gently with the flow of water that reacted with his but as he stopped the motion, he realized that he was not the sole reactor. In fact, even the floating ground was moving a little bit stronger than usual.

On the other side, Elowen was transporting herself via the vessel to one of the floating farms. She had been enjoying massaging the soil and singing to it softly with unrhyming lyrics adjusting to her mood then, good or bad. In response, the smallest particles of the ground were dancing along with the wind as her hands were still moving the surface. When she stopped however, she realized that she was not alone with the gesture, as her bare feet too could still feel the gesticulation.

Meanwhile, Phoenix was dealing with the limited capacity and resources issue he was hiding from the others, as he was sitting alone on a desk with his left feet on the table. The matter was rising as their number grew big. He took out the chip from his pocket that he took possession of from Wyre and always brought it ever since, spinning it whenever he could not help to start thinking if moving to The Earth was a bad idea after all. He even started to miss that Blue Chamber machine, wondering what it would say to him. He thought his trust for The World system had fully diminished, so why was he still holding on to that *brain* dancing with his fingers?

Phoenix dealt with his anger by doing what he knew best, swaying with his fists and fire. "I'm gonna kill them all with my bare hands in a flaming fire," he blamed the zombies this time, "and if I can't, my next generation will do it for me," he added.

"It is not genetic, you know, our fighting skills," his father suddenly barged in the open air at the edge of the port and further established his finding, "I've learned that it is instead our limitless desire to fight for what's right, whatever it takes, that we pass on generation to generation."

"You know, son, I begin to wonder. Is this, The Earth belief, really what you believe in? Or is it just because there is no other choice to where you could run into?" But as soon as he finished the question, the loam where they stood was suddenly shaking, not as strong as the irregular earthquakes often happening in the land, but at the same time not as light as being the impact from a flowing floating ground.

Something was wrong with The Earth, and none had a clue why. The reasons were much clearer for The World than The Earth, and at that point, the hurdle tree had had its branches growing from all directions, and any of them could be the impetus of the earth starting to be mad at them. If The Earth had stayed just the way they were, would this still all be happening? Phoenix blamed himself this time.

Mistral came to each of them one by one, started with Elowen, Wyre, then Phoenix, and invited them to the floating cave. She had been growing a meditation habit inside the floating cave and she wished for the others to feel the words the same way she had been.

"This is stupid," Phoenix found it the hardest than the rest to stay still with both his feet meeting shaping half a diamond and his skin guarding him from the cold breeze brought in by the ocean.

"Try to stay calm like the others, Phoenix, and don't let yourself be stray so far away to both past and future. Stick with the present for now," Mistral responded in clear irritation of a voice, but in words of the opposite.

"I'm sorry, I brought some friends today. I thought they could use some stress-free wind too to ease themselves," Mistral then spoke out loud.

"Who are you talking to?" Phoenix responded immediately. Mistral was able to strongly hold the temptation to open her eyes to give a snarl look at him, and replied instead, "Obviously, the wind." When she heard Phoenix laugh, she swore her face almost turned into a red tomato, but she was able to cool down by simply ignoring him. She then focused further on what the wind was saying on behalf of the earth.

She became aware that the earth was getting hostile with her thinking. The earth was still seeing everything and decided to wipe all the humans from her by telling all her organs to let loose, without knowing exactly the consequence told by the moon that she could hurt herself in the process. She was going to start with The Earth because she felt the hardest to kill them, but she thought if she could, she would certainly not hesitate to wipe those who hurt her, The World.

"They are getting more and more successful in getting their machines to do everything for them. As a result, they have reached hurting me to the core," the earth claimed, but she didn't stop there.

"It got me thinking, was there ever any possible way to separate between the good and evil on earth, and eliminate those evils once and for all so that the good could live in perfect peace and harmony until death did them part, not only after? I meant it, after all, why did the good get to leave my wounded body to live happily in the glorious heaven, and the bad to rot miserably in hell, while they looked down and up respectively on me coping and bleeding from the everlasting war between the living black and white forces of energy, using my organs as their resources?"

"Heaven on earth," the earth added again.

"Perhaps that could really be not just a metaphor, but an

actuality, a literal meaning, if the wicked humankind's time on earth was over without a trace, and I could finally be without pain every time I breathed in the air to my lungs and let it out. Maybe, just maybe, it would do both God and Satan a favor too, for killing the time in choosing their citizens."

Mistral unfolded both her eyelids in distress, but she saw the others were still closing their eyes in peace. She then realized she was the only one who could, maybe Hayes too if he was there with them. Thus, she screamed to get them to open their eyes, waking Phoenix from his sleep in the process, and told them what she heard, word by word she could remember.

At first, they found it hard to believe that what she said was accurate. Both Wyre and Elowen were trying to get their idea across without hurting Mistral, but not Phoenix, as his no-filter mouth already started to rumble in words as clear as saying she was crazy. But then, the ground started to shake worse than their body trembling from the impact. The wind came in to assist the earthquake, moving the water to start flooding all the floating grounds and farms for the first time in forever, with the size reaching quickly as tall as an adult's knee. Thus, they began to believe in what she said.

The four begged the earth to stop, kneeling and apologizing for all the mistakes they and other reasoning beings had blamed her into. It got her to calm down and at the same to wonder if they were really entirely to blame. But it was too late, she could not control her organs. They were no longer responding to her command for some reason.

The earth was coming apart at the seams once more, ready

to strike once again the same way she created the existing Modern Permian age. This time however, it was not her alone, and so the earth said, "This time, you should talk to the Creator, I can't help you anymore."

However, they replied unintentionally altogether instead with "The Creator?" Wyre then asked the others, "Which One is she talking about?" But the others lifted up their shoulders, unaware themselves who exactly she was talking about.

"How can we call out for help to Him? For He is too great to reach," Phoenix then asked the earth, but he still needed Mistral to translate the wind language for him.

The earth responded with the simple way she always did it, "I'll do it too," she added, and so the five of them called out to Him, known by His wonted name of "God," they screamed.

"It's been a while since the last time humans were reaching out to me," God responded so quickly, but more surprisingly, they all could hear His voice, without exception. They asked Him why, they wondered, but He replied, "As humans were trying to fix their own mistake themselves."

He then confirmed that the earth was going to die. Hearing this, the earth begged Him to spare her, her life. "Please God, spare me! Don't say it's too late, I'll do anything you want!" She further implored with high-pitched shrieks.

"There is mercy, but there are also, always, consequences, for every choice you make," He added.

"Then I beg you, spare the humans. It was my fault for starting all of these all over me again," she pleaded guilty to her crime.

God was quiet, thinking, looking at them, then looking to the earth's eyes without the humans' acknowledgment as they were not able to locate where He was, for He was all over both the earth and the universe.

"If your organs still want to live, they can," He then answered, but the earth did not really understand what He meant. Weren't her organs supposed to follow her command? That was how she always perceived it, as humans were supposed to bow to her too, she believed.

"It's actually the other way around," He fixed her judgement, that the humans were her ruler instead, then added, "but they should have learned how to respect you, as they should have loved one another."

"Where a king and his army stand, the soldiers can choose to either follow their king until their end, choose to save themselves, or kill the king when they change sides of where their loyalty lies. Like so, each of these elements has their own mind of their own where they want to go or do. They can have the option to follow whichever master they have their trust on, whether to serve itself or another," He added, sounding so calm, almost like He had been in this exact situation, as if it really happened the same way before.

From there they realized, each of the elements had lost their trust to humans, then the earth. In the end, they had to find a way to gain their trust back. They questioned Him how, but God answered with only a simple phrase, "Ask them."

So, they tried.

XXXIX

Chapter Thirty-Nine

The End of The World

Four people rushed to the top of the floating cave in desperation. The pointy rust of the rock torturing their skin and the strong blow of the wind dragging them to fall as they climbed were the least of their concern. The unusually striking heat from the sun was mirrored by the outer layer of the hollow, making their bare feet blister by just trying to hold on to their stand, but it was also nothing compared to what they were seeing.

A flame was born out of the parching crops that were losing from the constant sunlight. The fire was acting out with turbulence in a circle with the help of the wind and they shortly took control of the whole floating farms. Afterward, the ocean floor was splitting up then clashing altogether like they were in a fight, causing quivers throughout the floating houses. By the law of physics, the water that jumped out of the blue surface should have folded the whole of The Earth; nonetheless, it diverted its direction to go the other way unexpectedly, either because it did not yet want to kill the people that were hiding in the floating houses and cruise ship or they wanted them to die in a burning pain instead.

"I command you to stop!" Phoenix shouted. He was the first one out of the four to find back the voice to speak up, after being speechless witnessing the whole thing. "What are you doing?" Mistral responded in great annoyance then she added, "He said 'ask them' not ordering them to."

"Let's work together," Mistral spoke to the air that was whirling the flame horizontal and afterward lifted both of her arms up high for it to follow. It seemed to not be working but she did not rest her arms one bit, her focus was to gain the respect back from the wind by showing it how.

Her tenacity inspired Elowen and so she said the exact same thing, to ask for them to work together, except that she spoke to the soil instead, the one she was most familiar with, with the only way she knew how. She slid down the thorny rock quickly, swiping her arms to bleed in the process, and headed to where they all once tried to grow the Eucalyptus tree but failed. She pulled herself down to fall on both knees and placed both of her hands on the ground. She screamed once because it was very painful on her leg and palm skin, but she kept them intact there, even when Wyre was trying to stop her. Realizing from Elowen's eyes that she too believed it might be the only way, he threw himself into the water and tried to balance himself so as not to drown by pushing his left arm to the left and right one to his right.

"This is stupid," Phoenix shouted, but instead of getting angry at him, Mistral smiled and reminded him of something, "Phoenix, the fire should come first, remember?" Seeing how hard the other three were trying, his heart melted and so he set aside his pride and tried to follow what the others did with his own way. He flickered five fingers to his front to get the fire and the wind to notice him, then five others at the back in where Wyre and Elowen were. Thereupon, the other three were smiling at him, and subsequently Phoenix to the others, because they realized each of the elements were standing before each of them correspondingly, looking like they were interested to hear what the humans were proposing.

The fire's figure was of a mighty dragon and its wings shaped like a giant umbrella that was cut in half and put on each side. "Please," Phoenix said while looking it in the eye, and its bearded head flickered to the right, asking Phoenix to ride on its back. He followed its request half-heartedly but was in a disbelief that he was not burnt or fell right into the water. In fact, for him, it was like sitting on a horse where its flaming skin felt as smooth as that too, and even though it looked like it was burning, he did not feel the heat. The dragon flew to all of the floating farms and all the fire in there was coming with it. It then hovered on the surface of the sea and watched as all the other fires were jumping into the water, as Phoenix and the others too with widened not-blinking eyes.

The air that was standing in front of Mistral was of an eagle with the color of a wind. Its head was suggesting the same way as the dragon, as its body was moving closer to her too, and so Mistral followed its request. Similarly, it flew to all the floating grounds where the lonely gale that was left alone by the fire in the floating farms moved into. It headed to the cloud afterward with the others and together formed more and more clouds that blocked the intense sunlight.

The substance of the land in front of Elowen was growing drastically in a matter of seconds from a single dust, then little cuddly bear she could hug to a colossal size of a twenty-story building, just similar height to the other two. Its color was very dark brown on its arms and legs and very light beige on the others; almost like a giant panda in resemblance, but with some little branches and leaves still attached to its skin. It then sat down floating in front of Elowen, waiting for something to come out of the water.

Seeing the three creatures grown out of the other elements, Wyre suspected that his turn would come very soon, and he was right. Soon enough, his body was rising with the water that shaped exactly like a flying fish. Once it came out of the water, the giant bear stood on the water surface, still floating, hugged all of the floating grounds and lands with its arms extended like a tree that grew very fast, and lifted them all up. The fish then moved its body near to the cruise ship where its flap managed to move it with the flow of water. Together with the bear, they moved them all to the other side of the ocean where it was calmest, even further from where The World was.

Afterward, the dragon came back and put his feet on each floating farm, one by one. It was followed by the eagle whirling its wind with the dragon. As a result, excess flames came out of the soil and united with the dragon's body. It was then the bear's turn. It put its hands on each too whilst the fish flapped water to where the bear's palms still rested. Every time they did it, crops were rising from their burnt bodies and flourished quickly back to what they were.

A miracle, they all called it; truly everything that had been happening were. The four humans managed to take part in saving all of The Earth members and their abode from disaster, and like an orchestra, they played beautifully with their own instruments. The four creatures representing each of the earth's elements did not leave their sight. They stood forming a guardian muster, with the humans watching cluelessly thinking everything was over, but apparently, it was not. The four humans who were still attached to their back, somehow could understand by looking at their eyes - they did not know how, assuring them that they were asked by the Creator to protect them from what was coming.

Meanwhile, on the other side of the planet, the earth's kidney still failed her but there was none to remind those who lived on it. Mother Nature felt the shortness in her breath was going more and more towards losing it. She felt defeated, tired, and eventually ran out of air completely. Whether she was going to faint or die, however, she was glad she was able to go back to sleep at least one last time.

The earth was losing her breath for only less than five seconds.

The day was supposed to be a bright sunny one, perfect to go to the beach, and so it was where most of the Code Whites were at. Their feet were brawling with hot white sands and their body could not wait to jump into the water. It was exactly twelve o'clock in the afternoon, but the light in the sky was suddenly leaving them to the dark - the darkest, and no one had not even known what no-light meant until they saw what it really looked like, when there was really none of the light left. Though the sunshine was gone, those who were still in their sunbathing position had their skin burn like hell. Even those who were just as close as standing inside by the window, curious of what was going on outside with the sky, found their skin covered in flames too.

Zirilo was sitting not far from where he could see the outside world through the glass aperture. On the table lay a wide printed plan on how he was planning to bomb The Earth. On his hand however, leant back a golden frame with a picture of him and Hayes, smiling widely towards the camera, in the half-built House of Rules. "What I would give for everything to just be like the old days," he spoke to himself, but his wandering mind was distracted by the loud havoc going on outside, and so he stood up and walked closer to the wide window. "Aah," he screamed as he realized the closer he was to it, the more his skin was feeling the heat. In response, he moved a few steps back, but he could still see what was going on. The horror.

Flying objects in the sky fell onto the ground immediately. Even vehicles rolling on the land crashed onto each other and ignited fire from the impact. All the brain scanners in all the chambers clamored in their own tempo and starting sequence saying, "Something to think about," before breaking down altogether into fragments and pulling each other's materials following the rest of the metals from other kinds of machines and robots, sticking into piles.

The face of The World's leader turned ghastly as he witnessed water particles evaporating and flying back into space, then all the buildings and houses crumbling down into ashes from losing oxygen that glued them together, including where he was. He felt his inside was exploding from ceasing the air pressure that he was not even able to scream and before his skeleton even hit the ground, his soul was already gone.

After almost five seconds had passed, the oxygen was finally coming back to earth as she was gaining back her momentum to breathe in her peaceful sleep, just before all of the remains were almost exploding into foggy hydrogen gasses. Nonetheless, everyone in The World was dead without a single survivor.

The earth was only running out of breath for no longer than five seconds, but that was all it took to end The World as they knew it.

XL

Chapter Forty

Heaven on Earth

The Earth's dwelling was moving gently towards the only land on the planet that was once used to be under the great The World's authority. Driven by the four beasts who were protecting them against the apocalypse, the floating grounds reached the side of the port where their cruise ship had been when they were first banished.

Phoenix and Mistral flew over the land thoroughly and after a short while, they realized there was no hope for survivors. Phoenix then took a short detour back to what was used to be the House of Rules. He closed his eyes for a moment there and opened them up again to see in more detail the piles of what was left, then came back again to meet the other three. That day, they officially moved back to the land, along with the rest, planning to start over humanity with what was left of them.

With the help of the four magnificent creatures, all the people got together to remove all of the corpses one by one. "The last time I did this, I was alone," Hayes spoke to Mistral who was staying by his side out of worry. "One thousand and seventy seven... one thousand and seventy eight," the old man continued his last count from decades ago, on purpose, and insisted on helping even though his body could not bear the weight any longer.

Mistral wanted to ask the air to help lighten the weight for Hayes, but she did not want him to hear it. She looked at the wind that was everywhere around her, put her palm against each other to show vividly that "please" gesture when Hayes was not looking, then said the words without the voice, hoping the air would understand what she meant.

The air understood and agreed. It moved so the corpse Hayes was bringing on his arms was hovering above his two upper limbs just half an inch in the intention so he would not notice. "What did you say to the wind?" Hayes seemed to detect but then smiled and went along with pleasure. Mistral was glad, and so did the air. It felt much lighter after the event and so it vowed to itself to cooperate so long as its invisible wings could accommodate, continuing its start by helping the others too.

The air helped a great deal in moving the remains to a proper place far from any land and closest to the sea, in the ultimate quietness out of respect. The peace was cut short however, when a group of ten people ran towards Hayes and Mistral screaming "Monsters!" Without even seeing them themselves, both trusted the group and ran back to where the other three were.

The great big walls that were once keeping the forest out of reach had collapsed alongside the apocalypse and cleared the path for them to come through. "How can they still be alive? That's impossible," Phoenix bellowed out his frustration.

"The bunker," Hayes suddenly responded to his shock himself, "that must be it," he added.

"What? Shouldn't that be destroyed too alongside the others? Who's protecting them?" Phoenix responded with continuous rage.

"What bunker?" Elowen was confused, but as she was trying to remember for the word sounded familiar, Phoenix and Mistral were already on their way up in the air with the dragon and the eagle. Wyre and Elowen then followed via the land with the fish and the bear.

"There's too many of them in the forest," Wyre screamed as he circled the shore.

"I can take care of those between the rumbles, but not the forest, the fire will burn everything," Phoenix screamed.

"Quick, this will do," Elowen then asked the land to separate itself from that of the forest to buy them some time. Mistral afterward asked the wind to help push the forest miles away from the land. Meanwhile, the dragon's breath aimed by Phoenix were cleaning up those unwanted beings that were running to bite the flesh out of the living, and the flames were put out by the hard thump Wyre's fish waggled against the surface of the sea. The mainland was finally free from disturbance once more.

"What should we do with the forest? Can those humanly-monsters swim?" Mistral asked Phoenix, who was watching them too from above.

Phoenix tapped gently on the dragon's head and it seemed to really like it. His face then came closer to its ears, whispering - no one knew what he was saying to it, then when he lifted his body back, he spoke to it another word in an assertive tone; "Carefully. If you can, then the others are able too," he said. The dragon nodded then flew circling the forest island while breathing out its edge with flame.

Understanding what he was trying to achieve, Elowen then asked the bear to get her near to the land, and on the shore near where the fire stood, she drew a circle instructing the soil to build itself a deep hole a meter after the fire. Wyre next gently rubbed the fish on its back and so it flapped its tail on the sea surface so the water would jump over the fire and into the hollowed ground. Lastly, Mistral proposed the wind to guard over the fire so it would stay tall and on where it was, not spreading, not burning the forest, always.

"Thank you everyone, that should do for now," Phoenix smiled and prompted the others to leave the island alone for good.

When they got back, they were surprised that the wind was still helping with cleaning the land. Not just the air, but all the people were also standing side by side helping each other.

"The air, they're still helping?" Wyre commented with disbelief.

"So it's not just us then," Elowen pulled her lips wide to each side.

"Maybe they started with trusting the four of us, and they're growing to believe in every one of the others," Mistral was speaking in tears, happy tears.

"Maybe God is speaking to them too, telling these elements to help us. Imagine, if things are going to always be this way," Phoenix was talking with a trembling voice, trying to hold back his true feelings. He used to be the most skeptical of the bunch, but he seemed to slowly change the way he thought.

"We have been living in a world with no conviction; too no mercy, no faith, and with limited imagination; directionless without further pursuit for knowledge that things like this are possible; blinded by what couldn't, and I wish that these beautiful things we're seeing can be the start of something true," Hayes' words were traveling from their behind, louder as he got nearer to where they stood.

"We need to make sure no one will ever forget this. I think I know what to say to my group, let me hear yours," Phoenix put his left palm on Wyre's right shoulder, waiting for his answer, but knowing what the first meant, the latter rested his the same way on top and responded, "I think they'll need just one leader to proclaim that, Phoenix, considering we are all one now."

"Are you sure?" Phoenix replied, and Wyre answered, "Besides, remember, the fire has to come first?"

"I'm sick of hearing that," Phoenix laughed, then the others followed. After hearing all that however, Phoenix formed his grip harder and promised not to let him and anyone else down the best he could.

"I mean, look at all this, the magic before our eyes. Who's going to forget this anyway?" Elowen shouted, as she believed she would not even forget any second of it for the rest of her life.

"I did, and look what I once built," Hayes responded with a slight smile but Elowen and Mistral shook their heads quietly to each other as they didn't think he put all that in the book, "but I still hope that someday a literal heaven on earth could really exist."

The world with no evil.
Is that even possible?

Phoenix believed that the only way for the people to live peacefully with each other as well as the earth was to trust that they would be able to always work together. All technologies that were invented by the scientists were no longer standing by themselves automatically, fully depending on the elements that moved them instead. Airplanes and cars that were moved by the air without fuel, houses built and crops grown straight from the ground regardless of the season, seawater desalinated by the fire in control for daily drinking, and everything else alike was constructed for helping the life of people with full consideration and respect to and from the elements that were surrounding them. No more natural disasters. The partnership had built the country like they thought they could never before.

A few years later, the established king of the land that remained intact with floating grounds and cave on its side as well as the remote banished island, Phoenix, was married to Kindra and they were blessed with a son.

One usual day, Phoenix sat down with Mistral, his advisor, and they watched their sons playing together. "Look at them," Mistral spoke, and Phoenix responded with a simple smile.

"My mom is the air's best friend; she can fly anytime she wants!"

"My dad can control fire and he doesn't even get burnt when he touches it! The only one to..."

"Mika!" Phoenix suddenly raised his voice on his son and came towards him. He kneeled before the little boy afterward and held the back of his hand gently with a warm look, then said, "We do not control these elements. One can only control when the other does not have the option. No one can control them. Instead, they are listening to us, and they choose to agree. That is how we can live peacefully like this. We do not harm them and thus, they do not ruin us."

One thing Phoenix was missing though, people can still hurt each other. It was not long after the conversation with his son, that two guards were running towards him. "A murderer on the loose," one of them spoke up first.

One night, Phoenix asked Mide Holmes to come to his work chamber with an old chip he spun with his fingers.

"You've still got that?" She looked horrified with what she saw, as it brought her to the horrible side of the past in a flash.

"I've never thrown it out, just in case," he responded. "I think we might need this again, but not to judge, just to help this time," he added with his eyebrows turning down on each side towards his nose, looking very serious.

Mide did not look very happy with Phoenix's idea, but he assured her that the idea in his mind was to only use the brain scanner to determine who needed 'help' the most, so he could keep the people safe. If the result showed Code Black, the subject should not be put to death immediately, but nurtured to be good. Otherwise, the world would still be occupied with evils.

"But there is only one thing I worry about, with this *brain*," he confessed to Mide, "What is this chip telling us about the definition of evil? I want you to find that one first for me," he enquired further, and afterward, Mide looked very pleased. Besides feeling her nervousness loosened by what he actually implored, she herself too always wondered what it was that made the *brain* able to determine which one was with the evil intention and which one was not.

In the end, they never figured it out.

Why were the Code White people, though they did not harm each other, still harming nature while at the same time blaming the earth for the unexpected natural disasters? Was that evil? Furthermore, was being evil towards nature never considered as an evil behavior?

Actually, what is really the definition of evil? Isn't it written by humans too? So, who can really define it except God?

Meng and Phoenix might be right. Even the good ones always have a bit of a devil inside of them. 'Bad' in the brain scanner, did not mean they were not capable of loving someone, and we all know 'love' is a good thing. 'Good' in the brain scanner, still could be a devil, probably that was why they needed the rescan policy. They were just being good out of fear of being caught as one of the bad ones, as they did not want to lose the privileges offered by simply being one of the good ones. Imagine if those entitlements had been honored to those who were bad instead, The World would have been full of evil.

So maybe, evil or not is heavily supported or affected by fear as well. A system that shows fear; fear from being sent to a place without such luxury that drives people to be good, fear of being restrained that they forget about the consequences, and many other things. Thus, evil or not becomes a very complex query to answer.

Remember how those little evil things people in the Code White area still did at the time? No one is free from evil temptation; it is in every one of us. We just have to accept the fact that it will likely be with us for as long as the world still stands, come and go in many forms.

I hope you, my precious daughter, will remember this long lullaby that travelled out my vocal cord, when your time comes to unite back this kingdom that your great grandfather first ruled in unity, for the duty is always in your blood to begin.

The fire that lives in us, the water that surrounds our ground, the earth where we stand, and the air that never leaves; ask them.

The Creator whose existence covers even the whole universe that He always seems invisible to mere mortals; ask Him the loudest and never forget Him.

Though the *brain* says you breathe with no empathy, remember that it is never the permanent measurement for anything. You are not evil; you are just different, and you will eventually learn what it feels like to care. Humans become fouls not only because they find blinding temporary pleasures in the suffering of others, but because they forget how to love their own enemies, which are never always limited to other than themselves. That is what you need to be more scared of, not to never be loved, but to never love.

This is not the final piece of the puzzle however, no, this is not even the first. These are what matter for you to realize the importance of a history for the future, to find knowledge in the past and hope in uncertainty, to see the glass-embodiment of a trust, and eventually, find the bravery to start and persevere - because what I am about to ask you is not for the lighthearted.

Whenever you are ready, without the reluctance to leave and with the fact steady - you need to find the dragon first.

AUTHOR

Priscila's writing journey first started when she was just a little kid who had just woken up from what to her at the time was the most wonderful dream that made her longing to go back to sleep. Realizing that no matter how many times she closed her eyes she still could not go back to where she left off, she wrote her own version of the full story in her mind, only to forget all about it when her next peculiar dream came.

Ever since, she has been writing short stories of her reveries that she does not want to omit, as a way for her to get out of this small town she calls reality - heading back to imagination city. One of those, she decided to continue to hundreds of pages long, and publish it.

She sincerely hopes you would enjoy reading it as much as she took pleasure in writing it.

PriscilaK.com